MR. RIDLEY

ALSO BY
DELILAH MARVELLE

THE WHIPPING SOCIETY

Book one, *Mr. Ridley*

Book two, *The Devil Is French*

Book three, *Reborn*

MR. RIDLEY

A WHIPPING SOCIETY NOVEL

DELILAH MARVELLE

FOR THOSE WHO LIVE IN THE SHADOWS.
YOUR DAY OF LIGHT WILL COME.

My dearest Reader,

Unlike most historical romances that feature a hero and heroine whose journey and love for each other ends at a mere one book, I am extending a unique invitation for you to join in on a much bigger love story.

When Ridley and Jemdanee first appeared to me, and their pages started to go beyond what two books could hold, I realized they needed three books. This begins *The Whipping Society Saga*.

While I will ensure each full length book ends without dangling your hearts too far over the edge of impatience, please come to this book and those to follow as you would to an episode of your favorite TV show. Many questions will be answered, others not. Each book will be wrapped up in its own way, but obviously... for there to be more, not everything can be resolved.

Please note this is still very much a historical romance, simply done on a three book scale. It's my hope you enjoy spending an unusual amount of time with Ridley and Jemdanee as each book brings them to closer to the people they must become to embrace what awaits them: true love.

I thank you for being a reader.

Much love,
Delilah Marvelle

GLOSSARY OF TERMS

Arrey—Expression of surprise in Hindi. Like 'Hey!'

Bhang lassi—a drink made of yogurt or milk, spices, rose water and cannabis (weed).

Bidi—Indian cigarette made from tobacco rolled in an ebony tree leaf.

Blackamoor—offensive term for a dark skinned person.

Challo—'Let us go' in Hindi.

Chowkidar—guard in Hindi.

Coca/Limestone combination—prior to the first known extraction and isolation of "cocaine" from coca leaves back in 1859, crushed limestone was used to draw out the "high" from coca leaves. The coca leaf by itself gives the user a heightened effect of modern caffeine.

Écritoire—a piece of furniture used for writing.

Goonda—thug or miscreant in Hindi.

Haan—Yes in Hindi.

Ici—There or Right Here in French

Ipomoea Alba—Known as a moon flower given the white flowers only bloom by the light of the moon at night and close when sunlight touches it. Native to tropical and subtropical regions of the New World.

Ipecacuaha—the dried root of a shrubby South American plant.

Phaujee—Soldier or male constable in Hindi.

Jee—A formal response to a yes or in answer to a question in Hindi.

Kali—Also known as Kalika, is a Hindu goddess.

Kancha—a favorite game for many young boys in India using marbles.

Katar—a type of dagger that sits on the knuckles originating from the Indian subcontinent.

Knee Splitter—two spiked wood blocks placed in back and in front of the knee. When turned, they destroy the kneecaps. Originally used during the Inquisition.

Laudanum—an alcoholic based solution or morphine/opium used for pain.

Maa—mother in Hindi.

Memsahib—a white foreign woman of high social status living in India.

Nahin—No in Hindi.

Pita—father in Hindi.

Rhus acuminata—A sumac similar to poison oak. Grows in China, Bhutan, India and Nepal.

Saali—expression of disgust, derogatory in Hindi.

Sahib—An Urdu honorific as a term of respect that is the English equivalent of 'Sir'.

Sepoy—an Indian soldier serving under British or European orders.

Shiva—One of the principle deities of Hinduism.

Shrew's Fiddle—2 pieces of wood or steel for the neck and wrists that is locked with a hinge. Originally used in the Middle Ages to punish women caught bickering or brawling.

Sonti—a rice-based Indian alcoholic beverage similar to sake.

Spilanthes—Spilanthes Acmella (known as the Toothache Plant, Paracress). In history, its medicinal usage was related to pain relieving properties.

Ullu ke patha—Son of an owl or idiot in Hindi.

Yeh lo, saaph ho gaya—'Here, it is clean' in Hindi.

HISTORICAL CHARACTERS

Eugène François Vidocq—Born in France, July 24, 1775, died in Paris, May 11, 1857. Considered to be the father of modern criminology. He is regarded as being the first private detective in history. After leading a life of crime, he converted his acquired skills as a delinquent to assist police in capturing men like himself. Countless writers in history modeled characters after him. Victor Hugo's *Les Misérables* (1862) featured a reformed criminal Valjean and Inspector Javert, are both modeled after Vidocq. Other works he inspired include *Moby Dick* by Herman Melville, *Great Expectations* by Charles Dickens and the very first detective created in fiction by Edgar Allen Poe, C. Auguste Dupin in *The Murders in Rue Morgue* (1841). Surprised that it wasn't Sherlock Holmes? Edgar Allen Poe beat Conan Doyle to the quill by almost 46 years! This is why I gave Ridley a raven. It's my homage to Edgar Allen Poe whose brilliant detective, Dupin, is never given the homage he deserves.

Mrs. Theresa 'Elizabeth' Berkley—Died in London, England in September of 1836 (year of birth and age unknown). She was a British dominatrix who owned a high-class flagellation brothel at 28 Charlotte Street. There is no source pointing to an actual name of the brothel or any depiction of what she herself might have looked like, only that she was 'attractive' with a strong 'disposition'. She earned a sizable fortune by becoming the Michelangelo of torture devices and designing contraptions for men and women who derived pleasure from pain.

The 'Berkley Horse', as an example, was designed by her in 1828 to be able to flog a man's backside whilst another could pleasure his front side. Bald-cunted Polly and Ebony Bet are actual names of two women that worked for her. After Mrs. Berkley's death, she left a valued estate of £100,000 (today's sum of approximately $3 million!). She bequeathed it to her brother who was a missionary man in Australia. When he realized how his own sister had earned her substantial fortune (for the naughty thing never told him…), he refused to take a farthing of it, relinquishing his rights. The entire estate went to the Crown.

PROLOGUE

London, England – 1810
A tale without a fairy.

Sometime between the hour of one and four in the morning, a frayed slipper was left on the marble stair of an opulent house.

The heel was covered in blood.

So was the massive bedchamber, where gilded mirrors had been smashed and ornate furniture overturned, revealing an endless maze of rare books and a blood-smeared floor.

It was there the constables found renown philanthropist Bartholomew Edgar Ridley lying in a pool of blood that fingered out in endless streams, soaking parchments as old as the Crusades. His nude body had been cleaved with an axe, pieces of him flung as far as the ceiling.

Nothing had been taken. Not even a wad of bank notes left on the *écritoire*.

Yet tucked into the gore of Mr. Ridley's broken sternum was the feather of a black raven.

Its macabre meaning was examined by many but understood by none.

Whatever truth was lost by the gruesome broadsides everyone now sought to purchase for halfpence on the street, it did not change the tragic events now known as *The Black Raven Murder*.

Mr. Ridley's twelve-year-old son was all that remained. His head had been bludgeoned and his body stuffed into a trunk whose lock had to be smashed to get to him. Miraculously, he survived.

His French-born mother, who had been separated from his father, rushed to be at his side.

From that moment forth, Evan Oswald Ridley became London's greatest preoccupation.

Bystanders and journalists crowded at the gates of his mother's abode shouting endless questions about the gruesome murder and what the boy did or did not see.

Little is known about Evan after that.

Some insist the incident had deranged him, forcing him into Bedlam. Others claim he was sent to France to reside with his mother's cousin, a 'police spy' known as Eugéne Vidocq.

What *is* known is that many years later, an estate lawyer delivered a sizable stack of documents to this unusual young man living in Paris who had inherited an equally unusual legacy. An astounding collection of rare books worth over a quarter of a million stuffed into a massive house, which had been locked up since the murder, now belonged to Evan Oswald Ridley.

To the horror of polite society, he returned to London and moved into the abandoned house.

It was there, at 221 Basil Street, Ridley became the whisper of every woman's fantasy and every criminal's living nightmare.

CHAPTER ONE

London, England – July 1830, late evening
Millbank Prison overlooking the Thames

This rot of an English prison reminded her of the forty-three nights she had once spent beneath a manure cart as an orphan in Calcutta. With the exception, of course, that she was only on day *three* of her imprisonment in a country that was not her own.

Aside from the stone walls and the roaches and the thick, murky substance dripping from the low ceiling reeking of human sewage, what made her incarceration doubly intolerable was that every last one of these blue coats treated her like a buffalo in need of intelligence.

Last she knew, she was the only female back in India to have THE prominent and highly-educated Parsee, Limazah, navigate her through the world of botany. All of it enthusiastically and generously paid for by her guardian, Dr. Peter William Watkins.

Phytology was a field dominated by men, yet one she could snap her fingers at both above and below her head to provide answers half of them needed a book for.

She, and no other, had an extensive collection of flora from over sixty-three countries that filled over thirteen massive greenhouses with specimen most of these warders had never even heard of. All of it labelled. All of it categorized by its classification and taxonomy like books in a massive library on a shelf that never ended.

That alone ought to be respected.

She had already briskly informed the sour-breathed British authorities more than twice that she was a proper lady and they ought to remove their hands if they knew what was good for them. Never mind the prostitutes, goat herders and shoals of hawkers she'd grown up with as a child who would have probably laughed hard enough to rattle the lice right out of their hovels.

She *refused* to incriminate herself by admitting that ten years earlier, her curtain of black hair had to be shaved to the scalp to permit regrowth without intractable knots and that her malnourished and filthy body had to be scrubbed and fed and fed by Dr. *'pita'* Watkins.

She was proof that no life was expendable, no life was hopeless.

It took her ten years to perfect the reading, writing, and speaking of the English language.

It took her ten years to perfect mimicking the prim, pert-nosed memsahibs surrounding her.

That wasn't to say she had forgotten her past.

Far from it. Prior to traveling into London, she still snuck out late at night to smoke *bidis*, played *kancha* for money with sepoys, floated naked in the river watching vast copper-colored skies smear into dawn, and took pleasure in kissing countless young, Persian merchants who considered her blue eyes exotic.

She should have never agreed to leave India.

"Move along," the British warder bellowed.

To ensure she remained calm through whatever interrogation lay ahead, Jemdanee steadied her breaths and dug into a strength far mightier than despair.

She dug out what few did in their darkest hour: hope and humor.

A hope to make it to another day and humor to ensure she didn't cry.

"Rattle those chains already," the warder called, rolling his hand. "Move!"

In an attempt to maintain her pace, Jemdanee grudgingly trudged onward against the substantial weight of the chains, clinking and staggering forward as she maneuvered down the lantern-lit stone corridor that led to the custodian office.

It was a ridiculous amount of chains. She was only five feet in height and eight stone.

"I am not an animal, *goonda*," she pointed out, in case the warder had any doubt. "I am the legal ward of Army surgeon Dr. Watkins who has worked under the jurisdiction of the Crown since eighteen hundred and fourteen. Do you have any idea how far his reach lies? He once removed a bullet from the Field Marshal's own chest on the same riverbank where crocodiles gather for amusement. No small feat given open wounds invite the wild to indulge, and yet I was there delivering gauze and tonics into his blood-soaked hands given no other man would. Together, we saved his life. I doubt you ever saved anyone."

The warder snapped toward her, his bulbous features reddening.

She decided to desist lest he backhand her. "That was uncalled for. I apologize and will say no more. You are merely doing what you are paid to do and I can and will respect that."

He grunted and waved her on.

The iron manacles burned her chafed wrists as the iron bar strapped against her corseted waist strained her shoulders and forearms with too many chains, clanging against every movement.

Jemdanee bore each thick, weighing ring with whatever panache she could.

Somehow, barely minutes after arriving into the elbowing crowds of London three days earlier, she had accidentally been separated from Dr. Watkins. Carpet bag in hand, she had hurried over to a display window full of bonnets, chuckling at how ridiculous it was of women to wear bouquets on their heads as if women were vases, then gaped at all of the people and the looming buildings without any regard to where she was going and... lost sight of Peter.

She couldn't remember the street of the hotel they were supposed to be lodging in, so she did what any intelligent person would do. She breezed into a magistrate building known as 'Scotland Yard' and had asked for assistance in locating the hotel.

The bindi spangle must have scared them.

Not one, not two, but *three* constables rifled through her belongings and demanded to know about the strange jars, copper instruments, and unknown substances that included a variety of rare indigenous seeds. Without any documentation (for Peter had it…), one of the constables grabbed her by the neck.

She had the bruises to prove it.

The *ullu ke patha* even charged her with indecent exposure for wearing a sari. They might as well have accused her of witchcraft.

The custodian room opened, revealing lanterns in the darkness. "Go in," the warder announced.

It was late and all of the other prisoners were sleeping.

It was the only warning she needed.

Much like she always did, she used the weapon of conversation for the purpose of civilized advancement, despite the chains weighing her wrists. "I do not believe we were ever properly introduced. I abide by the name of Miss Jemdanee Lillian Watkins. 'Tis a very fine British name that miraculously found my soul at the age of eight. Though my guardian will argue as to its meaning, *Wat* is a Buddhist temple and *kins* is an expression of an endearment. It reminds me to live up to its noble worth, despite my not being a Buddhist at all. And you are…?"

The warder dragged in a snot and then spit, eyeing her. "Jeremiah Samuel Flank. *Flank*. Like the arse of a horse I've yet to own given the governor ain't payin' me enough. Now be you done flirtin', blackie?"

Blackie? If she used the chains to choke him, Peter would probably do more than take the keys to her greenhouses. He'd burn them all down. "You seem like a very reasonable gentleman, Mr. Flank."

"Oh, I be that and more." His breath reeked of calves' foot jelly. "I be the most reasonable gent you'll ever meet on this side of the river."

Either he was being sarcastic or this was going very well. "Given I am only familiar with British customs through my guardian and what I have seen back in Calcutta, might I—"

"*Move the braid already!*" The warder grabbed the back of her neck and shoved her in. "Damn blackamoor be flirtin' with me."

Stumbling into the windowless room lit by lanterns, the warder slammed the door shut.

A grumbling breath escaped her.

She'd sooner flirt with a crocodile and fold both arms around its scale-ridden neck.

Unlike the other female prisoners kept in the north-west tower of Millbank, whose shouts she could hear through the stone walls on the hour like peacocks, she had never been one to scream. Too many nights spent alone on the streets of Calcutta had long cured her of that. She'd seen men do things to each other that made this British prison look like a festival decorated with silk banners.

Jemdanee paused realizing… she wasn't alone.

A gentleman leaned over the custodian's desk paging through a ledger. A satchel was set beside him. He disregarded the chair he stood beside, displaying an imposing height of over six feet. He continued to intently page through the ledger, spreading his knee-high black boots into a domineering, long-legged stance that announced she was now under *his* jurisdiction.

Despite the warm summer night not even the stone walls of the prison could vanquish, he wore solely black attire made of bombazine that displayed a muscled figure.

Dark chestnut hair fell into eyes he never once lifted from the desk.

She lingered, still chained, noting this particular breed of man was quite pleasing to the eye. Nothing like the burnt-red officers and wiry-haired men Peter sat about with discussing state affairs over port and most certainly nothing like the other warders and inspectors in the prison who could barely tie their yellowing cravats.

This one's flawless, silk ascot was styled into a sophisticated knot that whispered of higher European status. And his great coat with its fine, wide collar propped high, outlined an ample, muscled figure that announced he understood how to showcase his assets.

It gave her hope that she might be treated with the respect deserving of a lady.

Or at least a person.

He slowly chewed on something, deep in thought, but otherwise said nothing. Nor did he look up. The leather belt on his hips shifted, displaying two pistols and a blade sheathed in holsters.

One weapon hinted he expected a fight.

Two weapons hinted he wanted to display his might.

Three weapons, however, announced his intention to annihilate everything in sight.

It was like he was his own regiment.

Disregarding the notable distance set between them, Jemdanee attempted to align herself before him with the chink, chink of dragging chains and peered over at the desk's contents which held his attention so keenly.

Stacks of massive prison logs binding thick parchments had been unevenly piled onto the fading veneer. Stacks. Too many to count. "I find it very disheartening to think so many people are committing crimes," she conversationally offered.

He paused. His trained gaze remained on the sizable ledger before him.

That might not have been the best conversation for her to start with. "Not that I have committed any crime," she amended, adjusting her chains in a polite attempt to address her situation. "I have always been a law-abiding citizen." Not true. "Even when I was hip high and holding out a hand for others to feed me, I never took anything that was not freely given." That was true.

Shifting his shaven jaw, he paged forward and backward through stiff, warped parchments.

No one had beat her yet. Which made her bold. "There appears to have been a most *egregious* misunderstanding." Peter liked that word, so she used it. "Wrapping me in a stone's worth of chains for close to three days seems a rather harsh punishment for a woman who had only asked for directions to a hotel."

He set another open ledger onto the desk with a thud. "Have they been feeding you?" His deep, husky tone filled the confining space, a subtle accent hinting of years spent in another country.

That voice dripped with so much huskiness it scraped her own throat.

Her stomach growled on cue. It hadn't growled like that since… "I am a vegetarian. I therefore had to decline everything being offered except for the bread. It appears the fare here in England consists of nothing but meat, meat and more meat. Even the porridge had mutton in it."

She tut-tutted at the amount of grease it had leached into the wooden bowl. "The British may wish to reconsider its love for animal flesh torn straight from the bone. Plants have the ability to offer twice the amount of nutrients compared to what is found within the carcass of an animal who *might* have been your grandmother depending on your religion."

He said nothing. Nor did he look up as he intently paged through more thick bindings.

Maybe he thought her ungrateful. "Such life-sustaining offerings were nonetheless appreciated. I did not expect to be fed at all given it *is* a prison. I am, however, confused as to why I am not being permitted to speak to a barrister, especially given all of the testimony I have given. Surely, it would be in England's best interest to offer a more gracious form of hospitality to an Indian citizen whose own country has been... ah... *hosting* the British so openly for some time." To be polite. "Whilst I have not seen any progressive measures in India outside of—"

"Has anyone ever told you that you talk too much?" he rumbled out.

She pulled in her chin. Peter had always said she talked too little. "Perhaps I talk too much to ensure others know that I exist. For you, *phaujee*, appear to be ignoring me."

Still paging through several ledgers, he offered in a curt tone, "This *phaujee* is here to help. So limit the insults."

Sensing he was on her side (praise be!), she smiled, ensuring the crookedness of her teeth didn't show. "If there was any doubt, *phaujee* means soldier."

"Which, to me, is an insult. Soldiers are mindless."

This one needed a furlough. She edged closer with a shuffling chink, chink, chink. "Forgive the chains, but might I be granted an opportunity to contact my guardian? I have no doubt he is incredibly worried. It has been three days. I *have* been counting."

"You needn't worry. I've already spoken to Dr. Watkins extensively."

A much needed breath escaped her. Peter had a stronghold of governmental connections to get her out. "I am ever so pleased. Does that insinuate all is well?"

"No. He assaulted one of the constables who brought him the news regarding your incarceration and was *also* arrested."

Ay, ay. Peter did what he always did: he overreacted. No wonder women refused to marry him. That one was going to be a bachelor until dead. He needed to be reborn into something far more appealing: a goat. "Making him suffer for attempting to bring me justice would be incredibly unkind."

"I'll be certain to inform the constable whose arm he broke."

She cringed. "I will ensure he offers to set it. Bones within the arm heal remarkably well if properly tended to. I would also be more than happy to provide that constable with a body-numbing concoction of sedatives that will cure him of thinking he was ever—"

"Do you always show a casual indifference to what is better known as a dire situation?"

She gave him a pointed look. "Would panicking alter my reality? Would it erase what I already know to be true? I can assure you, *sahib*, I am fully aware of my own reality and that I am in a prison surrounded by other unfortunate women whose circumstance made them an aggressor. Unlike these British women, however, I am well-trained for this. For whilst they only ever see what *is*, I stand before you grateful for what is *not*. No one has taken a fist to my skull quite yet. If and when that should happen, we will revisit this conversation."

He said nothing.

She might as well have been talking to herself. "Where is Dr. Watkins being held?" She waited, but he didn't answer. "Is he here?"

"No. Unlike him, you are in a specially designated prison."

Of course she was. Peter breaks an arm, yet she is the one being doubly punished. "How kind of the British government to think of me. Do I get a water cabbage to go with the honor?"

A muscle quivered in his jaw as he flipped through more pages.

She pinched her lips and lingered, watching his large hands grip the leather binding. White scars of varying sizes covered the knuckles of each masculine hand hinting he used them often to break windows.

Or teeth. She eyed him. "Might I humbly plead for an audience with my guardian?"

"No." He continued to page through the ledger. "You belong to me until further notice. It's for your safety."

Her throat tightened. Whatever did that mean? Those scars and his inability to engage her beyond the ledgers hinted he was overly dedicated to work. "Are you a constable?"

His rugged features tightened as he kept paging through ledgers. "No. I work for the dead."

She lowered her chin. "I did not realize the dead hired the living."

"Oh, I have a steady clientele," he replied sharply between his teeth. "They pay me in bones." He paged through the ledgers more intently.

That dry indifference further faded what little optimism she had left. Especially with Peter now in prison.

The dolt. If not for her, he would have had a katar stabbed into his jugular years ago by her people for thinking a stethoscope was the equivalent of being Field Marshal. "Not to excuse Peter's brash behavior, or the arm he broke, but he has always been abnormally protective. I call it doctor syndrome. The need to help everyone. After all, what unwed white man of an upper class origin willingly takes in a brown child that only brings him trouble? Save me from saying it, but that one lost the last of his rational mind well before he ever met me and my woes. Was it the heat? I dare not fathom, but he abandoned wearing English clothes whilst donning a mustachio in some deranged attempt to be a native. Only… his Hindi is worse than my French and his skills as a father are over compensative. Not that I ever made it easy. Kali knows I have always been too curious for a mere one ayah. I needed four. And after this? He may employ a hundred and seven."

He paused. "Are you referring to Dr. Watkins?"

"*Haan*. I used to call him *pita*, which is Hindi for father, but he grouches that it makes him feel old. So now that I am a worldly age of eighteen, I call him Peter. Which is amusing, for it sounds the same given my accent." She dipped her voice. "He succumbed to his first grey strands and has yet to recover. I continue to assure him that forty-three is incredibly young and that forty-four is when it all ends." She smirked at her own humor.

Setting aside a ledger, he dragged over a new one.

Silence pulsed.

This one had no humor.

Curiosity getting the best of her, she leaned toward him trying to better see his face and eyes which had never once looked up. Why was he so anomalously focused on those logs?

Hopefully, they didn't have access to the government logs back in Calcutta.

She had been arrested two other times for very stupid things when she was younger and still adjusting to her life with Peter.

Once for smashing a bottle against the balding head of an officer who backhanded a servant (she got on a chair to do it) and another for setting fire to a fern hut used by local Indian men for fighting roosters they refused to let her buy.

Forty-seven aggressive roosters ended up taking over several streets and Peter was forced to pay damages for the furniture and the hut. Late though it was to admit, setting a fire to any building in India was incredibly stupid.

The whole country could have burned.

But it didn't.

"Is this about my passport or documentation?" she queried innocently.

"No. I already have both." With the turn of boots that sent his great coat billowing around his broad frame, he rounded her and the desk and yanked open six drawers one by one by one.

He glanced up and paused, their gazes locking.

She almost shrank back, the intensity of his stare crawling into her skin and mind.

Mercurial amber eyes skimmed her appearance, weighing her for the first time since she entered the room. The harsh lines of his rugged features strengthened as he continued to asses her from face to hand to elbow to shoulder to head and back to the hem again.

It was as if he were ticking through every finger and every toe and every strand of hair on her head to decipher what sort of a person she was.

Methodically returning to and removing more and more ledgers, which he piled onto the desk, he flipped through its warped pages. "Either you are incredibly deranged or you are utterly oblivious to your own peril. I genuinely hope it is the latter. You mentioned being denied a barrister. Has *anyone* informed you of the extensive charges filed against you?"

She felt her booted feet sinking into the stone floor, especially given the way he had earlier surveyed her like a display window in need of rearrangement. "I am confused as to what you mean by extensive."

A ragged breath escaped him. "Jesus, what a mess." He shifted from boot to boot and eyed her.

Dread dragged its fingers down the length of her spine. Peter only ever said 'Jesus' when there was a problem and divine intervention was needed from the Christian side.

The silence tore through her chest like a cannon shot.

Leaning over the desk in exasperation, his dark hair fell further into his eyes as he intently compared the ledgers with the impatient thudding of open palmed hands. "The name is Mr. Ridley." He squinted and paged through more ledgers, scanning written notes. "A higher placed contact at Scotland Yard which I cannot name, given he is violating the law, asked that I get involved due the complexity and severity of the crime."

She gaped. Severity? *Complexity*? She tried not to panic. "What charges could have possibly been invoked? Are you insinuating that asking a constable for directions to *legal* lodging is *illegal*?"

"I'm *insinuating* you were carrying a sizable amount of death-dealing substances that have never passed into our borders before."

Oyo. This was about her indigenous collection. "I wish to assure you, Mr. Ridley, every one of those jars were handled responsibly. They were collected seven months earlier from the Madhu forest west of Yamuna for the sole purpose of showcasing its effects to the Royal College of Physicians here in London. Peter insisted on parading my talent in the hopes of nudging me into a university. 'Tis a fanciful dream of mine and Peter is enough of a fool to think he can actually influence the professors into considering me as a student. To better explain his mind is this: when he points to a stallion and announces to all it is a pig, by Kali, it *has* to be a pig. Stallion? What stallion? All he sees is a pig."

He surveyed her for a prolonged moment. "Him and pigs in a pen aside, *Watkins*, Scotland Yard believes otherwise. Hence the charges and why I'm here."

This did not bode well. He was calling Peter a pig and her a Watkins. "Are these charges being crudely based on my being an Indian?" she demanded, knowing full well it was.

"It doesn't help."

"I do not understand," she argued. "I have done nothing! *Nothing, nothing*. Why would Scotland Yard think I have?"

Ridley's large hand tapped the desk. "Because none of them have an ounce of intelligence even in their pricks. Pardon the language. Rest assured, I am on your side and will get you out of this mess. The Royal College of Physicians where Dr. Watkins was scheduled to present your findings on uncategorized indigenous seeds has been verified. Apparently, you tinker with botany."

How typical of yet another man to think her plants were a hobby.

Hobbies didn't save lives. "Tinkering is for fairies, Mr. Ridley. I specialize in medicinal botany. Haphazard and nefarious though it may seem to those outside my horticultural sphere, one cannot offer solutions in reversing the effects of a poison without understanding the poison itself. Much like humans, nature savagely protects itself from predators, and plants are no different. I have studied and recorded well over eighty-seven instances in which—"

"No need to cite numbers." His voice grew ominous. "Here are the real ones: A gentleman and his wife walked into their viewing box to see a theatrical and never walked out of said box after what appears to be a lethal poisoning administered before the eyes of several hundred people. How does this relate to you? Their deaths occurred at the Surrey Theatre on Blackfriars Road, which happened on the fourteenth and you strolled into Scotland Yard on the *fifteenth* with a sizable bag of poisonous substances inquiring about a hotel across the street from that same theatre."

Her eyes widened.

The cackling accusations of superstitious women cradling fruit baskets as they whispered to each other, *Challo—her eyes are of the white man*, scraped into her head.

Everyone had always judged her for reasons that went far beyond her culture. She belonged to neither side. Her mother, whose dark, beautiful face had long bedimmed and disappeared like the veil of hers found floating in a river with no body, had once admitted to Jemdanee as a child that her father had been a British soldier who 'died' before he could offer marriage.

Being older, Jemdanee now knew her mother had knelt to what so many women in the hovels did to supplement a non-existent income: sold sexual favors.

So here she now was: a walking sexual favor being accused of murder.

Life had a very morbid sense of humor and she was no longer laughing.

Determined not to let the accusations or the panic crawl into her head, she remained what a street urchin of time gone by would be: calm. Deny, deny. "I would never use the secrets of the natural world against anyone. Not even those who deserve it, and there are quite a few that do."

She... probably should not have said that last part.

Cracking his knuckles one by one, Ridley angled the ledgers before him. "You appear relatively calm. Usually, this is about the time women sob profusely and drape themselves on the stone floor."

This one was accusing her of murder. "Why are you here, Mr. Ridley? Did Scotland Yard send you to further interrogate me?"

He snapped up a hand, whilst still paging with the other. "Let us be clear in one thing. I don't work for Scotland Yard. I only step in when their oversized thumbs no longer fit up their rears. They have an annoying tendency to do things differently here in England than they do in France and have too many regulations preventing them from doing what I do best: slamming heads against walls."

That explained the scars.

He gathered more ledgers. "I've been following a spattering of deaths over these past few weeks similar to what had occurred over on Blackfriars Road. They share one glaring common element and it isn't you."

Her stomach churned.

"A case like this has to be done right. Which is why I'm here. I know you didn't do it."

That was a touch reassuring coming from someone she didn't know. "Then why am I being held?"

"Because I don't represent the Crown or the court *or* Scotland Yard. But I do represent justice and there is one upper tiered man in Scotland Yard who does, too. He has arranged a two-hour lockdown of the theatre starting tomorrow night at eleven. At that time, you'll examine a tray of segmented oranges and the corpses who appeared to have consumed them. It's my hope you might be able to provide an assessment of your own related to whatever poison might have been used."

She lowered her chin, astounded. "I specialize in plants. I am *not* an anatomical physician."

"But you understand the effects of poison on said anatomy, do you not?"

This went far beyond anything she had learned from Limazah. "I have only studied deaths relating to animals brought to me by my Parsee teacher. We never studied its effects on humans."

"Yet Dr. Watkins insists your vast knowledge of botany is impressive enough to be applied before the Royal College of Physicians. Isn't that why he invested all of his time and his money into bringing you to London?"

She dragged in an adoring breath for the only soul who had ever respected what few men did in any female: her mind.

Peter held so much faith in her and was now *in jail* because of her.

She tried to demonstrate she was no longer a child, but life ruled over her like the wind blowing through a stack of papers. They never landed where they were supposed to. "I am confused as to what you are asking me to do."

Ridley shoved aside the remaining ledgers. "You represent a new generation capable of making the impossible possible and that is what I need right now. The question is: if I were to set the source before you, would you be able to identify the poison and how it was administered into the oranges? Could you do it? Is it possible?"

That would require more than a double boiler and... no. "Once a plant leaves its natural state, it makes it very difficult to decipher what it is. I am able to do it with ingredients that are steeped, but only through the sampling of non-lethal plants by way of taste. The tongue. Lethal ones, as you might imagine, make that impossible. What further complicates your assumption is that poisons are plant based, but there are countless toxins that are mineral based and I only specialize in flora."

He paused. "So there would be no deduction you could offer?"

"No. None."

He thudded a fist against the desk, still paging through ledgers.

Sensing she had more or less hanged herself, she cringed.

"Unto every god I believe in, Peter and I only arrived into London from Southampton on the morning of the fifteenth, not—"

"I know." His voice was resigned. "You were never on my list of suspects."

People were dead and Peter was in prison.

She *had* to right this. "If an assessment is what you require, Mr. Ridley, I would be more than willing to attempt one. Depending on how a plant or seed is steeped, dried kernels, roots or leaves might be present, but that is still hoping for too much. I might not—"

"You needn't worry." He shoved aside more ledgers, still looking for something he clearly could not find. He paged through the ledgers faster and faster.

She eyed him. "Whatever are you looking for?"

"Your log. It isn't where it's supposed to be." He dragged over another ledger, thudding it into place, and paged through that one.

He paused and hit the ledger. "They recorded you coming into Millbank a day later." He squinted. "I will look into that." Ripping out several other pages, he tucked one of them away and then slapped the remaining stack of shorn pages onto the desk. "*These* connect you to this prison."

He slung the satchel from the desk onto a chair and deposited the remaining ledgers into each drawer, slamming them shut one by one until the desk was clear. "By the time they decipher you've been erased from the logs, I'll ensure this conviction doesn't touch you. Scotland Yard was given ticking orders that everything in that theatre, including the bodies, be respectfully delivered to their families in two days. Which means tomorrow night, once you've rested well enough outside of this prison, you'll have a few hours to sift through a possible assessment of what toxin *might* have been used. I'm asking you to try."

A flicker of apprehension coursed through her. "A few hours? If there is anything to be found, it will take weeks."

"Weeks you do not have. The trial is in five days."

Trial?! "What realm of logic do you live in? Assessments take time."

"I specialize in defying logic. It's how a mind can crawl into the abyss and solve a crime without having ever been there." Removing a box of match sticks from his waistcoat pocket, he struck one against the attached flint. Hovering his bare hand unnervingly close over the flicking flame he cradled, he gathered the entire pile of parchment he had ripped from the ledgers and held their corners to the flame.

It smoked, curled, ignited and singed all the pages, smoke rising toward the low ceiling.

Jemdanee gaped at the fire and him, her pulse roaring. It was obvious he wasn't removing her legally. Which meant... they were going against the entire British government.

A government that didn't require very much to hang a Hindu who already had prior convictions.

Her mouth made an O. "Whatever are you doing?!" she rasped. "Unburn it. Unburn it, lest they think I have something to hide. *Unburn it*!"

"Trust in what I do, not *how* I do it." He tilted his head, observing the flames he still held in his bare hand before tossing it to the stone floor, scattering embers. "Accountability is in the eye of the beholder, and in this particular instance, I have to gouge out the eyes of those who disagree with me. The governor denied my request of issuing you a two-hour release to examine evidence in that theatre, so I am hereby arranging it myself. Trust me, Watkins. I have done this before."

She didn't like the way he kept calling her Watkins as if they were long-time colleagues in agreement as to what was about to happen next. Furthermore, his indifference to his own government superiors and an indifference to the fire on the floor made it very difficult for her to conclude that he was in any way trustworthy.

Optimism only went so far. "What level of deranged are you? There is no need for a fire parade that will bring in the brigade! You could have easily tucked those parchments into your coat and walked us out."

"Carrying evidence that proves I assisted in the escape of a convict is *not* advisable."

She gasped. "Turning me into a fugitive and burning down a building full of women is not advisable, either!"

He rounded the remaining flames of curling parchment on the floor, using his large boot to gather the fiery chaos into one neat pile. "Oh, yes. Heaven forbid we should ignite a building

full of prisoners who deserve to die. *That* would be criminal."
He half-nodded as if seeing it all in his head. "Though highly
entertaining and it *would* reduce the taxes."

'Twas obvious he saw humor in the suffering of others.

It riled her. It riled the anger of the eight-year-old scrapper
she had always, always tried to bury but never could. "No. *That*
would be murder," she choked out, rattling and rattling her
chains for emphasis. "For I have seen and spoken to these
women. Women, who I can assure you, are here for crimes that
involve a desperation to crawl out of a poverty few will *ever*
understand. You with your-your... *expensive coat*. A coat that
could easily feed twelve people, yet one you hoard like a pig by
wearing it on your back. We are not animals you can cook into
the porridge you so openly eat. I have no need to be rescued by a
man wearing two pistols and a dagger but no heart. Let all of
England file its charges and call me a Hindu witch. Let them! I
am not the first Indian to hang for such an injustice and won't be
the last, you son of an owl. Now take me back to my cell. Take
me, take me. For I want no part of this. *No part!*"

Raking his hair back with a rigid hand, he swung his massive
frame back toward her.

She froze.

The harsh lines of his rugged features strengthened as he
stared her down.

Her body and mind rippled from unwanted awareness.

She *might* have overreacted.

Knee-high leather boots slowly thudded against the stone
floor toward her. Holding her gaze, and one by one by one, he
fastened the brass buttons on his great coat, burying the two
pistols and dagger on his leather belt beneath the expensive
fabric, announcing a man of his power needed no weapon at all.

She braced herself for the strength the back of his hand
would bring.

He rounded her, looming like a temple, the tensing of his jaw
hinting at too many unspoken thoughts. "Never accuse me of
being heartless, Watkins. Although I drip calm, *inside* my rib
cage is *splintering*. All twenty four bones surrounding my heart,
not including the sternum. They cracked because of your
unkind words." His overly flat tone hinted he wasn't joking.

She swallowed, her palms growing moist as she attempted to

shut out any awareness of him lest the weakness in her knees give way to the trembling in her soul. Had he yelled, had he grabbed her, had he shook her, had he swore, had he acted like every man she had ever met who sought to claim power over her using any physical means, she might not have been so... affected.

The lethal and feral calm he exhibited was unnerving.

It was like a jaguar resting on a boulder high above her with its paw hanging over the edge, seeing her, yes, but having just eaten, decided to spare her from the intentions it had been born for.

He lowered his chin. "Are you calm enough to have a conversation?"

Jemdanee focused on the five brass buttons of his coat to keep herself calm. "*Haan.*"

"Good." He lingered for a pulsing moment. "You haven't been on the streets, but London is writing stories worthy of a gothic penny novel and they all think it's you. *You.* A brazen, nefarious, magic-wielding savage out of India carrying enough poison in her mystical carpet bag to take out an *entire* theatre full of 'respectable' people. That is the only evidence they need to put before a jury. Because barristers will do what they do best—lie—and... *off to the rope you go.* Do you understand?"

She averted her gaze, sensing her life was about to spiral toward a place she preferred not to mentally crawl into. For it was a morose place where pain was far greater than what her limbs were capable of holding. One that harbored a wretched helplessness of a time when people blankly walked past her outstretched hands, ignoring her existence and her suffering.

Whilst she had always, always tried to see the light and the good of people and in life by drowning in the beauty of nature's foliage and its vast wilderness that yielded so much promise, *this* was the reality she'd been born unto.

That she, a Hindu, could be hanged at any moment.

Ridley tilted his head downward and toward her. "Breathe."

Her vision blurred, mentally reliving when she was a child and her head was being held into a bucket of water against her will on the street and she *couldn't* breathe and she knew she was going to die. If it hadn't been for Peter, an Army surgeon, who had been passing through in his rickshaw when he hollered and staved off the group of adolescent Bengali boys who had been holding her face into water until she lost consciousness, Jemdanee knew she wouldn't have lived past the age of eight.

It was one of many teeth-clenching junctions of her life that threatened to shatter the strength of what held her soul together.

Everything compacted into a single breath that hit her like marble at full speed.

A disbelieving sob she'd been holding in for too many years escaped her, as she staggered against the chains holding her. People were dead and everyone thought she did it. A flurry of Hindi escaped her, a part of her needing to cling to all she had left: herself.

Ridley lingered, then leaned his head further downward and in, tapping up her chin. "Ey, ey. None of that. Look at me."

The genuine thaw of his deep voice made her lift her blurring gaze from his waistcoat up to his broad shoulders and up to his rugged face.

Remarkable amber eyes further restricted what little she had left of her own breath, prolonging a painful but intimate moment that could have taken place, not in a prison, but in a vast mosaic hall behind a banyon-carved screen.

The heated scent of peppery woodland cologne overtook her half-breaths between the wafts of burnt parchment that still smoked the air and made it hazy.

The gold in his soulful eyes flickered with intensity. "I already have two names and a motive. I'm merely hoping for a hatchet to drive it all into the wood. So stay calm and do your best to make an assessment, but don't panic if you can't."

Tears traced her cheeks and dripped toward her trembling lips and chin, realizing her life depended on naming a toxin out of a list of *thousands*. She fought against another sob, doubting what fate had planned. Very little water and too many useless hardened crusts of bread brought on a sudden delirium she could no longer fight.

Her knees buckled and she fell.

Ridley jumped and caught her in the bulk of his arms, jerking her upright with the rattle and whipping of iron. He swept her close, thudding her hard into the solid warm of his chest.

Chains draped between them, she quietly sobbed, collapsing all weight against him.

Large hands firmly held her in place. He smoothed her hair but said nothing.

Jemdanee pressed her cheek harder into his coat, trying to dig through blurring emotions of knowing proof of her innocence lay within a theatre hosting dead bodies. "What if I... cannot... find the source or... how it was... administered?" she choked out.

"Optimists die first." Ridley's taunt muscles shifted her against himself. "Once you accept and imagine the worst, everything else is easy. I do it all the time."

"Imagining the worst... helps... with... *nooothing*."

"Imagining the best won't prepare you for Armageddon." He smoothed her hair. "Worry not, little one. You will survive."

Little one?

Jemdanee paused, realizing the tensing bulk of his muscled arms were still around her and that her wet cheek was mashed into the solid warmth of his waistcoat as if she a lisping lady out of Belvadere in the anteroom of a Chowringhee district mansion with her pale feet on the sofa demanding the 'natives' tend to the swelling of her ankles.

She awkwardly pulled away and blinked away the wetness coating her lashes. "I am not little."

"Says the little one. You don't even reach my shoulder." Hooking fingers into his inner waistcoat pocket, he snapped out a handkerchief and angled it toward her. "Dig into that chatty optimism I earlier saw. Whatever it takes. Rattle it."

She half-breathed between lips that still quaked. The harsh set of that jaw and the lines of his rugged face bespoke of a man who had seen far more of life than she had.

Yet... he remained calm.

It was inspiring.

With a sniff that was anything but dainty, she attempted to lift her hands to take the handkerchief he offered, but winced against the heaving weight, unable to bring the chains above the thighs of her wool prison gown. "I cannot lift my hands." Her words sounded as pathetic as she felt.

His eyes grew surprisingly gentle. "Allow me." Angling closer, he set the soap scented linen near her cheek and smoothed it, his large knuckles guiding it. "I'll be removing your shackles in a moment. I am merely waiting for the key to arrive.

It wasn't in the custodian box where it was supposed to be."

The grazing of soft linen against her skin and the soothing yet peppery scent of his cologne tinged with cigars made her keenly aware that this one was extremely regimented and removed, but not unkind. His presence whispered of a dominating man with very high standards of sophistication edged with unnerving patience and... darkness.

She sensed many women found him attractive and knelt to that alone.

Flashes of a taut, muscled torso dewing with perspiration that slowly, slowly evaporated his cologne gripped her imagination into pressing her knees together beneath her wool skirts.

Despite her own attraction to the mysterious darkness that ominously clung to his words, his tone and his eyes, hinting of an unending strength no human ought to possess, she knew that cross pollination with the likes of this one was not advisable.

She had trouble taming her own life.

What made her think she could tame this one?

Not wanting to engage the thought of how an overly serious man like him reached *his* crest during lovemaking, she edged back and back, rattling her chains in doing so. "I sense you are full of compassion and I thank you," she managed.

"Never thank me," he rumbled out. "In truth, compassion is a damnable flaw in my line of work. If offered to the wrong person, the result is a slit throat and hard landing at the bottom of a well."

And she thought Peter lacked the optimism to get through the hour. "It would seem you only ever think about Armageddon."

"Which is why I'm good at what I do." The subtle emotion in his rugged features faded. Removing a pocket watch by its fob, he noted the time with the flick of his thumb that opened the gold casing.

Rotating the watch back and forth against his thumb as if thinking, he shoved it back into his waistcoat. Brows still drawn, he scanned her designated prison gown and tsked. "How have you and that tiny, tiny frame not fallen over beneath all the weight of those chains and the wool?"

She tried not to grouch about being called tiny twice and little once. "If only the chains and the wool were the problem. A female prisoner was tasked to lace me into a most ill-fitting corset that is burning into my skin like red ants."

He rolled his eyes. "I never understood the preoccupation with corsets. There are countless other ways to restrict a woman's breathing and it doesn't require money at all."

She paused.

"That was a grand attempt at humor. Feel free to laugh in an hour."

She gave him a withering look. "You may want to avoid humor, Mr. Ridley. It does not suit the pessimism you cling to and only insinuates disrespect."

"You needn't worry. Unlike the rest of these Christian ankle-biters, you'll find me to be incredibly respectful of you and your culture."

"Yet you speak of restricting a woman's breath."

Lowering his chin, he pointed. "Don't make me admire your wit. It won't end well."

She met his finger and then his gaze. "It certainly has not started well, either."

"Fortunately for you, Watkins, I prefer my mangoes ripened."

Her lips parted at what she surmised was an insult. "Being that you are from London, I doubt you ever even *consumed* a mango."

"Oh, I've eaten all sorts of fruit. Though it has been some time since I've picked up a basket."

She almost leaned back but the weight of the chains prevented it.

"I wouldn't advise papayas," he rumbled out. "They're a bit *rancid*."

Her mouth opened.

"I am, of course, referring to my former wife." He remained serious but his expression was one of exasperated misfortune. "Nothing but yellow, orange and pink juice everywhere. That demon of a red-head once backhanded me with a vase and *that* was on a good day." He grimaced. "Parliament cored that one and pushed through the only good they ever did for me as a tax-paying British citizen: a divorce. I've been celebrating ever since with expensive cigars and champagne."

Jemdanee's mouth further opened. He was comparing his wife, his marriage, and his divorce to smashed fruit, cigars and champagne. All whilst remaining completely serious.

Stepping back, Ridley cracked his knuckles. "Forgive the rant. Poison-infused oranges sitting in a theatre made my mind gallop." Propping up the collar of his coat, he paced, the ankle length great coat billowing from each move. "I need the name of the constable who arrested you. For some reason it wasn't in your file. Do you remember the name?"

She lingered, her hands fisting. "All too well."

Ridley paused, glancing at her. "Did something happen?" He edged back in, intently searching her face. "If so, I need to know."

She swallowed knowing it could have been worse. She could have been raped. Instead, she was emotionally raped. "He had me stand naked for over an hour in a backroom where he left me. I was not given a right to clothes until a warder kindly covered me with his coat and hollered for prison attire to be brought in."

His features darkened. "I want a name."

Some men deserved to be backhanded. "Mr. Pickering."

He set his shoulders, remolding his rugged features to a gentlemanly calm. "Pickering is an opium addict and former soldier out of India. To explain his behavior would be to explain nothing, but he lost his wife and newborn child during an arson that occurred in Ambala at the hands of the natives. You needn't worry, Watkins. I'll rip his ear off. There are a few questions I have pertaining to your log."

A part of her felt honored that he would even bother.

"Look at me."

She did.

"Did he attempt to touch you?"

She shook her head and kept shaking it, grateful.

"Good. It means he gets to keep his other ear." His masculine face marked with resolve as he thudded a fist to his chest in mock greeting. "Meet your personal retinue compiled into one: *me*. As of two days ago, your name and likeness appeared on every broadsheet sold on the street. You can read about it in *The Morning Herald*, *The Times*, and *The Observer* at a mere seven copper pennies. Congratulations. You have achieved the highest level of infamy in London since the Radlette Murder that inspired the rhyme for crime: *They cut his throat from ear to ear, his head they battered in, his name was Mr. William Weare, he lived in Lyons Inn."* He leaned in and offered, "I can only imagine the whimsical little rhymes they will be chanting in your name."

She gaped. "How is that legal? How can they do that prior to a trial? How can they—"

"It's known as 'journalism'. They own everyone's name, regardless of the source or the lies they tell to sell papers, and I've been living with it since I was twelve."

She sensed he was not exaggerating.

He eyed her. "Given the public has a tendency to believe everything they read as if they were the tablets of God delivered by Moses, you'll end up dead if anyone sees you on the street. Which is why wherever I go, you go. When I ask a question, you answer. When I tell you to do something, you do it. Follow orders and you'll have the one thing few get: my respect. Agreed?"

She gripped her skirts hard to keep herself and her chains from rattling. What choice had she? Being lynched was *not* an option. "Agreed."

Turning, he stalked toward the chair set before the desk. Lifting it, he effortlessly swung it toward her, bringing it close, and set it with an informal clatter beside her.

Unbuttoning his great coat while holding her gaze, his hands curved over the back of the wood and on its top again. He tapped it. "We are on an uncompromising schedule and I know the weight of those chains are exhausting you. Come. Sit."

This man was *not* oblivious to his own intensity.

She awkwardly trailed toward him, trying not to wince against the iron dragging and digging into her skin. Not meeting his gaze, she turned and seated herself, a breath escaping her as the weight of the chains now rested against the chair as opposed to her body.

The raw chafing of her wrists pulsed. It didn't matter. She was getting out.

A knock came to the door making them pause.

He tapped a forefinger against his lips, signaling her to be silent.

She half-nodded, stilling the chains so they wouldn't make any noise.

Removing his pistol from the holster, he cocked it and crossed to the door, scuffing his boots to a halt. With the tightening flex of muscles that strained his coat, Ridley pointed the primed pistol directly at the closed timber panel. "*Enter.*"

Jemdanee felt her body coil in dread knowing she couldn't even help him.

She was chained.

The door edged open with a rusty creak that pierced the silence like a rooster getting its throat slit.

CHAPTER TWO

A warder peered past the oak paneling and snapped up a key. "Yardley had it."

Jemdanee almost sagged off the chair knowing it was the key to her shackles.

"Someone smack that idiot to *La Manche*." Ridley uncocked the pistol with the flick of his thumb and shoved it back into his holster. "The logs have already been addressed. The moment we leave, reorganize it back to what it was lest they be on to it."

"Yes, sir."

Taking the key from the warder, Ridley pointed. "Inform Turner we only have seventeen minutes lest we all get dirked and join the inmates. Where the hell is he?"

"Vacating the last of the posts. Flank turned into a bit of a nuisance. He kept asking about returning her to the cell, so I told him I was taking over and ensured he didn't come this way."

"Good. Keep him on the east-end. *Now go*."

"Yes, sir." The warder stepped out, closing the door.

Adjusting his open coat, Ridley strode toward her in silence. He rounded her, the faded leather belt on his hip shifting the weapons attached to it.

The discolored leather and the notches near its buckle were stretched.

It whispered of a man who stood at his own bedside each

night, fisting the end of the leather and yanking it loose from his trousers to set it onto a table. A table whose wood was probably as equally scuffed from the amount of times he had laid his weapons on it.

This one was a man dedicated to ritual habit.

His belt alone, heavily faded in its appearance, breathed that truth.

Ridley squatted before her, his muscled thighs expanding against his wool trousers as he chinked the manacles. Leaning in, his large scarred hands slipped up her restrained wrists.

His features tightened. "These were fastened wrong."

Was there a *right way* to fasten them? "I thought being in discomfort was the premise."

He stared her down. "Your skin shouldn't be rubbing off. Why didn't you say something?"

She swallowed in an attempt to ignore the heat of his taunt, muscled thighs possessively holding hers with his knees through her wool prison skirts. "If I were to announce my discomfort to the world every time it happened, my tongue would fall out."

A breath escaped him. He angled the bands of the shackles toward himself. "Even the bolt was turned inward. These bastards might as well have put you in a shrew's fiddle and a knee splitter."

A shrew's fiddle? *A knee splitter?* Yet her people were accused of being heathens?

"Hold still." Gritting his teeth, he turned the key in the padlock bolting her confined wrists together.

With a *clank*, it unhinged.

Setting the lock aside onto the desk with a *clack*, he quickly rose and, standing before her, slid her hands out of the iron, unraveling the long chain. "Lean forward."

She did so and paused. Her face now hovered near the flap of his trousers that had been uncovered by his open great coat. The textile fabric was form-fitted against a dormant but still very sizable indication of that male fertilizing organ consisting of a different sort of pollen.

Her knees instinctively locked together, unable to look at much else. That flap was the size of a map holding the world together with only a few buttons and… it was asking for directions.

She leaned far back.

Ridley jerked her back toward himself. "*Ey.* Hold still."

"Your stamen."

"My what?"

She scrunched her nose, realizing she had used a botanical term for his lower half. "Your reproductive organ. You keep wagging it in my face."

He rolled his eyes. "Pardon the wagging, but every man has one. Or did your plants never tell you that?"

She veered her gaze to his arm. He probably thought she was nose-to-the-book virgin. Little did he know her nose had been in far, far more than books despite her *being* a virgin.

Well before she'd even turned eight, she'd seen more cocks on the streets of Calcutta than she had *real* roosters.

Not all nefariously, of course.

Too many men in the district of hovels where she had lived went to the same mud wall to piss regardless of who had walked by. Some even tried to artistically draw things with their urine and then grandly gesture toward it as if they had discovered *uranium*.

She had stories. "My plants tell me more than you think. If they were here, they might point out that you unbuttoned your coat to flaunt your virility."

"I thought we were getting along." Angling his lower half away from her, his hand gripped the back of the chair behind her hard. He leaned down so they were almost nose to nose and directly eye to eye. "I'm thirty-two, Watkins. Count the years between us and be certain to include your toes. When I was eighteen, you were four. That turns off the imagination and everything below the nose. I unbuttoned my coat for one reason: *mobility.* These English coats are no different from a corset and are too expensive to rip. My advice? Embrace the maturity you lack knowing I have enough for the entire nation."

She wasn't doing very well transitioning into the Western world.

"Eyes to the elbow." He flicked her cheek hard with a forefinger and leaned over, removing the iron and remaining chain from around her corseted waist.

Her cheek now stung and she knew she had no one to blame but herself.

With a loud clatter he deposited the long chain and iron bar onto the nearby desk.

She rolled her wrists against the raw swelling and eyed him knowing she ought to say something. "I thank you."

"You're quite fortunate the bolts didn't gouge you anymore than they did. It could have damn well gone to the bone. Who put these on you?"

Oyo. "Mr. Pickering."

He said nothing.

With a loud clatter, he whipped the rest of the chain and iron bar onto the desk with the grit of teeth that had nothing to do with its weight, sending flecks of veneered wood from its surface into the air.

She jumped.

Turning back, he leaned in again and carefully rolled up her sleeves to ensure they weren't touching her skinned wrists. "He will know your pain."

She watched him, those cool, casual words unsettling her. She dared not fathom what happened when a man like him lost control. "Leave it be. I have endured worse."

"Many of us have. That doesn't make it acceptable." He stepped back, checking his watch.

He paused and tucked it away. Adjusting his great coat around his muscled frame, he fastened all three buttons, tugging it over his trousers and glanced back at her, his profile illuminated by the lantern. "*Up*, little one. Your prison attire has to be removed."

She stood, her pulse roaring. "You wish for me to remove it now?"

"Yes. Now." Ridley rounded the desk and opened the satchel, removing a well-folded gown. Stalking back toward her, he held it out. "Put this on."

She snatched the clothing from his hand, the billowing material unraveling like a sail.

He swung toward the door, his great coat swiveling against his large frame, offering her his broad back. Pulling out a hemp rope, he knotted it twice. "You have three minutes."

Recognizing she had better rustle as much clothing as possible, she frantically stripped her assigned wool dress that had been stitched with a prison number by untying all strings binding it together and let it drop to the floor, leaving on the tightly laced corset.

Her wrists burned. They were a touch more raw and reddened than she realized.

Pulling the calico gown she'd been given over herself while her long black braid kept falling in between the fabric, she grudgingly pushed that braid back out. She shimmied into the rest of the plain taupe gown, adjusting it into place.

Eyeing him, she quickly sniffed under each arm and cringed. Any hint of jasmine oil had long faded and given way to an earthy scent she hoped he couldn't smell.

Realizing the hooks were in the back of the gown, she paused. Western clothing had never made any sense. In her opinion, they had been designed by a loon in need of a monkey.

The hooks fastened in the back.

As if any human arm could bend that far.

Her hands dropped against the awkward position. Noting the upper rounds of her bronzed breasts were still on full display, she tried to yank up her décolletage to cover both, but it kept falling given its weight.

How was she to even reach the back against the corset she'd been laced into?

"One minute," he rumbled out.

Eck! Clinging to the heavy, lopsided and ballooning calico gown in an attempt to keep it above her half-exposed rear (she had no chemise…), she puffed out an exasperated breath, recognizing she had no idea how to affix the gown or keep it up. She'd only worn a Western gown and a corset twice in her lifetime.

There was a reason.

She adjusted the massive weight of the gown, but could only keep it in place by setting her hands against her breasts. Which still did not address… the rear.

Western gowns ought to be burned.

At this point she didn't care if he saw her shoulders and rear. Others had seen worse given she always swam nude in the river and she wasn't staying in prison. "I require assistance," she admitted, molding the gown against herself.

He set his shoulders but did not turn. "Are you granting me permission to turn?"

She blinked. Was it too early to admit that this one *fascinated* her? How was it that he, a six foot three male in a position of power with three weapons strapped to his thighs, would even think to ask a female Hindu for permission in a world that never did?

Overly serious and grudging though he was, she liked him.

She didn't even mind that he was fourteen years older.

She'd been through enough in life to be at least thirty-two herself. Maybe even thirty-three.

Pinching her lips, she pertly tugged the front of the gown down just enough to reveal a sliver of her upper breasts to showcase she wasn't his version of four.

She set her chin regally. "Permission is granted and yours, Mr. Ridley." *I am not by any means four.*

Tucking the knotted rope back into his pocket, he swung toward her. Skimming her bare shoulders and the exposed upper rounds of her breasts sitting above the corset, he paused.

Their eyes locked and her heart seemed to rush to her head and every toe.

His steady gaze bore into her with the heat of sandstone.

It was the only acknowledgement she needed as a *woman.*

She almost, almost smiled but thought that would be over-flirting. "It must have fallen."

His eyes grew flat and unreadable. "Along with whatever respect you have for yourself. Wit over tit, Watkins. Pull it up."

It wasn't in the least bit fair that the first white man she genuinely didn't mind flirting with, refused to even flirt back. The gods knew how to laugh. "I cannot attempt to cover myself when I am asking for assistance in garbing myself." She was now trying to argue her way out of being silly. "Look, look. There is more of this gown than there is of me." She rustled it twice for emphasis.

Ice crusted into those feral eyes.

She drew in her lips, awkwardly tightening her hold on the dress. How was it without even a word he could make her scramble to do what he wanted? Peter would insist she marry this one for that alone.

Jemdanee dragged the gown upward, securing it into place. "Armageddon."

"Exactly." Rounding her, he leaned in from behind, towering well above her and gripped her gown, further holding it into place. "You may want to reconsider your earlier commentary about meat. It reduces cravings."

An unwelcome heat crept into her cheeks.

He swept her unraveling braid out of the way and over her shoulder, his calloused fingers skimming her exposed brown skin.

She almost fainted as uncontrolled sensations radiated down to her breasts and to her belly and well below it. A shaky breath escaped her.

It sounded loud even to her own ears.

With the tug of both hands, Ridley jerked her back toward himself against his body hard, startling her. "We battle gravity, Watkins, so try to do a better job holding it up. Less of that heavy breathing or you're likely to faint and I already have a satchel to carry."

Although her ear and cheek tipped toward that alluring, dominating heat, she yanked up enough of the gown to permit him to continue. "Why do you continue to call me Watkins?"

"Is that not your name, *Watkins*?"

"No. I only embraced Peter's family name out of respect for all that he has done for me. This mere Watkins business, as you use it, insinuates I am a man. I prefer you respect that I am not. You may address me as Jemdanee. Few have that honor."

He yanked the gown of her back together. "I prefer we not become overly acquainted. My profession blurs too many lines as it is." Hook by hook from the bottom, he fastened everything into place. His large warm fingers moved fast, making her fully aware that he was trying to speed his way through it.

Glancing back at him, curiosity made her ask, "Why were you tying knots into that rope?"

His profile remained reserved. "It's how I think."

"With knots?"

"The world is full of them." He tugged some of the hooks a bit more vigorously, maneuvering the last of the hooks together. "It may fall from your shoulders given your small frame." He wedged the material together. "I swiped it from a corpse."

She froze, her skin crawling.

"This is where you laugh. You know... ha, ha? I was joking."

And she thought her mind prevented her from being normal. "*Arrey*. That was *not* amusing. Nor did you deliver it with the pun it so desperately needed."

"I disagree. Humor is born of darkness. Crown me." He patted her dress. "*Ici*. I know another language, too. Four, actually, not including one I invented myself. So don't think you're singular." He turned her around with the nudge of her shoulders, rolled up her sleeves again to ensure they weren't touching her skinned wrists and stepped back.

She eyed him, her skin still crawling. "This had better not have been stripped from the limbs of a corpse, Ridley."

"'Tis *Mr.* Ridley, if you please. Respect your elders."

She almost stuck out her tongue. "Karma is real."

"It certainly is." He tapped the sleeve of her gown. "I'll leave its extensive history to your vast imagination. Look for blood spatter. Last I knew there was plenty of it."

Ha. Ha. Haaaaaa.

He paused, as if hearing something, and swung toward the door.

It creaked open, revealing a very young, lanky warder. "All posts have been vacated."

"I owe you, Turner." Ridley gestured toward the desk. "Clean up the room and sweep it before you let anyone back here." Swiping up her gown from the floor, he rolled it and shoved it into the satchel, swinging it over his shoulder. "Watkins. Prepare to move."

She almost said, '*Yes, sir!*' as if he were a sergeant and she the cadet.

She bustled after him.

Ridley stalked toward the door, his great coat billowing as he approached the warder. "Any complications?"

"None. Though I do suggest avoiding Newman. That one can't be trusted not to ring the bell, even if paid. He'll be making his way through the corridor in a few minutes, keeping to his usual round. There is a small side hall and door for you to dart into and wait. The moment he trudges through, round the corner and wait in the storage room on the far end. No one ever goes there and it's removed from the main corridors. Stay in that room until I knock. After that, you're free to run."

"Excellent. I'll have Shelton deliver the agreed upon coin to you and the others. Go buy that dog of yours a full leg of mutton and a turkey."

Turner eyed him. "I don't have a dog, Ridley."

Ridley paused. "Who the hell are you living with?"

"My younger sister. She came in from Bodmin. You met her

briefly. Remember?"

"But you always mention feeding a poodle."

"She *is* unwed for a reason. I call her 'my poodle'."

Ridley tsked. "Never insult your sister, Turner. All women are beautiful until they become your wife."

They both snorted.

Jemdanee almost crossed her arms. This Ridley clearly thought he controlled wit, the universe and everyone in it.

He pointed at her. "*Se dépêcher*. That, Watkins, is French." He disappeared.

Astounded that she was getting out of prison with the blessings of every warder, she scrambled out after him lest anyone decided otherwise. Noting he was already half-way down the narrow corridor, she gathered her cumbersome heavy skirts and bustled after him, wishing for the lightweight flow of her sari.

In between bustling, she attempted to daintily wedge herself beside him.

When he didn't say anything, she whispered up at his towering frame, "I am humbled and honored by everything you are doing for me. If I may be of any service to you outside of—"

"Watkins?"

She hesitated. "*Jee?*"

"Quiet." He swung the satchel onto his other broad shoulder.

Footsteps echoed down the adjoining corridor before them.

Jerking to a halt, which made her collide into him, Ridley grabbed her and shoved her back hard toward an inset doorway, pressing his own body against hers and the door. "Don't even twitch," he rasped, the heat of his breath grazing the top of her forehead. "Everything echoes."

She froze.

The leather belt holding his weapons and the pulsing heat of his muscled body dug into her harder as the footsteps continued.

This man was no different from a god.

He was molding the world around them to bring her justice. For her.

For someone he didn't even know prior to this moment.

It was inspiring.

Her softening gaze lifted to meet his and to her exasperated dismay, the fluttering of her heart further betrayed her nail-scraping, lip-biting, knees-digging attraction.

It was getting *worse*.

The curve of his strong throat which was hidden beneath the knotted silk of his cravat beckoned as the heated peppery scent of his cologne seemed to drag itself across her lips. She felt like she was nestling against a sun-scorched wall and setting both hands against it not caring if her skin blistered.

If they weren't standing in the dim, dingy corridor of a prison, she would have grabbed him by the hair and kissed him until he admitted eighteen was the new thirty.

He lowered his gaze to hers.

Jemdanee swallowed, dreading he could hear her womanly thoughts. What did a man like this see when he looked at her? Brown skin? Crooked teeth? Or her lapis lazuli blue eyes that hinted of a white father she would never know?

Wobbling on her booted heels, her hands jumped to his waist to balance herself against the awkward position they held. She winced at the shuffling sound.

Her fingers twitched at the echo.

The footsteps paused.

Ridley's rugged features wavered as he searched her face, his breaths mingling with her own.

Her pulse roared.

The footsteps kept moving. They faded and disappeared.

She sagged.

Ridley gave her a pointed look and pressed his belt into her *hard* in reprimand. "You almost gave us away."

She winced against the pinch and poked his chest hard with two fingers, ensuring he felt each one. "Cease using the belt like a poker. I could have sneezed but *did not*."

"I could have left you in this prison but *did not*." Thudding the door behind them twice with a rigid hand as if displeased with her, he pushed away and kept walking, his great coat sweeping back into the narrow corridor as he disappeared.

The tingling in the pit of her stomach continued well after he had turned the corner. She rubbed at the area beneath her breasts where his belt had pinched.

He was as elusive as he was damnably rude. Why did she like him?

"*You were supposed to follow,*" he called in a riled whisper. "*Bustle it.*"

She cringed and rustle, rustle, rustled the oversized gown and herself around the corner after him, feeling like a balloon in need of inflation.

He yanked out a wad of black lace from his satchel and snapped it out. "Cover those blue eyes."

It was the first time he hinted he had noticed her eyes at all.

She couldn't tell if it was a compliment. She set her chin in case it was. "I am more than a pair of eyes."

"That you are. You're a fugitive wanted for the murder of seven people *with* eyes."

She winced at the body count the poisonings had amassed. No wonder they were looking to hang her. Taking the veil from him, she draped the black lace over her head with the turn of her chaffed wrists, burying herself in the fabric that barely allowed her to see through. She lingered, now eerily feeling very much like a harem girl in a sandstone palace awaiting inspection.

He adjusted it and leaned back. "It blurs enough." He gave her a pointed look. "Now pray to your gods we make it out of Millbank without having to use everything attached to my belt."

A breath escaped her.

He grabbed her hand and tugged her toward a door at the far end of the wall. Guiding her inside, he shut the door and leaned against it, encasing them in pulsing silence.

They were now in a small lantern lit room whose walls displayed racks of chains, shields and hip-high swords.

Because a prison wasn't imposing enough.

"We wait." Removing a cigar from his leather casing, he struck a match and lit it, the shadows and light playing against his rugged features. "Feel free to talk, but keep your voice low." The glint of a gold ring flashed from his finger.

Jemdanee blinked realizing the glint was a wedding band.

He paused. "Would you rather I not smoke?" he asked from behind the flame he held.

She shook her head. "Plenty of men smoke hookahs before me. I myself smoke *bidis*." When Peter wasn't looking.

"Then what is it?"

She scrunched her nose and leaned in. "Are you not divorced?" Not that she was curious. *Yet she was.*

He tossed the match and puffed on the cigar to further light it, the tobacco hissing. "I am." His jaw tightened as he released smoke through his nostrils. "I divorced Elizabeth on the grounds of adultery three years ago. She was involved with five other men."

She lowered her chin. What sort of woman would go to five others after meeting him? *Or dare to*, for that matter? "*Saali*. It would seem she created her own harem."

He drew in more smoke. "I'll leave the irony of that out of this conversation."

"Did your heart have a need to love again?" she ventured, gesturing toward the ring.

He eyed her. "I never re-married. A man like me only chains himself once."

A grand statement made in a storeroom full of chains that hinted every woman on every continent had lost their opportunity. "I do not understand. Why do you still wear her ring?"

"I honor what once was." He tapped it. "It's a tombstone."

How very, very… Ridley-esque. "Why honor her memory if she violated your physical and spiritual being?"

He dragged in a mouthful of smoke before misting it out. "Passion comes in many guises." His expression became one of pained tolerance as he fingered his cigar and tapped the building ash off. "The greater the passion, the more outrageous it gets. The vase I didn't mind. It was the men."

There was something wrong with this one. "None of that speaks of passion or love, *phaujee*. Using an object to physically hurt another is better known to the world as *violence*. Have you been to India?"

He leaned in. Lifting her veil, he wound a lock of her loosened black hair around his finger and tugged it. Hard.

She winced against the sting of her scalp and slapped his hand, glaring. "Why not fasten the chains again and attach what you British call a knee splitter?" she hoarsely whispered, gesturing to the walls around them.

He dragged in another breath of tobacco, his eyes flickering with an amusement the rest of him did not show. "Don't lecture me. I've seen too much of life and I am what I am because I am. People drown in lakes all the time, but it hardly keeps the rest of us from enjoying the water."

Jemdanee squinted. "I do not understand your analogy."

He puffed on the cigar again in agitation, the tobacco hissing. "Pray you never will." He checked his watch again. Taking in another quick drag of his cigar, he turned his head and breathed it out between teeth, keeping his voice low. "I had the servants put fresh linen on the bed. For your safety, your room will adjoin mine and the door will remain open at all hours except for when you're bathing or dressing."

Her lips parted. Heat rose from her chest to her face. "You insist I cover myself and eat meat to reduce the cravings, yet I am to slumber in a room adjoining yours?"

"I'm not that sort of man. The only time I'll ever go into your room is *never*." He stuck his cigar in his mouth, letting it dangle. "So don't beg."

She slowly shook her head, knowing however many days they were going to be together was going to bring trouble. "What about Peter?" she whispered.

His features darkened. "What about the arm he broke? Your Dr. Watkins deserves at least four years in prison for that."

Four years? This one didn't appear to like Peter. "He has duties in Calcutta and the Field Marshal made it very clear that his position depends on a timely return. It is how he earns his money given he no longer has his inheritance. Can you not help him in the same manner you are helping me?"

He quietly thudded the boot, gesturing down toward it. "He stays beneath it."

The problem with this man was she didn't know when he was or wasn't being serious. "I am quite certain he did not mean to break the arm of the constable," she whispered.

He dragged in a breath of smoke. "You don't appear to know your *pita* very well do you?"

She swallowed, not at all liking the direction this conversation was going. "I know him far better than you think. Peter is a very well-respected Army surgeon. How is he even being held in any prison given his rank in the government? Do you know how many lives depend on him? Too many to fill a prison. I feel nothing short of guilt knowing he brought us into London given they refused to give me a seat in a classroom back in Calcutta. A seat I know they will *never* offer me here in London, either, yet he stubbornly wanted to give me what no one else would: an opportunity."

He shifted his jaw. "Is that what he told you?"

She blinked. "Did Peter do something other than break an arm?"

He said nothing.

Peter, what did you do? "He is all I have and compassionately enabled me to survive the disappearance of my mother. Please. I would be grateful for any assistance you might offer him. I am not one to beg, Mr. Ridley, but for him, I would."

No longer meeting her gaze, he rolled his cigar between fingers. "I'll send a missive to Finkle."

"*Finkle?*" She almost snorted but feared it would echo out of the small room they were in. "I might have met his cousin, *Flank*," she whispered. "You British certainly have names deserving of yourselves."

He tapped off more ash. "Finkle isn't his real name. He and I pretend we don't know each other in the name of getting things done. Much like I'm going to pretend I don't know you when this is done."

This was promising. "Dare I ask how long I will be bound to you?"

The rolling of his cigar stopped. "Bound isn't the right word, Watkins." He released smoke through his nostrils. "Whether you find the source or not, we aren't taking any chances by letting you go to trial. The newspapers have already tainted enough minds to ensure no fair outcome will result, leading to a biased jury who will only see a poison-toting Hindu. Sadly, that is your reality, Watkins, because too many people on the vile side of bigotry seem to forget that in the end, we all turn the same color in the ground: *bone white*. Which is why in three days, I'll be packing you on a night ship to Calcutta all paid for by yours truly with paperwork granted by your fairy godfather Finkle. He and I have already had this discussion. You're not hanging for someone else's crime and London can kiss my middle finger because *that* is where this is going. So chin up. You're in good hands."

Kali only knew she wanted to lift both hands to the glory of his rugged face and touch that overly serious countenance in reverence. He had earned it.

Not that she would do it.

A knock made them pause. "You're free to run," Turner called.

Ridley dashed out the cigar, shoving it into his satchel and yanked open the door.

Getting out of the imposing massive brick structure and its multiple towers proved to be one that required a map that was clearly in his head.

They walked in fast silence until eventually, they merely walked out into the night by unlatching a massive door and letting it shut behind them.

He propped up his collar and jogged past. "Move."

She glanced around in disbelief. There was no one in the walled portico. It was as if he had erased every human in sight. "Are there no *chowkidars*?" she whispered, glancing around, half-expecting them. Realizing he probably didn't know what she had asked, she added, "Guards."

"They are all where they should be: indisposed. *Now move.*"

She darted after him, clinging to the veil which the night wind threatened to pull.

A liveried footman opened the door of an unmarked carriage just outside the gates.

Ridley tossed up the satchel to the driver. "Razor the gown and everything in it."

"Yes, sir."

"We ride to the farthest outskirts and then back again. Only pull into the carriage house once assured we haven't been followed. Signal me of anything and have additional pistols primed and on the ready."

"Yes, sir."

It was obvious that Mr. Ridley was the master of a very dark and very twisted universe. One he controlled with the flip of a collar and the thud of his leather boot.

She liked him!

CHAPTER THREE

Peering past the open door of a sizable, luxurious, black-lacquered carriage worthy of a dark prince sent by Rahu, Jemdanee noted through the lopsided lace hanging over her face that no one was in it.

Not even a Hyderabadi cricket.

Why did the thought of them being alone unsettle, entice and thrill her?

Ridley veered in and grabbed her waist hard from behind, hoisting her high up and into the carriage, startling her. "It's not that complicated." He released her onto the landing and tugged her skirts down into place over her legs, smoothing them.

She seated herself near the window and eyed him. "Where is our destination?"

"The longest route to rest. Nothing happens until tomorrow night." He hopped up, swaying the carriage with his weight, and snapped his fingers, pointing her to another area. "The other side, if you please."

She scrambled over to where he had pointed.

The door slammed behind them, encasing them in the lone flickering kerosene light within the coach that barely illuminated the velvet-lined space.

Leaning over, he ensured the curtains on the windows were closed.

Falling onto the seat next to her, he adjusted his leather belt and stretched muscled legs out, thudding his large leather boots on the seat across from them. He picked up a wool cap laid on the cushion and pulled it onto his head.

He held out several bundles wrapped in handkerchiefs. "For you. Eat."

The carriage rolled forward, swaying them.

Food! "I thank you." Her hands grabbed the bundles as she frantically unwrapped each one. With trembling fingers, she shoved the fresh cheese (mmmmmmmmmmm), an apple (divine, divine, divine) and a massive loaf of fresh soft bread into her mouth, glorying in its overwhelming combination of uplifting flavors.

It was like being eight again and realizing food was real and that it had flavor.

She chewed and chewed frantically and shoved more and more bread into her mouth. It was all there was left.

"Don't choke." His tone softened barely enough to hint that he meant it.

She paused, glancing toward him, and felt like an animal shoving its head into a bucket of slop with saliva dripping from all ends. She slowed her chewing to a far daintier appearance and tucking the last of the bread into her mouth, swallowed.

She winced against the discomfort which the dryness of too much bread had brought.

"Eating too fast will result in esophageal constriction." He held out a flask with the tilt of his wrist.

This one thought of everything. Including the nuances of the esophagus. "Is it tea?"

He snorted. "No one carries tea in a flask."

Offended, she countered, "They do in India."

He rolled his tongue against the inside of his cheek. "It's brandy." He held it out again. "But I give you permission to pretend it's tea."

Permission, indeed. She hardly needed two fathers. "Have you nothing else?"

"No." His mouth thinned. "I didn't think to bring my chef and a sideboard. Maybe the next time you get arrested."

She tsked. "I am not being ungrateful. I simply prefer not to partake in any form of inebriating drinks. I am overly wild as it is."

He gave her a withering look. "Your idea of wild is my idea of boring."

She poked his arm. "You would be the first to tease, but I once made a *bhang lassi* from the buds of a cannabis out of my greenhouse, and lost more than a day and a night. Apparently, I climbed a tree and refused to come down. I remember none of it and *that* is no easy feat. I blame myself for being what I always am: overly generous. I crushed in far more *bhang* than I did *lassi*, so to speak. Peter was livid. I could have chosen a river instead of that tree and this conversation would have never taken place. I have since learned to avoid anything that might alter the state of my mind. My mind is already altered. By life. I therefore only, only partake in juice pulp, tea, cow's milk or goat's milk. No others."

"*Goat's milk*?" The shudder in his voice was apparent. "Here. You've earned it."

She shook her head and kept shaking it. "Not unless you want all of the trees to bend from my weight."

The gold of his eyes flickered with renewed interest. "Do you fear yourself or the brandy?"

She puffed out a breath. "I have never tried brandy, so I cannot say, but I do fear another episode of *bhang lassi*. A part of me knows I will only do what I always do: overindulge. I call it overcompensating for a time when I had nothing. I can never take one sliver of cheese. I need fourteen in both hands and in every pocket. I apply that to everything in my life."

It was why she was forever getting into trouble. She tried to nudge boulders over a ledge whose distance she couldn't always gauge. "Few will ever point out their own flaws, but I will be the first to admit I carry the greatest one of all. I deny myself nothing and regret everything."

Ridley quirked a brow. "Allow me to introduce myself. My name is Control."

She feigned surprise. "Allow me to introduce *myself*. My name is None."

He unscrewed the flask and held it out. "I think it time you learn how to trust yourself. You have bread lodged in your throat." He leaned in. "If you never learn the art of control, you'll always be up in that tree and those branches won't hold you for long. You don't want a broken neck."

That was a challenge if she ever heard one.

He leisurely swigged it as if drinking water and held it out, holding her gaze. "Temper it."

Jemdanee eased out a breath and grasped the silver flask. "If I am to temper, do not permit me to drink any more than…" She widened her fingers by an inch. "No more than this. If I do more, swat me."

His expression become one of pained tolerance. "Where shall I swat and with what? How many times and how hard? Marks or no marks? Be specific."

She eyed him. "The responsibility is not that great. You may return to the deranged darkness from whence you crawled from, you…" Strange man. She sipped at the mouth of the flask, fully aware that her lips were now scandalously touching what had moments ago been in Ridley's own mouth. Liquid gushed into her own mouth as if punishing her for even thinking of it.

Jemdanee choked, gagged and then coughed, swallowing the bread no longer lodged in her throat. The brandy surprised her. It was a smooth burning liquid that tasted divinely of a buttery, berried spice. She likened it to savoring berries set on fire.

Flavorful.

Permitting herself another sip, she relished being in the presence of a progressive man who didn't mind her drinking at all. Peter wouldn't like him. "When a noose no longer awaits my neck, you must come to India so I may repay your kindness with a tin cup of *sonti* from a very darling old Indian who does nothing but ferment rice for the drink"

She paused, realizing the offer sounded like a marriage proposal, and added, "Not that you need to come. I am merely extending my gratitude." What was the point of inviting him to India? Was the brandy already making her insensible?

Ridley gripped his knees, searching her face. "A four-month journey for a single drink won't fit into my schedule, but I'm no less honored." The tilt of his head emphasized it. "Vidocq travelled there once for an assignment. India is all he ever talks about. It was the highlight of his career."

My, what a name. "*Vidocq*?"

"My mother's cousin." His voice warmed. "Brilliant, brilliant man. I lived with him in Paris for almost nine years and was privileged enough to attend an exclusive academy he oversaw. I was the youngest in attendance at thirteen."

Jemdanee lowered her chin. She dare not fathom what sort of deranged Frenchman could have possibly created *this* man. "What sort of academy was it?" She sipped more brandy.

"Not one he ever advertised. It was done behind closed doors given how dangerous and involved his lesson plans were. He was and is an informer for the *Sûreté*, and his approach to the prevention of atrocities against humanity is nothing short of revolutionary. He has overseen thousands of arrests and reduced crime exponentially in Paris. Criminals of even the highest rank refer to him as *le Vautrin*. The wild boar."

She had no doubt Mr. Ridley had a name, too.

With unending curiosity, she prodded, "Do criminals refer to you by a certain name, as well? Not to digress, but I imagine the fear you impose on them."

His tone grew wry. "They only fear my ability to see into their minds and snap their necks in the dark. They call me *L'Homme de L'Ombre*. The Shadow Man."

The Shadow Man. That was overly ominous for a criminal to say.

Jemdanee hesitated, wondering how much of what she saw was him and how much was a façade that hid *other* things. Far, far darker things that made any man this permanently serious. Too serious to whisper of.

She swallowed the brandy still floating in her mouth, needing its warmth against the chill overtaking her. "Why did you leave France? Did you no longer wish to assist him there?"

He shrugged, "I returned to London after inheriting my father's estate and decided it suited me. Much like Paris, London never sleeps and neither do its animals. Someone has to put them in cages."

How did his soul survive the burden of being responsible for every loon in the city? "Noble though it is, why choose such a disparaging profession?"

A distant look overtook his features. "'Tis the irony of what I do. I deliver justice to everyone but myself."

Her heart squeezed. Its deeper meaning meant… "Did someone hurt your family?"

Something disturbing replaced that distant look. He averted his gaze. "My father was murdered. They wouldn't let me see him given I was only twelve when it happened, but apparently, he'd been cleaved into so many pieces, they found fingers ten feet from his body."

Jemdanee felt herself shrinking, which was no easy feat after everything *she* had seen. She tightened her hold on the flask. "Was no one apprehended?"

"No. By the time Vidocq got involved, they had already scrubbed the evidence. It was well before Scotland Yard was established, so there wasn't anything in place to oversee a crime of that magnitude. The Bow Street Runners are naught more than overpaid fops with very little to no education. Ascertaining suspects based on evidence requires a learned mind and the ability to crawl into an abyss that blurs those lines."

The burden of carrying so much darkness in one's head overwhelmed her, blurring against the brandy warming her breath. Though she had always hoped otherwise, she knew her own mother had most likely met a similar fate.

For once upon a vast copper-colored sky smeared by time that was now ten years ago, her mother, who had worked as a basket weaver back in Calcutta, had disappeared.

The woman had never returned from bathing in the river and no one could find her.

Those and countless other sordid memories defined Jemdanee. Ones tainted by the hardships of poverty and the strange disappearance of her *maa* whose beautiful dark face had bedimmed and became only the scent of crushed jasmine grabbed from a nearby shrub.

It was why Jemdanee always rubbed jasmine into her skin. To honor and to love and to remember *maa* in a world that didn't remember her at all.

How did one survive being unable to erase what could never be changed?

One didn't, but one tried.

Conviction overtook her tone. "Atrocities of murder are high in India, as well. It goes well beyond what the British are doing. Far too many are touched by carnage, though not in any guise one might imagine. Peter struggles to convince the government to regulate certain poisons there, but given the wilderness it is all too easily accessible. Countless plants are nefariously used by the natives at every turn, regardless of the caste. There is one plant by the name of *cerbera odollam*, which grows freely and is used so often against others, it is known as the Suicide Tree. The kernels hold a toxin that results in death in less than three hours. I can only imagine the assistance needed in deciphering such lethal sources."

He searched her face for a long moment. Leaning toward her, his large fingers brushed hers as he took tugged the flask out of her hand.

She stilled, that touch tingling and warming her fingers like the brandy that clung to her lips.

He twisted the cap back on and tucked it into the satchel. "You went four sips over."

She dropped her hand, realizing he had been gauging her intake.

The swaying shadows within the carriage and the incoming lantern light that shifted his frame and face in and out of gloom, seemed to personify who he was: otherworldly.

Realizing the linen napkins on her lap now only held crumbs, she folded them one by one to ensure she didn't scatter them onto the pristine velvet cushion surrounding her and set them onto his left knee. "I thank you for the nourishment."

"You are most welcome."

She hesitated. "Do you think about your father's murder often?"

He set the linen napkins back into the satchel and adjusted the worn leather belt hosting his weapons. "Not as often as I once did. Work knocks it out of my head."

Work. Being able to earn a wage was indeed a path to freedom. One she had always wanted.

Whilst she had always 'worked' alongside Peter who depended on her vegetative knowledge for tonics whilst she ensured his medical valise was always ready for the grab, there was never a wage and her own gratitude prevented her from ever asking for one.

It made her curious. "Are there any opportunities in London for a woman of color to be able to earn a wage?"

He paused. "Why do you ask?"

She shrugged, feeling awkward. "I have been dependent on Peter's generosity for too long. Getting arrested is a humbling reminder of how reliant I am on him. He has hinted that he wants me to marry now that I am eighteen, but... I have experienced too much freedom to ever think it would suit me. A wage would give me a chance to pursue a life outside of marriage."

He said nothing.

This one probably thought she was setting standards too high for herself. Standards no woman, yet alone an Indian one should waggle fingers at. "Do you think my wanting independence outside of a marriage is outlandish?"

"Not at all. In my realm, outlandish doesn't exist. I've seen it all."

Why did that not spark hope?

He shifted and paused, his brows coming together. Patting his coat pocket, he dragged out a small glass bottle whose label, which had been crookedly pasted on its side, had been stripped, leaving a residue of glue. As if astounded, he turned it over in his large hands, preoccupied with what he held. He uncorked the bottle, despite it being empty, and held it against his nose.

He squinted, as if trying to decipher something and punched the cork back into its opening.

Sensing it was important, she asked, "Did you find it at the theatre?"

"All wrath, no. It's from a case I resolved a while ago." He rolled his eyes. "I didn't realize it was still in my pocket. I haven't worn this coat in a while."

She picked at her fingernails trying not to squirm at the thought that it may have been found on a dead man and he'd been sniffing it. "I can only imagine the story behind it." It was her attempt at being polite.

He rotated the vial. "It was surprisingly uneventful. Only one person died."

"Ah..." His idea of uneventful clearly didn't meet her standards.

Rising, he turned and seated himself across from her, dragging the wool cap on his head further down over his eyes toward the bridge of his sharp nose. Leaning further back, he held up the vial between large fingers. "Are you up for a game? Do you enjoy the art of speculation?"

What an unearthly soul. "Why not offer to pull out marbles whilst we ride away from prison?"

He tsked. "Marbles would only get lost under the seat. You

and that fancy talk of wanting an opportunity outside of matrimony speaks to me. Especially given the sort of marriage I had. A young, intelligent Indian girl with no prospects and the entire world against her represents a future that will never come unless the right person invests in what few see: her soul. How about we step into the prospect of offering you something bigger?"

She squinted. "If the mobs do not find me, yes?"

He tapped his boot against her own. "Cease thinking on that. You will be on that boat either way, and fortunately for you, Finkle holds enough power to scrub the books and erase what the public is thinking." He held up the vial. "Here is my offer. If you can ascertain one of the ingredients in this vial, I'll toss nine books into your hands to take to Calcutta. Because you don't want to stay. There is no bearable life here for an Indian or any person of color in London and your arrest is merely the beginning of the hardships you will endure. Ascertain one of the ingredients in this vial and those nine books are yours. It will give you an opportunity to start a life apart from Dr. Watkins in the realm you belong in: India."

What an odd demon. "How will nine books assist me to live a life apart from Peter?"

He rotated the vial. "Most men have currency in a local bank, whilst mine consist of rare books stuffed into every corner of my house from cellar to attic. The books I'm referring to are worth about ten thousand pounds."

She frantically adjusted the veil against her face in an effort to better see him. Ten thousand pounds. That was… *two hundred and thirty thousand rupees*! That could buy her the-the… *land* she wanted to invest in and-and… more greenhouses! And-and… rarer specimen for her and Limazah to work toward creating the apothecary they often spoke of!

More importantly, she would no longer be a burden to Peter who did nothing but spend, spend, spend his own money to ensure her a happiness that had never been his to buy.

Jemdanee paused, her initial excitement… fading.

It was too much money to take from a man who was already doing so much for her. It wasn't right. "*Nahin*." She shook her head and kept shaking it, refusing to even think on it. "I thank you for the unexpected offer, but I cannot."

"Why not?"

"Your generosity has already extended past saving my life."

"Let me save it twice." He pushed up his cap, his gaze settling on her. "Those books are collecting dust and there is no reason you should, too."

She shook her head. "You are already doing too much for me."

"Your definition of much needs to be reassessed given the situation you're in. It's an opportunity to be your own person. Take it knowing you owe me nothing."

That only made it worse. She would feel obligated. "No. *I cannot.*"

His tone hardened. "This is why most females don't ever get far in life. They're taught that imposing on others is wrong and then live well beneath what is worthy of them which is what is truly wrong. Take the money, Watkins. If I can better your circumstance, you had better damn well let me."

Was his fortune that vast that ten thousand pounds meant so little to him? "I appreciate your generosity, but am already blessed with the offerings Peter has given me throughout my life. I refuse to disrespect the gods by asking for more."

He swiped his face and leaned forward, adjusting and re-adjusting his broad shoulders as if his coat was about to be thrown off in agitation. "You listen to me. Is your mind *listening*?"

She stilled, noting his intensity had risen. "*Haan.*"

"You're in a situation you can no longer afford to be in. Fate has stepped in and dropped you into the lap of someone who has the ability to change your life: *me.* Fate does that sometimes. It saves us for reasons we'll never understand, nor should we question it. Bow to its offering knowing your arrest was the best thing to have ever happened to you."

She pulled in her chin. "Are you touched in the head? This arrest is not a fate I would have ever raised my hand for."

"No one willingly gets chosen. It's called being plucked for the greatness we cannot see until it's done." He dropped his hand into his lap. "I suggest you dart out of that forest and into the pastures, because your nose is too close to the bark to see the ax that is about to strike."

It was obvious Mr. Ridley enjoyed carving out fanciful analogies by the dozen for the purpose of entertainment. "If I were to understand what the bark was and where the ax was coming from, I *might* have time to dart. Instead, I have no idea what you are even referring to and can do nothing but blink."

He leaned in and pointed at her head. "I've dealt with your Dr. Watkins *very* closely these past two days. Enough to say his intentions are vile and beyond nefarious."

She pulled in her chin. "Beyond nefarious? For being vile is not enough of a slap to his good name."

"What good name? He intends to drag you into his bed."

Her startled gaze snapped to his. Her throat tightened. "That is not true." She almost spit at the thought. "He is a father to me and my love for him is that of a daughter. We have always been that to each other."

Ridley leaned far back, draping an arm across the back of the seat and crossing his boot to his knee as if their ride was going to take a while. "It takes a man to know a man. What he sees is what he invested in: a young exotic girl born to serve a white man."

She gasped. "Given the sort of white men you associate with on a regular career basis, I have no doubt you think the worst of *everyone*!"

"Ey. A little *less* on treating me like I'm the culprit here. I'm merely pointing out the jagged pieces of his mind. Do you really think he brought you here, all the way from India, merely to showcase you at a university that will *never* take you? No offense to you as a young girl or your culture, but you've been played like a deck of cards without any aces. He only brought you here to settle the last of his estate and chain you to his side."

This was outrageous! "Of course he brought me here to settle his estate. He and I are family."

His eyes grew flat. "Unlike most, I follow the path others fear to see because they think it's too deranged. Unfortunately, when it comes to human nature, the deranged is a lot more common than people think. Your Dr. Watkins never married, nor has he ever sought to associate with any women since you came into his care. Do you not find that odd?"

What was this? How did he know all of this? And *why* did he know all of this? "You appear to be digging into lives that are not yours to dig into. His profession has always kept him from meeting anyone suitable."

"Is that what he told you?" His eyes grew assessing. "How far is your bed from his back in Calcutta? Hm? Down the hall? Or do you and he share a wall and a door?"

She blinked.

Peter had her move everything into the room adjoining his shortly after she turned eighteen. It wasn't something he had insisted on. She had asked for a bigger room. They had always freely entered into each other's bed chambers at night and often lay shoulder to shoulder reading books.

Much like a father and daughter would.

On their journey over and on the boat, they were only forced to sleep side by side, given there were no extra beds, and whilst yes, his arm had been around her every night, it was because she was the one to always tug him close.

Much like a daughter would.

She refused to believe it. "In the ten years I have been in his light-loving care, he has never once attempted to touch or kiss me in that way. Never. Not once."

"That once is at hand." He spoke with cool authority. "In his sterilized surgical mind, he sees nothing wrong with it. He invested his time and his money incredibly well given he couldn't find what he was looking for in the women around him. So he created the sort of woman he wanted. And there you sit. Most men have to justify whatever lines they cross and he hasn't justified it yet by announcing his intentions, but based on what he did to that constable and that he had an engagement ring in his waistcoat pocket *etched* with his name *and* yours, you're about to have a mess beyond murder on your hands."

She choked, her eyes widening. The ring. The one he bought in Calcutta. The one he refused to let her see. Numbness overtook her body, mind and soul. Shiva. Shiva, Shiva. Shiva, Shiva, Shiva.

He pointed. "What you do with the information I gave you is yours to keep and apply in whatever way you see fit. I merely wanted to say it bothered me. The man is in his mid-forties and you're a mere eighteen and completely dependent on his generosity which he has groomed you into feeling since you were eight. You have the whole world tipped against you right now. One warped axis spins on a murder you didn't commit and the other on that of your guardian's intentions you never invited.

It seems cliché for both to find you at once, but life does this to people. It crops not one side of your jaw but both in an attempt to knock you out."

Her nails pinched into the skin of her palms. This wasn't real. Not these charges of murder and not Peter's intentions. It was as if the world had finally revealed its true self and decided *this* was all she, as a Hindu, would ever be good for.

Murder and copulation.

Murder and copulation.

Murder and… copulation.

"The charges filed against you I will overturn," he confided in a low tone. "That I vow."

Her nails pinched into her palms harder knowing what Peter wanted. He'd been grooming her all along. He'd been grooming the perfect surgeon's wife. One who tended to extensive gardens and made medicinal tonics whenever he asked. One who listened for hours about his work. One who spoke Hindi to be able translate everything in a world that was India. One young enough to survive having his… children.

She couldn't breathe. She couldn't breathe knowing she had become the very thing her people were fighting against.

"Do you want a life apart from Dr. Watkins?" Ridley finally rumbled out.

She was choking on the air she still couldn't pull in.

He held up the vial, drifting it upward to eye level. "Do you want a respectable way out?"

It was like holding up a key to the rest of her life. "Yes."

He nodded. "Given you are at a delicate turning point in your young life and need to learn how not to be further dependent on the generosity of others, especially men, how about I let you earn this? *Hm*? That way, it feels more like an accomplishment earned as opposed to a gift given."

Rotating the glass vial between bare large fingers, he offered, "You and I will play a game of deductive marbles involving the mind where you get to keep every last jasper. Guess one of the ingredients steeped in what used to be a tonic and those nine books and the money those books will fetch are yours. That way, you get to invest in your own future apart from any man. You become your own man, so to speak. Does that appeal to you?"

Her breaths edged to a calm, no longer being sucked in

through nostrils. She half-nodded.

His voice softened. "It's quite all right, little one. Unlike those around you, I hold out the hand you need." He continued to rotate the corked glass tube. "Ask me four questions about this vial to make a deduction. Make all four count."

Uncertainty twisted more than her mind. It twisted her soul. "Why are you doing this for me? Why are you... helping me? You know nothing of my worth."

His eyes grew hooded like a hawk. "My history makes me understand your worth. I know what it's like to be trapped in a trunk you were bolted into against your will. You can't breathe. You can't see. You can't move. You can't get your fingers past the wood that surrounds you as your nails have already scraped so far that blood smears the darkness and your skin and your mind. Take your way out, Watkins, knowing you owe me *nothing*. Nothing but a promise to run from every man who tries to own you. Run knowing I am smashing the lock and opening the trunk for you to get out. Don't look around lest you get shoved back in. *Just run*."

Her throat tightened sensing this would be her only chance at knowing true freedom from every white man. Her mind was its own maze and its own garden and it had already survived more than this. *Run.*

Holding up the vial, he prompted, "I await your first question."

The pulsing of her fingertips were eerily bringing to life his analogy of being locked in a trunk as she scraped digging past that wood called life. *Run.* "Is it horticulturally based?" she choked out.

"It most certainly is. One question falls."

She eased out a breath. "How many ingredients?"

"Three. Your second question has fallen."

"And I am to... only name one of the three?"

He tsked. "I already told you that. Yes. You wasted a question. That only leaves you with one."

She almost smacked her own head for going too fast. *Think. Think, think, think and become Limazah. What would he do? What would Limazah do?*

She knew.

Jemdanee waggled her fingers toward it. "I will save my last question after its inspection. Might I see it?"

56

"I'm rather disappointed you didn't ask for the vial to begin with. Now do something people rarely do: *impress me*." He tossed it at her. Hard.

Her heart jumped and she with it as she caught the bottle with two hands, almost knocking off her own veil. Whatever was he— "You could have been more civil and handed it to me."

"Life rarely hands us anything. It usually throws it." He stared.

It was like being seated before the mortar and pestle again with her furrowed brow, all-knowing Parsee teacher hovering and expecting an answer.

She turned the vial toward herself, rotating it and paused. There was very little left within it. Barely a dappling.

"What?" He lifted a brow. "Is doubt your new god?"

"Not even a flame or a double boiler can extract a residue from this amount. Nothing remains."

"Is that so?" He set his shoulders. "Nine books from the late seventeenth century which are no longer in print is a lot of money, and if you want that money without the burden of feeling guilt, you have to earn it. There is more than enough in that vial." He dipped his voice. "Hint: break it if you need to."

She held it up, pointing to the lack of any liquid moving inside. "Breaking it would be pointless, for your definition of more is my definition of none. How am I supposed to—"

"In real life, sometimes the chance of amounting to anything in a world that offers nothing is contingent on believing in *something*. Do it knowing that it's either this or Dr. Watkins and countless other men who will want the same. What future do you want? Look into that crystal ball and let it roll."

She felt as if her composure were under attack.

As if her entire life was about to be decided by this. *This*!

Holding up the glass vial before herself with trembling hands, she angled its innards toward the dim lantern light set above. A thin oily residue spotted with liquid that refused to cling to the sides of the bottle hinted of multiple substances being mixed against nature's will.

The only way to make any sense of it was to do the one thing she did best: taste it.

She had her question. "Is it poisonous?"

He cracked his knuckles. "No and I'll even toss in an extra hint: it's a home-brew tonic."

"Home-brew? That means anything can be in it!"

He sighed. "If I didn't think you could do this, I would have just given you the money. I'm not evil. I'm merely trying to make this educational for a young girl who wants to get into a university. Regardless of your answer, I'll still give you a grade and the books."

She puffed out a breath in exasperation. All of that torture and angst for nothing.

Uncorking the glass bottle with fingers that still annoyingly quaked, she dragged its rim through the lace of the veil beneath her nose. The flowered acrid scents of alcohol brewed with other plants drifted through her mind. Rows of speeding shelves and the plants she kept on them tapped her memory as she methodically ticked through a massive list of possibilities.

She sniffed.

Two? No. It held more notes than that. He said three.

She turned over the empty bottle into her bare palm and dabbed the glass hard several times in an effort for the sides to release whatever drops it could. She was rewarded with a faint ring of a darkened reddish substance on her palm.

Bringing her hand beneath the veil, she sniffed it again and dipped her tongue to it, its sweet-bitterness stinging her tongue and... numbing it. *Isolate*. She quickly dabbed her tongue to the substance again before the numbing overtook her ability to decipher the other plants. And again.

The residue hinted at indeed three.

One biting. One sweet. One bitter.

One of the three being the rarest of them all.

She corked the glass bottle. "'Tis a very, very odd combination. Very odd. They should not have been tossed together."

"That tells me nothing."

She brushed her teeth against the numbness still prickling her tongue. "If I were to exclude the spilanthes numbing the root of my tongue, it appears to an odd confection of...." What if she got it wrong? Eeeeeeee. "Ipecacuaha? And laudanum." The laudanum was the only one she was certain of. That was easy. She could taste it. "Ipecacuaha would be the rarest originating from Brazil." She could see it in her mind's eye on the top sunlit shelf beneath her

South American plants. "I have several back in Calcutta."

His brows flickered. "You deduced all of that from your tongue? *All three?*"

She eyed him. "I could be wrong."

"You aren't." He weighed her for a long moment, then sat up with a riled thud and adjusted the cap on his head as if he could no longer sit still. "God blind me. It took my chemist *two hours* to decipher what you just did in a few minutes."

She gaped. "Do I get the books?"

He squinted. "All nine and an two extra for impressing the hell out of me."

To clap in the light of what Peter wanted of her would have been morbid.

What would have happened if this man hadn't appeared into her life?

Her eyes burned knowing the only person she had ever trusted and loved and adored was... a lie. When would the ache in her heart know peace? When? "Thank you." She swallowed, chanting to herself that tears would change nothing. She'd cried enough of them to know. "I have no words for what you are doing for me. I am genuinely humbled by your generosity."

His rugged features softened. "You have your whole life ahead of you. Fly that kite high and don't worry about hitting any trees."

Save her from kneeling before a noble man who clearly wanted nothing but her happiness. Her lips trembled against a smile knowing she had found an unexpected torch in her darkest hour: him.

She eyed the small glass bottle and did what he did to her earlier: she tossed it at him.

Only a bit too hard. She cringed.

He caught it with one hand, his gaze riveted to her face. "Don't tell me the vase is next or I'm dropping you off right here."

She shrank against the seat. "I was merely attempting to follow your lead."

"Don't. You're likely to lose your mind." He tucked away the bottle into his inner great coat pocket, still searching her face. His amber eyes bore into her as he cracked his knuckles one by one by one.

She sank further against the seat. "Might you please not do

that? The sound of bones popping beneath your skin makes me want to crawl out of *my* skin."

He sat up, still watching her. "Given where you were born and raised, I'm assuming you've already seen a dead body. Have you?"

That was random. She rarely permitted herself to crawl into the darkness she had come from. She preferred to pretend it didn't exist. "Yes, I have. Too many."

Just beyond the pristine grounds of the rows of Anglo-Indian homes at Chowringhee where she and Peter lived, filthy streets went on for too many miles that led to an equally filthy river. A river she used to bathe in as a child. One where the corpses of people and animals floated by like logs finding the current. Ones lost to disease and forms of brutality too horrid to name. They bobbed in those waters awaiting a justice that never found them.

It haunted her to think that her mother might have floated by without her ever knowing it.

He squinted. "So the bodies in that theatre won't be a problem? Seeing them, that is?"

This one needed a finger poked into his head. "The sight of any dead body unnerves me. That, Mr. Ridley, is normal."

He said nothing. Stretching his broad torso in an attempt to settle himself better into the carriage seat, he thudded his boots onto the upholstery beside her and observed her past his cap, but still said nothing. His rugged face, however, showed that he had a very long list of questions and wanted a very long list of answers by way of an essay.

Something had changed. "If you have questions, Mr. Ridley, I should hope you would ask them."

His head leaned back against the seat. He closed his eyes. "Who says I have questions?"

This one was a combination of hero and strange. Swatting at the veil that kept tangling against her face and hair, she tugged it off.

"Put it on." His head remained tipped back against the seat, his eyes still closed.

How did he know she had removed it? "It annoys me."

He opened his eyes and leveled her with a gaze of bleakness. "You let me save you once when you agreed to take the books.

Now let me save you again. Put in on."

"You draped the windows." She waggled both hands toward them in exasperation, demonstrating no one could look in. "As such, there is no need for me to—"

"When I say there is a need, Watkins, there is a need." His tone turned lethal. "Do you know many Indian women are jostling about London? Not. That. Many. And with those blue eyes set against the darkness of your skin you might as well holler murder. It's for your safety and I didn't spend the past two days orchestrating your release merely for you to end up dead. Now put it on."

Murder? "Comparing my skin to murder is rather crude to say."

"Facts don't give a damn about your feelings and neither do lynch mobs." He stared. "I can take on three men, easy. Anything after that, we're both dead. Put it on."

It wasn't worth arguing over.

Using two fingers, she plucked up her veil from the seat and yanked it back over herself. "Might you cease calling me Watkins? It unnerves me given Peter's intentions." She shuddered at the thought of his greying mustachio tracing its way up things it shouldn't. "I prefer you call me Jemdanee Kumar. It was the name I was born unto."

The clattering of wheels of the carriage prolonged the moment.

The line of Ridley's mouth tightened a fraction. He pushed up his cap, further revealing his shadowed face. "'Tis a pleasure to formally meet you, Kumar. You should have never taken his name. Kumar is who you are and who you will always be. Kumar it is and Kumar you are. Kumar, Kumar. I like that."

She lowered her chin. He was missing the point of this conversation. "I prefer you call me *Miss* Kumar or Jemdanee. Not a mere Kumar. I do not like it on its own. Kumar is supposed to go at the end of a name, not the beginning."

"An unconventional girl deserves an unconventional respect. I am offering you esteem and am addressing you as I would a colleague. For you to object insinuates you have no understanding of how men address each other."

She half-coughed and almost snorted, knowing he was being utterly serious. He was taking equality to a level no man should. "I have no understanding of such esteem, Mr. Ridley, because I am not a man. Despite its long list of hardships that do not include my being an Indian, I take pride in what I am: a woman. If you prefer to remain formal, and I agree to respect that, you may call me *Miss* Kumar. I insist."

"Never," he bit out as if offended by the prospect. "Society has a horrid tendency to define a woman based on the man she belongs to. 'Miss' parades that she belong to whoever plays the role of her father, and 'Mrs.' parades that she belong to who? Her husband. Only socially ambitious women needing to identify their lack of marital status use 'Miss' and they do nothing but annoy me. If you genuinely feel the need to be defined by who you belong to, why not start calling all of the men around you 'Master'? For *that* is what they try to be to anyone who lets them, be they woman or man. Is that what you want for yourself? To be controlled even by the leash of your own name? Because I, as a *Mister*, belong to no one. Don't you want the same for yourself, *Kumar*?"

The pulsing heat of that gaze made her feel like she was back in the jungle.

Deranged as she was, it made her want to reach out a hand and push aside the ferns. Those soulful eyes reflected a granite-like strength that were as charming as they were feral.

Very few people knew that crocodiles had soft bellies.

And this crocodile had the softest belly of them all.

Kali save her from falling in love with him for she knew he was too dark to ever love her in any normal way. It was there in his eyes which taunted. His heart was slumbering in the deep cave of his chest, yes, but it had not seen much light for it to grow into anything normal.

Not once had she seen this man smile. Not. Once.

It unnerved her. It was as if he were denying himself even that one pleasure. "I thank you for surprising me in a way few ever do," she admitted, softening her voice to reflect her sincerity. "Not to pry, but... are you known to smile?"

"I think you answered your own question."

It saddened her. For overly serious and wry though he was, he was also profoundly generous and kind. Such a strange, strange combination for a man. "Confining one's self to a shadow-ridden existence without ever smiling, Mr. Ridley, cannot possibly be good for your constitution or your heart."

He tsked. "You needn't worry about the vitality of my organs. They do what they always do: function."

Which meant he didn't care.

No longer meeting his gaze, she veered her eyes to his sizable black leather boots which were still set beside her. An angled scuff on the otherwise well-polished leather tip was revealed by the faint lantern light of the carriage.

Odd though it was, it bothered her. For it was like seeing the scar on his soul that was made completely of leather.

Lifting the corner of the veil draping her shoulder, she moistened the black lace with the dab of her tongue. Angling his boot toward herself, she drew it beneath her veil and quickly used the moistened lace to rub and buff at the leather.

His leg stilled.

She didn't care. In between the tilt of her veiled head and a few more buffing measures against the scuffed leather, she offered, "Your boot required attention, Mr. Ridley. Much like your soul. I therefore wish to acknowledge both." She patted it. "*Yeh lo, saaph ho gaya.* May one day, you learn the art of true joy and how to smile given what you do for others. That is my wish for you."

Sitting up, he dragged both boots from her, letting them thud against the floor of the carriage. His face swayed in and out of shadows and lantern light. "If a smile could erase all that I have seen, I'd be doing it on the hour like a clown who'd been given paint. There is a reason I offer my mind and services to others. Assisting humanity in a world as *pissed up* as ours enables me to do something far more important than smiling: it's called breathing. The problem with you, Kumar, is that you seem to think all this world needs is a bit of sunshine sprinkled with humor water. But as you can see by the night you're having, the bramble has long overtaken the dirt that choked out the tulips. Everyone, right down to the pastor, is telling humanity lies. They try to hide the crimes of mankind behind the veil of 'faith' but 'faith' doesn't keep death from making a visit. There is only one god and master of this universe and his rightful name is death."

She edged down her chin realizing darkness and bones was all this one saw.

It was *not* a path she preferred to take. For she knew it led the mind into places it never returned from. She had touched more than a finger to it when her mother had disappeared and she herself had almost disappeared with her mother because of it.

She was all she had and all she would ever have in a world that tried to take everything.

Even now, knowing she had lost Peter (Peter!) whilst *also* being sentenced to the crime of another, she *refused* to swallow what the world wanted of her to feel: hate, despair, and misery.

The world choked on it enough.

"In my culture," she confided, "there is not any one way to believe in the path we take under the Supreme God and its pantheon of divine beings. I choose to believe in all of them for a reason. In a world such as this, one divine being is not enough. They assist each other in their duties and it is a lesson we as humans must draw from. For even a divine being has limited power and relies on the strengths of its fellow consorts. And you, Mr. Ridley, with your dark talk, are in dire need of not only faith but a consort. Though I highly doubt you know it."

"Oh, I know it." He removed his cap, scattering his hair into his eyes. He pushed his hair back with dragging fingers, then bent the rim of the cap forward and back as if wanting to break it. "Sometimes, even I forget to be vigilant in remembering I am human."

Neither of them said anything for a long time.

He tapped at the worn edge of his cap. "Vidocq gave this to me a long time ago. He was wearing it whilst waiting for me at the docks at *La Manche*. My mother didn't want me being raised in London after what happened to my father, especially when I became suicidal at thirteen, so there I was in Paris standing before an imposing man who by the steel of his hand redefined my path given I had none. He tugged this cap on my head and said, '*Welcome to the life you never wanted. Now live it or die.*'"

Ridley half-nodded. "I wear it to remind me of exactly that. For I didn't choose to be this, Kumar. It chose me. I don't take pleasure in being in the presence of the dead. I don't need them. They need me."

He lifted his gaze from the cap and after rotating it a few times in his hands, he snapped it out. "For as long as you are in London, it's your burden to carry, as well. Toss the veil given it bothers you so much and when I ask you to, you'll tug it down over your nose. Welcome to the life you never wanted. Live it or die."

She eyed it, sensing it was his way of announcing they were acquaintances. Real acquaintances. The sort only men were to each other.

Aside from Peter, she never had any male friends. And with good reason. The men of her culture were no different than the men of the white culture: women were an accessory to procreation and their pleasure at a woman's pain.

In all but a few breaths this Mr. Ridley had already taken *her* breaths proving to be what few men ever were: a paragon of virtue.

It was humbling.

"I thank you." She removed the veil with a rustle, setting it aside, and took the cap as if it were a crown. After rotating it in the direction it needed to be in, she tugged it on.

It swallowed her head like a monkey swallowing a whole orange.

It sank alllllllllllllllll the way down to her chin, leaving her to see nothing. Nothing but fuzzy fabric. She felt stupid. "*Arrey,*" she chided from beneath it. "I might as well be in your head. Darkness is all I see."

"Don't make me take it back." Leaning toward her, he quickly removed the cap. "Learn to problem solve." Dragging up her waist-long black braid, which made her pause, he bundled it onto her head, never once meeting her gaze and yanked the cap back on hard into place. "*There.*"

It fit. Perfectly.

He leaned back against the seat, setting his shoulders. "Get some sleep."

She adjusted the cap and heaved out a breath. "Welcome to the life I never wanted."

"Keep saying it."

"I will. I will, I will." Lowering herself against the corset that made her feel like a piece of timber being laid on its side, she awkwardly set her head on the seat, tweaking her neck far into her shoulder in doing so.

It was a miserable position for her to try to sleep in.

It reminded her of mud walls and dirt, despite all the velvet. There wasn't even room for her to pull her legs upward *or* fit all the fabric of the heavy gown she was wearing.

She missed India. She missed her greenhouses and the wild

land that always sought to make its presence known to anyone who thought they were civilized. Even the home she and Peter had shared with its recreation of western comfort had the carved wooden legs of furniture set into porcelain filled with salt water to prevent termites from burrowing into what nature always found: itself. The unrelenting heat of the summers she was so cursed to love lulled everything into an eerie calm where the dust ruled and even the horses became too overwhelmed by the weather to swat their own flies.

Peter. Oh, Peter. It gouged her soul knowing she no longer had a father or an actual home in Calcutta.

She would have to make one on her own.

How could he do this to them? Yes, she loved him, yes, but not in that way. Never in that way. He was and would only ever be what she never had, a father.

Wincing miserably against the corset that had not been shaped for a body at all, she shifted against the rigid seat. Jemdanee kept shifting and shifting and shifting, attempting to set her bum and hip, left and then right. Then left again. "What I require in the name of any rest is a hammock, the sun and a tin of pineapple pulp."

Holding her gaze, he slowly edged his head from side to side. "However did you survive prison?" His voice softened. "Hm?"

Sensing he was trying to relate, she searched his expression from where he was angled sideways. "By never sleeping."

"Wise on your part." He unbuttoned his coat button by button, using both hands to push it wide open and away, exposing his weapons, waistcoat and trousers. He removed his weapons, one by one, setting them into a mahogany box he had opened by lifting its lid beside his head. It had been cleverly inset in the side wall paneling of the carriage. He shut the case and latched it.

He patted his knee. "Come, Kumar. Take my knee. It will be more comfortable."

Astounded by the offer and that he had put away his weapons in her honor, she eyed him from where she still lay contorted against the seat. "I thought you did not want us to become overly acquainted."

He lowered his chin. "It's a knee. I'm not asking you to kiss it."

Her heart flipped. "You do not mind if I assemble myself onto you?"

Shifting all the way over against the seat, he offered, "You require rest or that botanical mind won't blossom."

Her lips twitched, sensing it was a compliment. "Few men care to compliment the mind of a woman."

"Few men have the right mind to be able to acknowledge education is the only barrier separating a man from a woman." An inexplicable look of withdrawal came over his face. "Do you want your hammock or not? Pineapple pulp is currently unavailable."

An exasperated smile touched her lips, sensing this was their first step toward… something. "I will take the hammock, Mr. Ridley." She staggered to sit up against the corset. With her cap still in place, she pertly settled into the seat next to him, wondering how many other women were granted the honor of his knee.

No matter the direction.

Nestling herself against the velvet cushion of the seat, she lowered herself onto the warmth of his lap. She set her head onto the heated firmness of his thighs and felt like a marigold chosen for display. Welcoming the divine scent of his peppery cologne tinged with sweet tobacco, soap and freshly starched wool trousers, she melted and dreamily closed her eyes.

The earlier brandy made her soul further flutter and sway.

He lifted his muscled arm and adjusted it firmly around her, his large hand resting on her arm. He tightened his hold to keep her into place.

Every inch of her *swooned* at being transported to windy hilltops knowing he was holding her. Mr. Ridley was holding her. *Her.* As if she were worthy of the honor, his knee, his arm and his protection.

Whatever this was, it felt… *different* from anything she had ever known.

Kissing dashing Persians was like falling into mud water compared to this.

For Mr. Ridley was beyond divine. "May the stars kiss you for sheltering me from harm and giving me more in one night than anyone has given me in years," she offered softly against his knee. "May they also kiss you for making me feel welcome in a land that is not mine."

He said nothing.

Nestling her face and her head further against the heat of his muscled legs, she daringly slid her hand down toward his large boot, regally settling into a world that made her feel like his queen.

He didn't object.

It was nice.

The constant clattering of horse hooves and carriage wheels against the cobbled stone coupled with the sway of the carriage eventually gave way to her eyes getting heavy.

The night disappeared and she with it. It had been a long time since she had allowed herself to sleep without worrying about the world around her.

It was nothing short of bliss.

She dreamed of nothing.

Not of India. Not of prison. Not of dead bodies. Nothing.

It was the sort of rest her soul needed.

She slept for a long time.

The shifting of muscled thighs and his hands beneath her made her stir.

"*No*," Ridley whispered, the warmth of his brandy-tinted breath grazing her head and her cheek. "*Sleep.*"

She vaguely felt herself being lifted and carried, but was too devoted to the bliss of heavy sleep to do anything more than tuck her head against what she knew was Mr. Ridley's chest. The sensuous scent of his cologne and the heat of his massive body made her nestle closer.

He was carrying her.

As if life had always been like this.

As if his duty were to cradle and protect her and only her.

As if she mattered despite the world telling her otherwise.

Her fingers curled against the smooth fabric of his coat, making her drift into the anomalous reverie that maybe, maybe life could be what she wanted: a large cup of steamy happiness she could stir her finger into and gulp.

The softness of a feather-stuffed pillow met her head as his large hands slowly slid out from beneath her. Her cap was gently removed, dragging her braid out and her boots were unlaced and nudged off. His fingers carefully pulled up the soap-scented linen around her body and over her shoulders in the darkness.

A large hand smoothed her hair and skimmed her cheek.

She *melted* against that unexpected touch, wanting and needing the heat of that hand to skim all of her and make her forget everything that had ever been prior to that moment.

It was like meeting a different man.

The one whose work coat had at long last come off in her honor.

"Kumar," he huskily whispered from above and over her. "I'll be downstairs if you need me. Do you require anything else before I go?"

"*Nahin.*" She snuggled into the pillow and faded back to sleep in her haze, wanting to say more but unable to.

The bed shifted and creaked against his muscled weight. "We'll bathe and feed you early in the morning to erase your time in prison," he whispered. "Sleep. Stay in the only world where life is perfect: in dreams." He then tucked the linen around her, smoothing it around her body and chin, and stepped away.

It was as if she had met the man she was going to spend the rest of her life with.

He lingered for a moment in the darkness.

Edging back, he opened the door and left the room without closing it.

Jemdanee drifted back to the lush depth of sleep knowing a most terrible thing had just happened. In a single night her heart had been kidnapped and was being held for ransom by a man who wasn't even willing to set a price.

CHAPTER FOUR

1:07 a.m.
221 Basil Street

H e used to be so fucking organized.

If Vidocq saw what his study had turned into, the back of that gloved hand would have done what it always did best: hit him.

Between seven different newspapers he read every day (none of which he ever disposed of) and his own paperwork piled onto furniture, the floor, and random corners up to the waist, his study resembled the catacombs of Paris where bones had been tossed with no names.

He was used to it.

Extinguishing his half-smoked cigar into the ash pan, he paged through his ledgers, trying to focus.

"*Haaallo.*" His raven landed onto the wooden floor beside the desk with the folding of wings.

Without lifting his gaze from the pile of ledgers he had to get through, Ridley offered warmly, "How goes your night, Chaucer? The missing strip of wallpaper eight feet from this desk tells me you were being a prick again."

Rounding the desk with several hops, Chaucer eyed him with the turn of his black feathered head and landed onto the corner of the desk. "*Caaawww.*"

"No worries. Given Elizabeth was the one to choose the wallpaper, strip it to the plaster and turn every fiber of it into the dung that we both know she was. As long as it's not the books or my papers, you'll never hear any complaints."

Chaucer said nothing.

His 'relationship' with Chaucer was as equally macabre as everything else in his life. After the death of a well-loved dog that was cruelly taken, Ridley had decided to brush away the conventional keeping of an animal.

He purchased a newly hatched raven.

It was his way of further digging into the mind of the faceless woman who had created him.

The one whose overwhelming acrid scent of cheap rose water had penetrated his nostrils in the darkness that blurred everything. The one who had grazed his cheek with an ax, wordlessly commanding silence before gesturing to the trunk at the foot of his bed like death gesturing to a grave before hammering his skull into the shadows he never emerged from.

While there had never been another murder involving the feather of a raven, nor had she ever attempted to reveal herself or play with his pain, he knew by always, always keeping a lamp burning in the upper window of the room his father had been butchered in, that the justice he believed in would never die, regardless of the price he had to pay to keep the oil burning.

With the hobbling of quick feet and feathers, Chaucer peered up at him from the floor. He then flew up and lunged, spearing him with his beak.

"Ey." Ridley snapped his fingers at him in warning as Chaucer settled far back enough not to get swatted. "Be useful. Go organize some papers."

"*Caaaawwwww.*" Wobbling from side to side, while still staring him down, Chaucer further rattled and clicked at him.

Lifting his brow, Ridley countered, "Your lady bird can wait. I'll let you out in the morning."

Falling silent, Chaucer tilted his head, blinking. A soft, grating, "coo" followed.

Ridley's mouth quirked as he reached out and smoothed that soft head that burrowed itself against his palm. "I thank you for being the only one to never judge. Extra chicken for you in the morning. Now let me finish this or my head will never hit the pillow."

It rarely did, but he tried.

Gathering the remaining stack of his notes from what he had dubbed the *Barlow Poisonings*, he rearranged them, letting his gaze fall to the names of *James Jack Barlow* and *Emily Grace Barlow*.

Siblings. Ages sixteen and nineteen, with James being older and attending Cambridge.

The two came from an upper-class merchant family whose family empire had grown from importing oranges amongst other exotic fruits like papayas and mangoes. Emily was engaged to a much older gentleman, Mr. Richard Rubenhold, whose sizable income would have re-infused the failing Barlow estate. Unfortunately, Mr. Rubenhold and his elderly mother had died twenty days earlier after falling violently ill during a dinner party hosted by the Barlows.

Illness and source leading to their deaths had been undetermined.

Then there was Mr. and Mrs. Barlow, the parents to Emily and James.

The ones who *died* in the theatre.

After threading the names of every person who had 'passed' under suspicious circumstances revolving around 'food' that had spanned over the course of nine weeks, it resulted in a very convenient list of those affected.

They were family members all related to the Barlows and the Rubenholds.

It would seem the generation these days were getting bold about voicing their opinion on arranged marriages.

A knock against the door made Chaucer fly up and across the room.

Ridley glanced up from his disorganized desk, past the cluttered furniture piled with newspaper. *Jemdanee.* He sat up, accidentally sending parchments and missives flying. He shoved his hair out of his eyes. "Come in, Kumar," he called.

"Forgive me, sir," the butler insisted, opening the door to the study and peering in, his robe affixed over a nightshirt. "'Tis me."

Ridley couldn't help but be disappointed. Kumar entertained him. Which was incredibly rare. He'd seen too much to be entertained by anyone or anything anymore. "Shouldn't you be sleeping?"

The butler cleared his throat. "I was. Quite blissfully, in fact, sir. Unfortunately, Mr. Quincy came knocking at the servant's door as he is known to do past the hour of one and refused to leave. Are you at home? Or shall I convey the usual message of expletives?"

"Let us not be rude quite yet. What does he want?"

"He refused to say."

"Is he alone?"

"Yes, sir."

Ridley fell back against his leather chair and dragged his pocket watch out by the fob. He was about to lose an hour. Maybe even more. Fuck. *Welcome to the life you never wanted.* "Tug him in through the back door. Not the front."

"Yes, Mr. Ridley." Propping both doors open, the butler departed.

The corridor and marble floors greeted him, oil lamps illuminating patches of darkness.

Chaucer hobbled toward the door, then flew out of the room and into the corridor, disappearing.

Pushing his rosewood pistol off to the corner of the desk, Ridley flipped open another ledger with his notes from current cases. He reread them on a nightly basis to ensure every detail remained in his head for later use.

The Clover Stack case.

Male of about eleven. Freckled white skin in state of blue darkening, brown eyes, brown hair, lean, four feet and ten inches. Approximately seven stone. Signs of bloating indicating death occurred only days earlier.

Remains discovered under a clover stack in a stable, wearing only frayed, brown wool trousers with the left button of the flap missing. No button found. No callouses on either hand and nails unusually clean, indicating wealthier station despite frayed trousers. Notable indentation of the skin on the left, fourth finger evocative of a large ring no longer present.

Most likely stolen.

Based on minimal disruption surrounding the body, death took place at another location. Teeth untouched, yet jaw, side and back of skull fractured. Nostrils heavily coagulated with blood and uneven bruising on right shoulder and entire side. Broken ribs, shattered pelvis and dislocated shoulder all on same right side, indicating possible fall from an elevated height.

No signs of anal penetration. No witnesses. No motives. Lack of blood on trousers indicate victim was not wearing them during the time of death.

Steps echoed in the corridor, making Ridley sit up.

The booted stride wasn't in any particular hurry despite it being almost two in the morning.

Quintessential Quincy.

Leaning toward the desk, Ridley dipped the quill into ink and quickly wrote: *A reward of five hundred pounds has been offered and dispatched to designated columns in every newspaper.*

He set aside the ledger to let the ink dry, and inserted the quill back into its holder.

A rawboned gentleman with a swath of wavy black hair that fell into piercing green eyes strode into the room. "Do you ever sleep?"

"Do you?" Ridley countered. "Keep it to twelve minutes."

Quincy stalked in with his hands in the pockets of his posh tailored attire, well-polished leather boots gleaming against the candlelight. His expression was one of pained tolerance. "One of the girls was almost butchered. Geneva. They're threading her up right now."

And so it began.

Back to Elizabeth.

The one who needed a bramble woven crown to go with her name.

So much for twelve minutes or less.

Ridley gestured rigidly toward the butler. "Close the doors behind you, Fulton. Retire and remember to have every last servant follow the instructions I earlier gave you. No one talks to anyone outside of this house for three days, and above all, be welcoming. Overly so." He was referring to Kumar.

"Yes, Mr. Ridley." The doors folded into each other.

The room now hummed with lethal silence.

Quincy removed both hands from his pockets, revealing four fingers and a partial stump of a forefinger on his right hand.

It personified everything the man was.

For this son of a bitch had been born with a gift and a curse no man could boast and no doctor could cure or explain. Quincy could take four knives to his back, bleed out, and die without ever once feeling it. In a very literal sense.

It made him Ridley feel gloriously normal. It's why they got along. They both saw the world through a cracked glass that refused to hold the water. "I told her to hire more sentinels to protect those girls. Did she?"

Quincy eyed him. "You know how Elizabeth is. It wounds her sensibilities to think she needs a man at all."

He'd punch the wall later. "And now what? I'm supposed to do what she always wants me to do and spit shine another mess? So much for her not needing a man."

Wedging off the wedding ring from his finger, the one he wore to remind himself that what had once been love should never be hate, Ridley held it up, then clacked it onto the desk before him. "Inform her there isn't a single board of timber left of this three-year-old bridge to burn. The ring is purely ornamental and meant to remind me that murdering one's bondwoman is illegal."

"The incident regarding Geneva is only part of the problem. Elizabeth insisted I call on you and explain."

"*Quelle surprise*," Ridley breathed out. "What is there to explain? Are you saying your finger went missing between her thighs and now I'm being asked to find it?"

Quincy's features darkened. "Can we not do this, Frenchie? I only work for her."

Smacking the ledger shut, Ridley stacked it off to the side, causing one of his hemp ropes to fall of the desk. "What man doesn't?" he muttered.

One would think after everything he'd been through in the unending chasm known as life, he'd feel unaffected knowing that his former wife, whom he'd once entrusted with the darkest pieces of his soul, was now a birch mistress to thirty-four men and eighteen women.

It wasn't much of a compliment.

Quincy strode, further weaving into the study past stacks of newspapers, grazing his hand against the covered furniture as he passed. He tapped at the spines of the leather bound medical books on the shelves and paused only long enough to pluck up a mint from the porcelain bowl on a side table.

Flicking the mint into his mouth, Quincy crunched through

it on his way over. "So the complication is this: I accidentally killed the mudsill who attacked Geneva. He got in through a broken window in the cellar, and as you well know, my condition makes it difficult for me to gauge the force I use." That impersonal tone broke the stillness as if they were discussing politics. "Given you always vie for Elizabeth whenever Scotland Yard tries to wrangle her in, she is asking you to step in."

It was a good thing he wasn't holding a pistol or he would have used it. "Let me consult my conscience." Lifting his gaze to the ceiling, Ridley pretended to listen as if the silence were talking and then lowered his gaze and offered, "Fuck all of you. I'm not your personal guide to right and wrong. Because the answer is always the same: *wrong*."

Quincy stared him down. "I was doing what I was hired to do: protect the girls. The son of a diddle was waving a crucifix and roaring about God burning their souls when he lunged at Geneva. She almost *died*. I left him exactly where I tackled him on the floor. I think I snapped his neck when I bounced his skull off a piece of furniture. Christ, you know me, Ridley. I've done a long list of things no man in my condition should, but I'm not that. It was an accident. Would I be coming here to report it if it wasn't?"

Sometimes, he felt like he was dealing with the Spanish inquisition who thought itself to be the equivalent of a gallant knight. "For a moment, let us all sip port and believe this little tale you're telling me. Is Geneva all right?"

"Barely. That bilge rat removed a fucking knife out of his boot and started cutting her as if she had agreed to it."

Ridley slowly shook his head knowing the girl was only twenty. "Why wasn't the window in the cellar replaced?"

Quincy lowered his chin. "It was. But these self-righteous loons who think they speak for religion keep knocking it out. Now a foot of thread is being woven into her like a rosary through fingers. In my opinion, Elizabeth has to put bars on the windows. She has to."

"That would certainly complete the disparaging symbolism she brings."

"Ridley, be serious. Can't you send one of your contacts from Scotland Yard to ensure this is handled appropriately? Everyone at *Sérail* is panicking knowing there is a dead body two feet from the Berkley Horse that no one wants to get strapped to. They'll hang more than me. They'll hang every last one of those girls and two of them, as you know, have children."

A breath escaped Ridley. He knew that.

He wanted to blame Elizabeth who now went by the *nom de plume* of 'Mrs. Berkley' for the tragedies that continued to befall those living behind that black painted door at 28 Charlotte Street. He wanted to blame, blame, *blame* Elizabeth for creating a world no woman belonged in.

A world he and she had secretly shared before she decided to share her 'talent' with the world.

Deranged though it was to admit, her creation of *Sérail* was probably the safest haven there would ever be for countless prostitutes who would have otherwise ended up pregnant, diseased or dead. Because Elizabeth's one rule for every girl in her care was one no brothel could or would ever offer: no fucking.

It was all about the whip.

Ridley slid the ring off the desk and wedged it back on, knowing he had no right to judge. She had been through far too much prior to meeting him. "Are there any witnesses outside of Geneva and yourself?"

"Three. Elizabeth, Bald-cunted Polly and Ebony Bet."

All of them delinquents in need of a good hanging.

He thudded his boot against the floorboard beside his desk knowing he was going to do what he always did: save Elizabeth and her 'family'. "We need someone the magistrate would actually trust. The bigger the name, the bigger the gain. Were there any clients there who were titled? Anyone who might speak up?"

Quincy adjusted his coat. "Lord Bainbridge came to assist."

"*Bainbridge?*" Ridley tsked. "We might as well hang you now. He'll never admit to being there. The boy is seventeen and lives with a mother who invests obnoxiously large sums of money into her church. What the hell is Elizabeth doing letting a boy that age into the establishment? And why the fuck did you let her?"

Quincy glowered. "I help you with cases all the time, don't I? I help without ever asking for the 'books' I need and this is how I repay me? With a twist? With accusations?"

Ridley scrubbed his head knowing Quincy was one of the

few strongholds in the criminal community he could actually trust. "Leave the window broken and point it out to the constables. Before you turn yourself over to a magistrate—which you will, for it will further demonstrate your innocence—have Doctor Harris call on Geneva immediately. He and the judge are elbow associates, so it will work in your favor, and if Bainbridge can verify your story—assure him his testimony will be held private—you'll be released for a mere citizen defense."

"Can you guarantee it?"

"Nothing is guaranteed. 'Tis Bainbridge you must worry about. Did anyone touch the body?"

"No. I bolted the room after it happened."

He'd trained this one well. "Take the key straight over to Parker at Scotland Yard and tell him everything you told me. If he has any questions, have him send me a missive. At worst, I'll have Finkle clean it up. Anything else?"

Quincy eyed him. "Elizabeth sends her warmest regards. In those exact words."

Ridley opted to say nothing. There was a darkness within Elizabeth that brought out the darkness in others. A woman whose unending strength and intelligence had once awed him.

Until their sensual relationship of leather and rope turned abusive.

She crossed too many lines.

Always accusing him of not being the sort of man she needed. Always accusing him of wearing his gloves to cover his ring. Always accusing him of fucking other women whilst she shoved him into walls and gouged him with objects, trying to get him to do what he, as an overlord, refused to do: snap.

For she only ever wanted to meet the *real* Ridley.

The one who came out when pummeling criminals.

There was a reason he burrowed deep into his own mind and rarely left it. He refused to tap into that dangerous place called passion.

It was what made a man crack.

It was what made a man resort to picking up an ax and swinging.

And he knew he was capable of that and more. For one didn't crawl into the minds of criminals and leave unaffected. Their grime continued to smear itself onto the brain like mold spreading over aged cheese looking for blood.

Elizabeth had always tried to get him to push their relationship past the ropes and into barbed whips and beatings. Beating a woman had never been his calling. It withered his cock and insulted his level of intelligence.

So she attempted to rile him into wanting to do exactly that.

He never did which only riled her, in turn.

Whilst he forgave her everything, given her tragic history, his fist hit a brick wall when she started fucking other men in the hopes that he would sail over the edge and kill them all.

He almost did.

After which, he filed for divorce. He'd endured enough mental stitches in his lifetime to have scars on the inside his skull and didn't need to start cracking past the bone.

Ridley eyed Quincy who was still casually crunching through a mint. "Must be nice having a mind like yours. Why the hell are you still here? Aren't we done?"

"Elizabeth was hoping you might call on her at *Sérail* this week."

Thus began her need to dominate the one and only person she never could: him.

The last time he had attempted to have a civil conversation with her at *Sérail*, his shirt had been soaked from the contents of a chamber pot tossed by a client of hers named 'Pincher'. She'd told Pincher to do it and so poor Pincher met Ridley's fist full of knuckles, earning Pincher a new nickname of 'Punched'.

It's what happened to bondmen who didn't think for themselves and let their birch mistresses control them too much. "Nevermore. I rather like my linen shirts, given I import them from France." Ridley leaned toward him across the desk. "If she has something to say, have her send a missive and sign it in blood. If it isn't written in blood, I won't read it, because I stacked her twenty-seven trunks on the doorstep for a reason."

"Yet you continue to help her whenever she asks for it." Quincy heaved out a breath. "In my not-so-humble opinion, and I'm not one to comment on what either of you shared given I think everyone at *Sérail* is deranged... you're enabling her."

Ridley pointed. "If I treated her in the way I really wanted to, I'd be arrested. Unlike her, I'll always be what she never was to me: *civil*. Because I'm around enough delinquents and hardly need to start leading them all by example. Feel free to write that down and tuck it into her cleavage. Or her cunt. You decide."

Quincy held out a hand. "She needs a stack of forty. Her supplier died."

Jesus Christ.

If only he didn't feel the guilt at having failed her as an overlord.

Agitated, Ridley yanked open a drawer, bottles tinkering against each other and opened a large mahogany box revealing a compressed stack of dried coca leaves. His fingers gripped a smaller stack than requested, which he snapped out. "Have her gauge the intake. They aren't chocolate truffles rolled in walnuts."

Quincy grabbed it. "Do you have any limestone to go with it?"

As if he was about to doll out death. "No. Coca on its own she can chew until her jaw falls off without any effects. But the limestone is my game. Not hers." Ridley grabbed a few coca leaves for himself. Using the open tin that had fine shavings of limestone, he pinched a good powdery finger of the gritty white substance into the coca leaves and rolled it, then folded it over. He shoved it into his pocket for later use given he was going to be up for a while.

Slamming the drawer shut, Ridley used his hand like a broom. "No more of this. Time is something I have too little of as it is."

"Yet you always make time for her and this. Why do you—"

"Because trying to do the right thing sometimes feels wrong, but in the end isn't. As I said before, I prefer to be civil." He eased out a breath. "I have to finish these notes by three."

Quincy veered in. "I saw you carrying in a woman. Is everything all right?"

Damn the man for being a hawk. "I carried in no one."

A gruff laugh escaped Quincy. "I'll be sure not to tell Elizabeth or she may roll out the black carpet and tell the woman stories you don't want her to hear. Like that time you got arrested for bashing the head of her lover through fourteen windows on Regent Street." He gave him a pointed look. "She said it was the only time in her life you showed her you cared."

Shifting his jaw, Ridley bit out, "I'm not known to bend. I snap. It rarely happens but when it does, not even death will save the world. You tell her that."

"Duly noted. So when do I get to meet this enigma you carried into the house in the middle of the night like a vandal?" Quincy smirked, his green eyes dancing. "I'm *endlessly* curious as to what your taste in women has warped into since the last one."

That wasn't funny. "Permit me to emphasize something," he said in a low tone that hinted he was restraining himself from putting a hand on the pistol that was angled on his desk. "I carried in an assignment who happens to be seven months over the age of eighteen. And her yet-to-be-lived life is hanging by a thread for lack of evidence that has to be delivered to Finkle in less than nine hours. Evidence I don't think I'll be able to deliver, which is incredibly stressful to a man who can't set aside a cigar until it's done. No one can or should know she is here, because I need every minute of those twelve hours and another forty-eight to get her out of London should things go bad. And they will. Tap your ear and say it with me. *No one... can... know.* Not Elizabeth. Not Luc. Not James. *Especially not James.* Not even Paul or John out of the fucking bible. Is that understood?"

Quincy let out a whistle and walked past. "You need to get out more."

"You need to get out less. Stop killing people and giving me work."

"If it weren't for me, you wouldn't get out at all." Quincy cracked his neck. "I'll call on Parker before the body starts to rot and brings in the *real* freaks."

Ridley puffed out a breath at the thought. "Have him *also* send out missives so it doesn't end up in the papers. Above all, keep my name out of it. I don't need another article written up by another sleazy journalist who keeps telling the public my mother had whored herself to Lord Spencer and that the murder of my 'real' father took me to Bedlam."

"Can you blame the stories? You're living in a house your father was butchered in while openly inviting every criminal in London to peer through its windows. That to me spells *loon*." Grabbing the entire glass bowl of mints from the side table, Quincy walked across the room with it, as if to demonstrate who really owned the house. He paused in the doorway. "Fair warning. Elizabeth is a dog of the worst sort. She'll smell her and do something crazy: like befriend her."

"Not if you erase the scent and rub lard with crushed mints

on your chest. Maybe then she'll opt to lick you instead of the girl."

"To Satan's ears and into my bed. One day. One. Day." Quincy disappeared into the corridor and paused. "Where is this girl anyway?" he called, his voice echoing. "Upstairs? Did you and she already…?" He whistled.

Swiping up the pistol from his desk, Ridley jumped over stacks of papers and stalked out after Quincy into the corridor. He aimed his pistol at the glass bowl that was positioned on that hip. A squint, center and…

He pulled the trigger.

It shattered, the blasting echo of the shot thundering around them as mints and Quincy scrambled toward the wall. "*Jesus fucking Christ!*"

Ridley tossed the pistol, sending it clattering back toward his study. "If only the good Lord could save you from thinking I would ever buck an eighteen-year-old girl and be entertained by it. Unlike the rest of you pricks squirting seed on the hour, I'm a gentleman first and an overlord second. How is that hand of yours? *Hm*? I know you can't feel it, but is it bleeding? If not, stay right where you are. I'll attempt another shot."

Quincy glanced at his hand in exasperation and held it up held it up, showing off that it was bleeding from the shattered glass. "There is something wrong with you."

Resuming his gentlemanly façade, Ridley adjusted his coat. "Says the man who can't feel pain and works for Elizabeth. You two should buck each other and send me the bill."

With the roll of eyes, Quincy trudged down the corridor. "I forgive you. Now go take your coca-infused limestone, Ridley, and think about hiring a prostitute, because you're a fucking loon that needs to be guided through your own madness." He muttered something and disappeared.

Ridley cracked his knuckles, knowing yet another stack of leaves weighed the inside of his coat pocket which he hoped would get him through more hours.

Hours he never had.

Aside from a lack of time, he held too much self-respect to pay a woman to fuck him.

Which is why he fucked himself. Because no one knew what he liked more than he did.

It kept life pox-free and gave him more hours to do what mattered most: work.

A quick movement from the main stairwell made Ridley jerk toward it, snapping up a fist.

CHAPTER FIVE

Releasing the tension of his arm, he dropped it.

Of course.

There she was. There was little Kumar on the last stair holding a massive Oriental vase high above her head, draped in *his* cashmere robe. Her uneven breaths rose and fell as her arms quaked to hold up the heavy vase.

He eyed her. "Is there a problem?"

Her black braid swayed past her waist as she further tensed. "There was a pistol shot," she rasped in that heavy accent, searching his face. "A pistol! Did you not hear it?"

How charming.

This one had come to rescue him from a pistol with a vase.

And not any vase. *The* vase.

"At ease." He adjusted each cuff. "I can see you've already made yourself marvelously comfortable, because there you are wearing *my* robe and toting *my* vase. A vase that was the only thing in my father's room that hadn't been shattered during the murder twenty years ago. So don't drop it."

Her eyes widened.

A ragged breath escaped him. "What are you digging through rooms? You haven't even been in this house for an hour. What are you doing?"

She carefully lowered the vase and awkwardly set it onto the floor, wedging it toward the wall to ensure it was out of the way.

"I only went into your room. The door was open so I decided to make use of your chamber pot given I could not find one in my room at all. I then chalked my teeth using your mouth brush, towel bathed myself given I reeked, and re-braided my hair when…" She rose, turning back toward him and lingered.

A little too much information. "Now that your derriere has formally touched my porcelain and your mouth has christened my toothbrush, permit me to educate you on self-defense. *Never* go for vases. *Ever*. It's only effective once and they shatter. What happens after your only weapon shatters? Bash goes the back of your skull at the hands of your enemy and you're dead. Learn to grab something you can reuse. Preferably an object that will set as much distance between you and the perpetrator as possible. Like a curtain rod. Or you might as well not grab anything at all. At that point, run, because you're useless."

She hesitated, still intently holding his gaze. "Why was there a pistol shot?"

Those overly large upturned eyes were not at all the shape or color any female should have. They weren't even blue. They were a shocking pale blue verging on flecks of eerie white. Set against that dark gold of her skin, it was like beholding a magnificent medieval painting set in the corridor of a gothic palace.

The sort that a man silently prayed to like the Black Virgin in Cusset.

Her eyes hid nothing and it was fairly obvious they didn't want to. The bizarre playfulness retained within them, despite everything Dr. Watkins had shared about her life, both awed and annoyed him.

It was as if she refused to feel the slaps of life that enabled better thinking.

The whispering of hemp ropes clothing every inch of her body in the art form of weaving patterns until no skin showed on her arms or her legs or her breasts or her throat, and then having her regally sit cross legged on a velvet chaise and sipping champagne he drank from her lips whilst fucking her was an image he needed to knock out of his mother-fucking head.

"I was practicing," he eventually said, keeping his tone cool and flat lest he betray his overlord tendencies. "The walls needed it."

She lowered her chin. "Whatever did the walls do? Did they mock your level of intelligence?"

That humor needled him. She used it too much. "To clarify, I had an associate call on me."

She tsked. "Shooting at associates is not advisable. They will cease trusting you."

Damn her for turning everything into a joke. She was up for murder and had a lusty guardian and was *joking*. "I suggest you return to your room and tell your jokes there given no one here is laughing." He swept his finger up the stairs. "Keep the robe, as I have plenty of others, and go to bed. Go." He was still trying to get the image of her fully clothed in hemp rope out of his head.

She smoothed his robe against herself, tightening the belt around herself to further hide what the calico gown beneath didn't. "I feel very well rested."

This one had only slept less than forty minutes. "The shadows beneath your eyes betray you."

She lingered, her slim fingers sliding back and forth against the fabric of the robe as if waiting for him to command her to do something.

The wrong side of his brain noticed.

Yanking out his already rolled and folded coca leaves, he stuffed them into his mouth, chewing its bitterness and the wincing sharp sweetness of limestone. "I have to work." The warmth and numbness against the inside of his cheek started as his saliva dampened the dry leaves he needed.

She hesitated, searching his face. "What sort of vegetation did you put into your mouth?"

Vegetation? Hargh. It wasn't broccoli. "I only chew it when my mind needs to focus and a cigar isn't enough."

"That did not answer my question."

"Coca." He gestured toward the stairs. "Your inquisitive mind may now depart."

She squinted. "Only coca?"

He shouldn't have been surprised she would know the tricks of drawing out its effects. "No. I scraped a little sugar on it."

Her full lips parted. "You rolled a wad the size of eight coca leaves into your mouth *with* limestone?"

"Fourteen with limestone, since you appear to be counting. I get little effect from anything less."

She gasped. "*Are you deranged?*"

He slowly chewed to emphasize it. "Some say I spent countless years in an asylum."

"Your mind is blessed and yet you disrespect it." Her features tightened. "Spit it out."

She seemed to forget she was only five feet in height.

Maybe even a fourth of an inch under.

Veering in close, he wordlessly pointed out the sizable one foot and three inch height difference by lowering his chin *down*.

Her head rolled far back to look up until he saw nothing but those tiny nostrils and a chin.

"Never forget it," he said. "I never do anything I can't handle. I've experimented with enough to know what my limit is. If you ever see me grabbing a hundred and a whole tin of limestone, stop me."

She tapped at his chest with a forefinger as if she herself were now on it. "Limestone draws out too much of the toxins from the coca. Do you not understand what that means? It contains benzoylmethylecgonine alkaloids."

"I contain a hundred percent of I don't care. Understand that without the coca, there is no Ridley, and without Ridley, all of the cages will be empty and there will be panic on far more than the street. Now be a darling little girl and go to bed." He patted her small cheek. "Go."

She pushed away his hand. "I am *not* a little girl."

"So says the little girl." He stepped back, chewing into the leaves for emphasis. "Children whine about being put to bed all the time, too."

"You sound like a clock in need of winding."

"Tick-tick. It's the beauty of coca. It enables me to use every minute I don't have. Now go to sleep knowing you get to lounge about all day with a pot brimming of tea until eleven tomorrow night. Unlike me. I haven't lounged in eleven years."

"I will not retire whilst those leaves remain in your mouth." Despite being at his shoulder, she bumped herself closer, attempting to tap a brown finger up and against his bottom lip. "Spit. Spit before any more effects take you. Spit, spit."

Having a self-righteous Indian herbalist living in the house with him for three days was going to be more of a nuisance than he originally thought.

He stepped back, breaking the contact of her finger against his mouth lest he bite it off. "Before you assume the worst, these were prescribed to me by the best apothecarian in London. They're incredibly useful for long nights and keep me focused."

"That *apothecarian* ought to be hanged so he might be re-born as a pile of manure. English apothecarians are quacks! Their knowledge is acquired not through practice but reading books that have long since expired."

"Cease riling that mind or you won't be of much use to us. That was the whole idea of arranging the theatre lockdown for tomorrow night. So you could actually sleep, have a full day of rest, and think clearly. Had I known you wanted to stay up all night like an owl on coffee beans, we would have been *there* not *here*." He stared her down. "Now if you'll excuse me, I have to work."

"Not with those leaves in your mouth."

It was getting harder to stay calm. The coca was spiking his heart rate and making him talk faster than he could keep up with. "You appearing into my life for two minutes doesn't mean I give up what enables me to function whenever I have to work beyond what my physical body cannot do on its own past certain hours."

She lowered her chin, her blue eyes flaring. "You are addicted to coca."

He usually had more control over it, but the amount of cases he'd been handling since his new, under-the-table agreement with Finkle meant he had to keep up. There wasn't any room for him to fail given his reputation and what Finkle was now offering: immunity to himself *and* anyone he named in return for solving cases Scotland Yard couldn't.

After being arrested well over thirty-eight times since becoming a private inspector, he needed the immunity more than he was willing to admit. "I have to work."

"Between the two substances you are combining, Mr. Ridley, if ingested irresponsibly it *will* result in seizures and/or death. Peter and I have witnessed seizures so violent at the hands of coca/limestone that it bleeds the brain from lasting too many minutes. Did your quack ever tell you that?"

Death was the least of his concerns. The only reason he hadn't hanged himself from his own rope and done away with the uselessness of his sense of being was because he had promised his mother he would never attempt suicide again after she found him barely in time at thirteen.

Work enabled him to function and gave him purpose.

Work also erased his own sins. "I've been around enough death to know what my chances are. I'll take them."

"If you disrespect what I believe is right for you," she warned, "I will disrespect you, in turn. Is that what you want?"

He sped up his chewing to keep up with his thoughts. "Are you threatening me?"

"I will offend you for offending me and offending the body the gods have given you."

The maestro in him was awfully, awfully curious. "Go on, Kumar. Amuse the grim side of my soul and offend me. Simply know I'll keep doing what I have to do to be the best: *chew the coca.*"

A determined breath escaped her. "May Shiva help you. You may be twice my size, but I will take you down in a way all men fall." Bumping in close, she grudgingly held his gaze from well below him and grabbed him by the bollocks, twisting it like a rope.

His body bucked from the pain as his senses roared against the stabbing that flared his nostrils.

Eyes watering, he choked and almost gagged against the leaves he was chewing. He coughed. Shoving her away from himself, he attempted to push the coca leaves to the right side of his mouth, wincing.

He didn't need that.

Kumar's cupped hand breezed up to his chin again as she met his gaze. "You may spit or choke, *phaujee.*" Her tone indicated she was not going to do it with any pleasure. "I will permit you to decide how the coca will be relinquished. If you prefer to be uncouth, you will fall in pain against the nearest wall giving into what you are: a man. Now relinquish the coca or I will do it again knowing you are too much of a gentleman to backhand me for doing the right thing."

Mighty words for an eighteen-year-old.

Ridley swilled the juice in his mouth which he now felt too conscious of to swallow in her presence. "You certainly knew how to pull the lever," he said out of the corner of his mouth.

She crossed her arms. "I grew up seeing women do far worse in the name of saving those that matter. Now thank me. Do you think I enjoyed that? Do you think I enjoyed reducing myself to hurting you or touching your stamen as if I were a whore in a hovel looking for food?" Her voice cracked.

Numbness was overtaking his entire mouth and jaw as his bollocks ebbed from pain. He released a slowing breath through still flared nostrils in an attempt to control the overbeating of his heart *knowing* what she had resorted to in the name of her concern for him.

Why was his deranged soul endlessly honored?

Probably because he was usually at the other end of this, reprimanding others.

In kudos to her and that, he snapped out a handkerchief from his pocket, the one she had cried into (how symbolic) and spit the wad of coca leaves and limestone into it along with all the juice he'd been holding. "*Ici.*" He gave her a pointed look and turning, folded it and set it onto the side table. "Your concern is acknowledged given that I am first and foremost a gentleman. That doesn't mean, however, I will cease chewing. I simply won't do it in your presence."

She kept her gaze trained at his head. "I will continue to be the conscience you clearly do not have, Mr. Ridley. I will find those leaves and I will burn them right along with tossing every pinch of limestone into the street."

It irked him to hell that she was lecturing him.

He knew right from wrong. He defined it. "Those leaves aren't yours to burn. So be wary of overstepping your bounds. This is my body and I will do with it whatever I please."

"Do not chew coca and the limestone again. For if you *die* between this hour and before my departure to Calcutta, I will be left to hang! Or have you forgotten the charges being brought against me?"

Most women were too silly in the head to compete with his head.

And maybe that was why this one was so... marvelous.

For despite her age, and despite the antics that reflected that age, her mind was still sharper than most and that uncanny ability to sniff and taste plants as if she were a chef in the kitchen throwing nearby items into a pot was unnerving.

It gave him too many ghoulish ideas.

Ones that wanted to drag a very young girl to murder scenes as if it were the carnival in need of hot air balloons, ponies, and wood-painted toys.

She dropped her hand to her side. "There is a raven upstairs in your room," she grouched. "Why am I not surprised you have a raven living with you in your own personal cemetery? The way he kept staring at me whilst I attempted to use the chamber pot was unnerving. Nothing I did prompted him to leave. It was like death staring at my piss, insisting I cross over."

An exasperated breath escaped him. The cheeky bastard. "*Chaucer!*"

The raven flew out from his room upstairs into another room, giving him the tail.

Dragging back his hair, which kept falling into his eyes, Ridley flopped his hand to his side and offered, "For him to have stayed in your presence that long is a compliment. He never watches me piss."

She blinked. "Is that supposed to *be* a compliment, Mr. Ridley?"

The last thing he needed or wanted was a pea hen with downy feathers telling him how and when to spit. This was his realm and the overlord in him wanted to roar about it, especially after Elizabeth. Edging back, he gestured toward the open doors of the study behind him. "If you will excuse me, I have to finish my notes. By all means, break a few vases if it'll entertain you. All I ask is that you clean up afterward and above all… let me work."

"You will not be rid of me that soon. You owe me over two hundred thousand rupees."

This one needed to be roped. "If you keep at it, I'll let you and all eighteen of your little years marry all forty-four years of Dr. Watkins and what few hairs he has left on his 'stamen'."

"Cease using my age as an excuse for your inability to engage a woman in any civilized form of conversation."

Ouch.

Peering past him and toward the candlelit room beyond, she said, "As your associate, I wish to see your study."

"*Associate?*"

"*Haan.* You require my expertise tomorrow night, do you not? You are also investing in my independence. That makes us associates."

He didn't need to be a private inspector to know where this was going. "Let us be clear in this, little Kumar, lest the money I am giving you and the elaborate prison escape I conducted was not enough to translate your situation. You need me more than your plants will ever need the sun. *Don't* disrespect that."

"So announces the man who needs me to solve this crime. Given what I did in that carriage with a mere dappling, I believe my talents are far greater than anyone you have ever met. I am a botanical savant and if I were conceited—and fortunately, I am not—I would demand you bow."

Touché in French, Latin, Spanish and Italian. With a smack.

She angled past him with a head wobble. "If you must work despite the late hour, I will assist you so you may retire sooner *without* the use of coca. Is that not thoughtful of me? Given how young I am? Usually the youth of this day is accused of thinking of nothing but themselves and having no common sense. Yet here I stand before you providing you the two that you clearly lack."

Not even the fading remnants of coca humming through his veins could calm him.

Three days of this? And no coca?

Finkle I hate you enough to want to gouge you with a fork.

Because three days, that included, morning, day, and night, was a *liiiiiiifetime* in his investigative world. She and her chatter and her gorgeous eyes and her charming accent were going to be part of all four thousand, three hundred and twenty minutes of his life.

It was a lot of minutes.

And he had to work. He had to. Or he'd be up in the attic stringing rope around his neck waiting for the snap because he thought about suicide far more than any man should.

That was the glory of coca.

It muted those thoughts.

"Are you going to show me your study or not?" she prodded.

Ridley heaved out a breath. The entire world was against the poor thing, there was no reason he ought to join in. Fortunately, he didn't have to be anywhere in the morning or the afternoon.

They had nowhere to be until tomorrow night.

"As you wish. Touch nothing." He turned and stalked past her and into his study, angling past stacked books and newspapers and into the room. He jumped over papers and crossed the expanse of the room, weaving through furniture and stacks of more books.

Removing his great coat, he tossed it onto the bigger mess known as his desk.

Kumar pattered excitedly after him from the corridor with quick steps.

The level of that excitement toward seeing his study *was* mildly adorable.

Few appreciated what he did.

Lowering himself into the well-worn leather chair, he let it creak beneath his weight. With her tendency to do nothing but talk, talk, talk, he doubted he was going to get anything done tonight.

She veered into the cluttered piles of books and paperwork that covered the room and paused. Her full lips and eyes widened as if what she had stumbled upon a nightmare.

Why did he feel a need to defend his lifestyle? "It's far more organized than it appears."

"Is it?" Glancing around the lamp-lit space, she very carefully wove her way through stacked files, papers and old books that covered almost the entire floor up to her waist. She eventually paused before his desk, peering over a sizable pile of medical books separating them with the prop of her chin. "Your study is unusable," she pointed out.

Polite though it was, he knew she was pillorying him. "The books were here well before I was, but insulting the mess changes nothing. It represents eleven years of the greatest work this city has ever seen or known."

"You certainly know how to compliment yourself."

"If I don't do it, no one will. Not even Finkle."

Too many took him and his work for granted knowing he worked for free and lived off the estate. It was how he honored the vast fortune his father had left him. One that had been bestowed in a most unusual form of 'paper' currency known as rare books.

He sold them off to collectors monthly like the bank notes that they were. Ten massive rooms in the house, not including the entire cellar, were filled from floor to ceiling and corner to corner with an unusual array of books dating back to as early as 1291.

DELILAH MARVELLE

As with all things, his father had been obsessive and had spent his already vast fortune by re-selling antiquities scavenged from aristocratic estates in France during the revolution.

It was all blood money.

Since inheriting the house almost eleven years earlier and moving into it, Ridley had made some progress in organizing the house. His bedchamber and the one adjoining it were finally properly furnished with French pieces, as were the corridors and the parlor.

In between whatever time he found, and before he sold off every book, he read them.

It was the one pleasure he gave himself: reading.

Unfortunately, every time a section of a room was emptied, it only warned him that the money was limited to the size of the house. There was no doubt in his mind that his father's overly bizarre obsession with books and French revolutionary antiquities had resulted in the man's demise. For the objects he hoarded had always meant far more to his father than people.

More than his own wife. More than his own son.

And now the books and French antiquities were here but his father wasn't.

It was the very definition of irony.

Kumar peered toward the desk in renewed curiosity and gestured toward random, uneven piles of ledgers, newspapers, ash pans with several unfinished cigars, pieces of hemp rope, his shaving bag, and missives. "If this is what the inside of your mind looks like, I fear for you."

"Ha. Ha." He paused and added, "Ha."

Her lips curved in prim amusement.

Oh to be young again and find the world funny. He couldn't even remember the last time he'd actually laughed. If ever.

He'd always been an overly serious child even well before the murder. The murder simply tapped a few more coffin nails into place.

Propping his elbows on the chair he was seated in, he bridged his fingers together. "Now that you have seen it and commented on it and have insulted the man who is saving your life—twice—I hereby bid thee a good night and you may go. Rest well."

"I think not, Mr. Ridley. Your study is in dire need of attention.

'Tis fairly obvious you have no desire to address it on your own." Reaching out a hand, she picked up his great coat, ensuring she didn't knock over any of his ledgers, and folded it over her arm. She then turned with the flick of skirts and the robe and wove through the piles, hurrying over to the coat stand in the farthest corner of the room.

He squinted. It took Elizabeth two weeks into their marriage for her to even realize it was there. This one was observant.

The overlord in him liked that. A lot.

"I will organize everything for you," she conversationally offered. "Everything, everything. I will treat your papers as I do my plants. Which they once were. Wood."

Tilting his head, he watched her sling the coat onto the brass arm of the coat stand. His jaw softened noting that her black braid was coming undone.

The end of that braid brushed her round, tight rear.

He didn't like that he noticed. It made him feel like a thirty-two-year-old deviant standing at the window of a girls' boarding school waiting to see more than skirts.

She smoothed his great coat and glanced back at him over her shoulder, her pale blue eyes looking for approval. A lock of onyx hair fell further down onto the side of her bronzed face.

He waited for her to adjust it. *Tuck it back.*

Lifting her hand to her hair, she tucked it back into place.

It was as if she could follow a command without him giving it. Rare. Nice.

"What shall I organize first?" she asked.

It was almost two in the fucking morning. "I would rather you not touch anything," he confided. "Everything is where it needs to be. It may look like a mess, but I know where *everything* is."

Most of it.

Some of it.

A quarter of it.

She lingered. With her dirt-smudged stockinged feet peering out beneath his robe, she wove back through stacks of newspapers toward him and paused before the desk.

"You need new stockings and an hour-long bath," he pointed out. "For you, Kumar, still look like prison and that isn't a compliment."

She intently held his gaze and veered closer to the desk separating them. "Might you pretend to like me? Or do you not like women at all? Do you not associate with them anymore after your wife?"

A primitive warning sounded in his head.

He knew what she was asking: the wrong questions.

A part of him was deeply disappointed that an intelligent young girl like this would be drawn to an older morbid son of a bitch like himself. The last thing he wanted was to crush the idealistic petals off that little petunia. For whilst, yes, he was known for being incredibly generous in nature, and offered that generosity to everyone from sweeper to oyster shucker, he knew when to slam the door on a female nose when it tried to lean past the frame and see the rope.

Skimming her hand across the desk, she pursed her lips. "Given we have no choice but to co-exist over these next few days, I wish to know more about you, Mr. Ridley. I wish to know what the world does not."

She wouldn't be the first woman to be curious.

Too many tried to drape themselves across his cluttered desk with nothing but garter-tied silk stockings as if that was enough to grab the brain lodged in his skull. Give him *Micrographia: or some physiological descriptions of minute bodies made by magnifying glasses with observations and inquiries thereupon*. That he would fuck on the hour.

Because when he needed to thud out being a man, he lined delinquents up and punched.

For copulating with a woman who meant nothing to him changed nothing. If anything, it would only result in bringing a child into a world his own *dog* couldn't survive in. To the devil with that and no. Spraying his seed into linen he could easily wash and feel no guilt in causing it any pain suited him more than fine.

He chose his words carefully. "Everything you need to know about my 'functionality' is right here." He thudded the desk once with a fist. "*This* is my god, my church, the altar and bible I pray to on both knees at all hours. Everything else is rain pelting the window."

"May the gods never punish you for saying it." Skimming her brown hand over the hemp rope draped over one of the ledgers, she asked, "Aside from the dedication you grant your work, do you ever make time for other pursuits?"

He thudded his chest and arms. "I box twice a week and fence. It fills out the coat and extinguishes aggression lest I altogether kill these men before the jury can."

"Is that all you do from day to day?"

"Why? Are you needing a schedule?"

"I am merely curious."

"About what?"

She heaved out a breath. "Do you not do anything else outside of your work?"

Tsk. Tsk. Tsk. Curiosity never killed the pussy. The one known as Ridley did. "'Tis rather astonishing how busy these knaves keep me. They even commit offenses on Easter and Christmas morning. Not that you celebrate those."

She squinted. "So you do not even attend social gatherings?"

This one also seemed to think he had time for dinner parties. "Oh, yes. All the time. I attend the funerals of victims and make note of everyone in attendance should a perpetrator get morbid and show up. Afterwards, I partake in a meal with that family and offer condolences, but for some reason, they never want to dance."

She pinched her lips. "Cease being callous. I am merely trying to get to know you."

"And I'm letting you. This is me, Kumar. Me. Morbid, flippant, overly serious, real, intelligent and to the point. Always to the point. I hide nothing. Never. Why? Because I'm not a criminal."

She sighed. "Do you not do *anything* that is not in any way related to crime or the dead?"

Recognizing that he was being rebuked for not doing more with the living, he shifted his jaw. Too many seemed to think he needed to be lured away from what mattered most: justice. "Are you insinuating what I do is unimportant?"

Her lips parted. "Of course not."

"Then what? What is the point of you bringing up what I do and how I do it and when I do it? Are you now in collaboration with my mother? Did she send you over with a missive regarding the amount of time I ought to spend doing 'normal' things? Because last I knew she was in *Bordeaux* paging through books I send by the dozen to ensure that doesn't happen."

She rolled her eyes. "Work, no matter how gratifying, does not define the parts of us that lives outside of it. I have always been devoted to my greenhouses and learning, but I am also devoted to celebrating life. I attend festivals, dance, and visit other villages throughout India whilst racing toward anything new I can do." She hesitated. "Perhaps one day, when enough time has passed, I might be able to visit again and you might be able to grant me a tour of London. Or perhaps you might come to India. I would very much like that."

He knew where this was going.

Lever down. "Permit me to halt your one-seater coach right there, Kumar. I don't know if you have or haven't kissed a boy or rolled the dice for him, but this here *man* doesn't work in the entertainment business. Never have. Never will. For life isn't always about having a good time, especially when people are dying. I don't take women dancing, and haven't attempted to in years. To get to the point of this civilized rant: I don't offer walking tours to girls who barely reach my shoulder. Not unless you want a tour of every location in London where I arrested felons, donkey thieves and more. Do you understand?"

Silence overtook the room.

Kumar eventually half-nodded. "*Haan.*"

"Good. Now that you know everything about me, are you exhausted enough to retire?"

She eyed him. Gathering all of his half-smoke cigars, she stacked them into the ash pan one by one. "Your room upstairs is as much of a mess as this one."

Thinking about it riled him. He hated living in the clutter he never seemed to be able to crawl out of. "It's why I pay the servants double the wage. This particular room used to be very organized," he countered. "Hell, I used to file everything into trunks that were methodically tiered and labeled. I even measured the amount of ink that went into this here well, but it annoyed that woman who shall not be named. The one I divorced. It annoyed her that I spent more time in here than I did in her parlor. A parlor I had graciously cleaned out and furnished with obnoxiously expensive teakwood things, oval-backed sofas and gaudy bobbles *she* wanted. I gave her an entire room and sold off far more books than I should have."

If only he hadn't been duped into thinking he and his ropes

needed anyone in his life. For he'd chosen the wrong hell of anyone. The darkness in him had wanted a little light only to end up in a windowless basement and no key. "And do you know how she rewarded her king?"

Kumar lingered.

The sooner this one understood his position on women, the sooner whatever was going through her head could be buried. Deep. "Barely three weeks into our marriage, I arrived two hours after I said I would due to my negotiating a damn hostage situation involving children and she and her irrational screams had emptied every last trunk and drawer, shredding pieces I'll never get back. She did it on the hour like a cuckoo from a clock I never purchased. The servants and I would clean it up and there it all went back on the floor like a dog with a pair of shoes that wanted to chew through the sole. So I stopped organizing it, because too many cases kept coming in and I had to work. Which was damn difficult with that one."

Punishing Elizabeth by not permitting her to touch him or bed him did nothing. She'd lie on the other side of his locked door and talk to him allllllllllll night about what a prick he was.

If he had been a prick, he would have backhanded her to Madrid then to Russia then over to Italy and into the ocean, but never once did.

Roping Elizabeth to a chair and setting her in the corridor to keep her from ripping up his files did nothing, either. She would purposefully piss the rope *and* the chair like the animal that she was, *insisting* he hit her, *insisting* it was the only thing that would make her kneel.

He wasn't one to backhand women not even in the name of his own pleasure. For his pleasure was in the burn of the rope. She knew that going into their marriage.

She. Knew. That.

Unfortunately, their marriage didn't have a leather clause contract because he became something he rarely was: stupid.

Needless to say, it led to a hell of a lot of fights and him always leaving the house to pummel the only people he really could: delinquents. "It didn't matter how many times I took her dancing or shopping. It didn't. For some dogs kneel and others bite and kicking a dog regardless of its antics is wrong. I repeatedly set aside everything for her, *everything*—even the murder of a child one night—*knowing* she needed me more. Only it didn't matter. Because I could have slit my throat, pulled out my spinal cord and thrown in a bit of heart muscle and it wouldn't have been enough for her to think I cared."

Because Elizabeth and her dramatic need for Hades wanted nothing but pain.

Banging into her anally without lubrication while she screamed hadn't been enough.

Gagging her into unconsciousness while his cock rammed her throat hadn't been enough.

She kept pushing him to do things that had made him only hate who he already was: the devil.

Kumar blinked. "Why did you marry a woman who had no respect for you?"

Because he was known to rescue them all. "Let me tell you something about Elizabeth. That one knows how to wave a map and bury the treasure so deep, even *she* can't get to it. She used to be a novelty I met with every Tuesday night at an exclusive club. A novelty who could recite Socrates as if he were her father. Given the sort of man I am, I need someone capable of complimenting my mind, and that one did. She made this dullard believe there were words in the night sky written by Voltaire."

A breath escaped him. Note to self: never attempt to meet a woman in a flagellation club. It invited bigger hellions. "Too many demons reside in the caverns of her head, not to mention my own, and I'm not an exorcist."

Kumar said nothing. She merely picked at her fingers, looking so miserable, one might think she had attended her own funeral.

He clearly brought back a shadow, for he had spewed more about his life to her in one sitting than he had to anyone in years.

He was still edging down from the coca. "That was uncalled for. I didn't mean to shove an anvil into your arms and break the scaphoids in your wrists."

She squinted. "My scaphoids?"

He tapped his wrist. "It's a bone."

She eyed him. "Of course it is." She softened her countenance. "You need not apologize. I am honored you were willing to share so much with me. Few do. Even Peter has a tendency to limit sharing personal thoughts. Why do you think I talk so much? I have learned to entertain myself while attempting to prod out a measure of conversation from those around me. I sense their discomfort given I am not of their culture or color and do my best to erase it."

The earnestness in that accented voice which revealed her little vulnerable world made him nudge aside a stack of missives he almost *shoved*.

It riled him knowing Dr. Watkins had treated her like a pet. Snarling women like Elizabeth deserved to be treated like pets. Not bright-eyed angelic Indian girls who knew the taxidermy of plants like he did bones. "Never doubt the glory of a good conversation, Kumar. I live for it and will admit, it has been quite some time since I have had the unending pleasure and privilege of being entertained by a highly intelligent mind like yours." He meant it.

She brightened. "You think me to be intelligent?"

It was obvious she didn't hear it often if at all. Society was cruel. "You are *incredibly* intelligent. What you did with that mere dabbling of that vial goes beyond what any of top chemist I have worked with over the years can do. You're brilliant."

She smiled shyly. "I thank you for making me hum."

That humble charm was darling. "You do that. Hum."

Peering over the side of his desk, she deposited the ash pan's contents of stacked cigar stubs into the bin filled with ripped parchment, setting it on his desk and angling it into place. "I suggest a hookah. It makes less of a mess."

He stretched, cracking his neck. "Oh, yes. I can imagine myself on the streets of London now. Bumping into passing citizens while asking them to excuse the size of my hookah."

A bubble of a laugh escaped her. Her eyes brightened as her lips curled.

His chest tightened at the glorious beauty of that sound.

Laughter wasn't something he was used to hearing. Not in his field, not in this study and most certainly not in this house. This was the house that often whispered of things he still tried to catch. Like the creak of the door when a shadow and an axe had moved in. Like the shattering of glass outside the darkness of a trunk he'd been locked in for too many hours with blood running into his eyes as the thudding and the dragging of something heavy down the corridor moved past his ragged breaths.

It was something his mind would *never* unhear.

Kumar searched his face. "Mr. Ridley?"

He sat up. "Yes? What?"

"Are you unwell?"

His gaze snapped to hers. "No. Why?"

Those features softened. "You look haunted."

When wasn't he? He defined enough of the past to be a ghost. "My mind never lets me rest. It's the curse of what I do."

She hesitated and reached out across the desk to touch his face.

His pulse roared as he caught that hand to prevent its contact, his fingers pulsing against the heat of her soft skin. Her brown fingers trustingly curled around his and tightened.

The curling of those small fingers against his large hand whispered of what he already knew.

She wanted more.

For she wasn't a mere Kumar but a Jemdanee. A Jemdanee full of smiles and compassion which had miraculously not been stripped despite her upbringing. Despite poverty-stricken demons and a guardian who had been grooming her like a dog.

Ridley released her hand and scrubbed the thought. "Try to respect the boundaries of others."

She lingered. "It is not a sin to offer compassion to another."

The pulsing of his fingertips hinted at what he feared: a heightened state of awareness toward an eighteen-year-old girl. One he was responsible for. One that could end up dead if he didn't get her on that boat in less than three days. The hearing was in five. "I have nothing against compassion, Kumar," he rasped. He flexed his hand to rid himself of feeling her. "I admire that in you. I admire it in anyone who holds onto it despite the wrath of circumstance others use as an excuse to violate others. I simply prefer you respect yourself by not touching a man like me."

Because tucking her into that bed had been beautifully different.

The overlord in him had cradled her vulnerability enabling him to be protective.

It was the part of him that was still very human and still capable of being soft.

The part of him that tried to *be* human despite the countless beasts he associated with morning, day and fucking night.

She lingered as if hoping he'd say more.

He thought it was best to bring an already long evening to a lull. "I bid thee a good-night."

Holding up the hemp rope she had already removed from the ledger, she draped it over her upturned palm. "You had mentioned you use this to think." She brightened. "How do you think with it? Might you show me?"

Bwaaaaaaaa.

It was endearing but misguided.

He rose and rounded the desk. Fortunately, it was only his eight inch 'think rope' and not his one hundred and fifty foot 'overlord rope'. Holding her gaze, he tugged the piece of hemp rope from her palm and held it up for her to see. He knotted it twice, methodically ensuring each knot reflected each thought.

Duty. Tight. Himself. Tighter.

She peered up at him. "What are doing?"

"Thinking. I do a lot of it." He held the rope between them and snapped it, causing the two large knots to compact. "Whenever my mind is in a knot, these are, too. They represent random thoughts and keep me calm when I need it most. Because staying calm and focused in my line of work is an art. These usually stay knotted until I feel it's resolved.

"Permit me to guide you through it." His calloused finger touched the first knot. "This one, which is bound tightly to ensure it doesn't come undone, relates to the duty I feel toward you. It's who I am. So please don't confuse what I do for you with anything else. I deliver justice to everyone. For that is the definition of justice. To be evenhanded. Always. No exceptions."

She glanced up at him.

He moved his fingers over to the second one on the rope. "The second knot, which is tighter still, is the curiosity I know you feel toward me. It's a curiosity a lot of women feel toward me without realizing that my life comes with a very long rope. Not just this one."

She eyed him.

His chest tightened at facing the only reality he'd known since becoming what Vidocq had inspired him to be: a villain's nightmare. "I won't go into my personal use of it behind closed doors, but I have enemies that take pleasure in giving me pain. I've had a dog I loved dearly shot dead merely because he was mine."

That son of a bitch lost a lot of blood that night. He got

arrested. "I've had a footman, Charles Lerner, who had his throat slit merely because he was brave enough to serve me during a case that went bad. And over the seven brief months Elizabeth and I were married, she was attacked on the street by rabble because of me. Her infidelities made it easy for me to walk away, but knowing she was in danger made it even easier. Fear that. Heed that. And above all understand that what I do is real and unlike these knots, some things cannot be undone."

He eased out a breath between teeth. "You're eighteen, Kumar. I keep saying it, and I'm about to shove a lot of money into your hands *while* saying it, but there is a reason. What you do now will affect the rest of your life and will stay with you. Always. Like a knot. Only you'll *never* get it out. When you're older, you'll find your place and your stronghold which will include a man worthy of you. Unfortunately, that man won't ever be me. Aside from our sizable age difference, it's very difficult for anyone to belong to me. It was difficult for Elizabeth and part of why our marriage fell apart. For I will always belong to my profession first and to everyone else last. That is the contract that is wordlessly signed when it comes to me."

The deep bronze of her cheeks flushed.

"Do you understand?"

Her overly large eyes and delicate features softened all the more as if she were now looking up at countless stars scattered across an endless sky gifted by the darkest of nights.

Pile on the agony. He knew that look.

It was one that whispered of a renewed hope in men and humanity. "Can you not..."

Raising herself on her toes, she gently kissed his lower jaw with full, soft lips. "What you do for others is what few dare to even do in their heads. I admire that. Gruff and overly serious though you appear to be, you define every woman's dream."

He shifted his still tingling jaw, but otherwise didn't move out of fear he'd break from the honor she had just given him. "If that were true, I'd still be married."

"Some women cannot be saved." She squeezed his hand, transferring her warmth into his, before releasing it. "Just as you have given me hope during a time I needed it most, please know you have a friend in me. A true friend. One you can always rely on."

The wilderness of the country she had come from whispered

she held no fear.

Not a fear of him, not a fear of his life, not even a fear for her own life.

Even worse?

She wanted to do it with a smile.

It wasn't right. He had to shake this idea of them even being 'friends' out of her head before it took her down a very dark alley he wouldn't be able to yank her from. "Friendship is far too strong of a word for us to even share. Let us be passing clouds in the night sky so no one can see it."

She shook her head. "I will not settle for that. Especially given you fear being bruised by attachments. 'Tis a very lonely existence you attempt to cure with a raven."

There went his reputation. "I'm not *lonely*." God keep her from pitying a man who routinely masturbated to ensure he never crossed any lines. "Far too many people shuffle in and out of my life on a regular basis. Hell, I couldn't be lonely if I tried." Even married women attempted to wedge past his door holding up spice cakes in the guise of wanting more. As if he had carved OSCULATE ME on his forehead and cock. "I'm not lonely."

"One can be in a crowd and still feel *very* alone, Mr. Ridley. I have often felt that when in India and the population there is well over England's."

It was like trying to argue with a five-foot female professor. "Unfortunately, some people are meant to only watch the crowds as opposed to be in them. Ten years from now, I'll still be doing what I do best. This. And Chaucer and I are more than fine with it. It's who we are and it suits us and our feathers."

"I fear for you, Mr. Ridley." Her expression wavered. "You appear to have embraced your own murder and celebrate nothing but death. Why? Do you not want more for yourself?"

The silence loomed between them like a heavy mist.

That stung. Especially given it was coming from someone so young. Especially given how often he thought of ending it all when her life was barely beginning.

She hesitated. "I did not mean to offend you."

How could one forgive what was true and what remain unchanged?

Holding her gaze, he brought up the rope between them and tied another knot into it for her to see. *Regret*. "When I was your age, I would have loved to have had no responsibilities outside of a tying a cravat. I would have loved to have gone to parties, attend horse races, gotten drunk, played cards, been an idiot with no education and gone sailing, merely because I could. *Instead*, I was hovering over books and dead bodies in every morgue throughout Paris, determined to understand what made the flesh fall apart so I could put shackles on what was happening all over the world regardless of the culture: *murder*."

He pointed down at her face, gently dabbing her brown little nose. "You have a chance to do all of those things, Kumar. Do them. Right down to the sailing. That is why I'm saving your life and giving you money to run with. So you can *have* a life. Above all, understand that the grooves of my muddy road have gotten too deep and well below the knee, which means the turning of any wheel outside of that rut, snaps the elliptic springs holding the forebeds, futchells, bolts, and splinter bar of the coach I'm riding in. So whatever you do, *don't* think you can be like everyone else and try to take these reins by offering me your so-called 'friendship'. Because I'm the only one who knows how to drive this form of transportation at high speeds without killing the horse."

That was a bit long winded.

Even for him. "It's late and that was your bed-time story. It's called Pandora has a box and Ridley owns both so *don't* rattle it. One never knows what crawls out."

She held his gaze. "After a bed-time story ends, Mr. Ridley, it is usually followed by a form of affection toward the one who has quietly listened. I will retire, but only if a kiss is bestowed onto me."

There was no wavering in her voice or in those pale blue eyes.

Nor was she teasing.

Despite the warning.

Despite the rope still hanging in his hand that symbolized his life: *twisted*.

In between methodical breaths he took in an effort to remain calm, he stared at her knowing she and her wit and her buoyancy and botanical intelligence and youth and faith of better things to come in a world that rarely if ever offered it, wanted to kiss the lips of morbid Evan Oswald Ridley.

Though not in the way other women tried to.

She wasn't looking to seduce, corner, dupe, control, ply, grab or possess him.

She didn't even want his money.

She was merely attempting to hold out her hand as if it were enough.

His mind, which was impenetrable in its strength and pride and what it believed in and wanted, betrayed him. It spiraled him into an inner world better known to him as… dissections.

Coca leaves and limestone emptied out of the tin and the box, no longer in use.

An endless night of work alongside a keen, understanding face.

Gloved hands gripping tight in smoke-ridden crowds.

Passing off the cigar and waiting for it to come back after a drag from her own lips.

Stacks of paper filed, organized, ready.

Him dictating and her taking notes.

Her slicing foliage to determine a source.

It only barreled forward faster and faster and faster after that.

Her laughter.

Hours of conversation.

Her bronzed skin dewing from the mist that came in at night as they walked to an assignment.

Ropes that became her clothing whenever they were in the house as she paged through books.

Them fucking and fucking and fucking until pleasure was a nuisance and pain a necessity.

A pistol shot to the skull of any son of a bitch who tried to look at her or hurt her.

Bam, bam, BAM!

Ridley's nostrils *burned*.

They. Burned. Like. Fuck.

For he *knew* he was standing at the gates of hell with sulfur sweeping at him holding up the key that was going to latch every criminal into place.

It was the future known to his analytical mind as heaven.

He had peered into the future that he knew he would one day share with her.

A future his methodical mind had already measured, laid out and *set*.

It's how he saw the world. Through an array of puzzles known as dissections.

The more intricate the dissection, which included language and maps and paintings and books and people and murder scenes, the more everything warped into what could have very well been mounted on massive sheets of hardwood spliced into pieces he always put together.

And she was a piece.

One that would fit into the palm of his hand and click into everything he was and wasn't.

Only not now. Not for many, many years to come.

She was too innocent.

She needed to become what she still wasn't: a woman.

God blind him, how he wanted to hold onto that moment of knowing everything he saw in his head would be real, but his mind sped up and roared knowing if it did ever happen, it wouldn't be for a very long time.

Feeling his chest was no longer his own out of frustration that the future couldn't happen *now,* he gritted his teeth and snapped the rope across her shoulder, startling her. "Damn you into hell for making me wait."

She held his gaze, her expression wavering and gaping. "You... you hurt me. *Intentionally!*"

It took him a moment for him to register what he'd actually done.

The overlord had spoken.

He, who had remained calm throughout an entire marriage that had dragged his teeth across the pavement without ever once swatting at Elizabeth, had snapped a rope against the shoulder of a young, Indian girl looking for a hero.

One who would shape the future of not only his life but others.

Son of a bitch. "There was a point to that, but I still shouldn't have done it." He numbly dangled the rope before her. "Feel free to return the favor."

Welcome to the life you never wanted.

She took the rope, as if arguing with herself about what to do. Half-squinting up at him, she tugged it tight and— "*This* is for not kissing me like a normal man would." She snapped the rope against his chest, whipping it right on the nipple so hard that his linen shirt felt as if it had been slashed open.

He sucked in an astounded breath. "An incredibly well-delivered strike. Bravo and I felt it. Now—"

"*This* is for coca and limestone." She lowered his chin and snapped the rope against him harder.

The sting made him realize she was just getting started. "Uh... can you not—"

"*This* is for the room you do not keep which reflects your soul!" She whipped the rope, snapping it again and again.

He blocked the lashes and glared. "Ey. *Enough*," he bit out, hardening his tone to lethal so she understood she was overstepping bounds no overlord would permit.

A breath escaped her as she grudgingly held up the rope, dangling it between them. "I do believe my list of complaints are done."

Ridley slowly took the rope. It was fairly obvious he'd found a rope-swinging sort of girl ready to not only reorganize the study but his life. "I shouldn't have done that and you have my apology. I was annoyed. I was annoyed knowing..." *You're not broken.*

She squinted. "Knowing what? Do explain, Mr. Ridley. Do. For taking a rope to me was uncalled for."

Unraveling each knot in the hemp rope, he tied a new one. *Patience.* He shoved the rope into his pocket. "Why do you think I permitted you to return the favor? Pain for pain. Though somehow I ended up shouldering more."

"Speaking of shoulders..." She lowered her chin and tapped at her own shoulder, circling it. "I believe you owe it a kiss."

This one didn't know when to stop.

Ridley angled in, trying to remain calm lest his mind revert to the earlier blur he saw in his head. "Kumar. You are far too young and far too mirthful in nature to tie an anchor the size of mine around that little throat anytime soon. Ropes, ravens, murder, and poison is only the beginning. There is no happily ever after given the sort of man I am and you aren't ready for the life I lead. I require someone... *broken*. In pieces. So I can pick them up and put them into my pocket for later use."

She lifted her gaze to his and lingered.

Dropping his hand to his side, he rounded the desk and seated himself again, whipping the rope onto the desk.

She adjusted the robe at its collar, exposing the raw, skinned marks on her wrists from the shackles she had been in for days.

As if she hadn't endured enough.

Those poor wrists. Fuck.

Pickering had earned more than a visit. All forty-seven links that had been heartlessly weighing against those small wrists too tightly with a bolt turned inward were going to be punched into that motherfucking body.

After she retired.

For she didn't need to know about him being a loon. Which he was. It was the only part of himself that he tried to hide. For he enjoyed it too much and knew that his restrained and chained façade held back a mind that veered him burningly close to the very thing he arrested others for.

Quickly yanking open a drawer, he pulled out a tin jar of salve he used for cuts, scrapes and burns which he encountered during assignments. Opening the lid with a *ting*, he swiveled his chair sideways and gestured toward the open space of the floor beside him. "Come to me, Kumar. Your wrists need tending. Do they hurt?"

"Haan." She glanced down at them, then bustled over and regally knelt before him with the billowing of the robe and calico skirts, lifting her eyes and her raw-reddened wrists to him. "Kali praise you."

He pointed. "None of that. Kali and I don't know each other. You should also learn not to forgive people so easily. Stay angry. It's good for you."

She puckered her lips. "I prefer not to give you another case to work on."

"Your so-called humor has finally found its bounds."

She peered into the tin he was holding.

Sitting closer at his feet, she dabbed her brown finger into the cool, scarlet substance and held it to her nose which she crinkled. "'Tis bloodroot. How fitting you have a tin of a plant that relies on ants to spread its seeds and has no nectar. It might as well be your soul." She eyed him for a long moment. "It is only ever used by the Algonquins. Why do you have it?"

He lowered his chin.

If he weren't already sitting, he'd be kneeling. For if this was her mind at eighteen... the glory of what it would be at thirty almost knocked the motherfucking breath out of him. "My, aren't we a bit of a genius and hello, hello. A native from the Algonquin tribe came into London last year. He was gracious enough to share a gift devoted to healing. I use it all the time."

Damn you for not being broken enough to play with.

Digging a finger into the tin, he removed a sizable amount of the cool, thick salve and set the tin onto the desk. Taking her one hand, which was so damnably small and soft, he carefully applied the red-tinted salve around her entire wrist, tilting her hand in doing so.

She winced.

As if he didn't feel bad enough. "I promise it will heal fast." Releasing her hand, he leaned over to the desk and dug a finger into the tin again. Edging back to her, he took her other hand and carefully applied the salve to that entire wrist.

She winced again and hissed, her features untwisting and then flickering.

His voice softened. "Are you all right?"

She puffed out breaths, her small cheeks inflating and deflating.

Seeing her in so much pain was… *horrible*. Unacceptable. Why did he hear creaking coming out of the cavern known as his heart? What the hell? "*Guérid rapidement.* Heal fast."

Her expressive face changed as she watched him. She grew somber.

Too somber for his liking. "Does it hurt that much?"

She slowly shook her head. "*Nahin.* I was thinking about…" Her voice cracked.

He clicked on the tin, trying not to focus on her pain. Pickering. Cane. *Tonight.* "Yes? What?"

"Given what you do, if someone had disappeared over ten years ago and there were pieces of that puzzle that were still remembered by a few, is it possible to investigate that person's disappearance? Perhaps even find the one responsible for it?"

He knew she was referring to her mother. The one Dr. Watkins had told him of when they were sitting across from each other in prison trying to dig through ways to keep her from getting hanged.

It twisted his breath. "The more time passes, the less likely anything will ever be found. With no evidence, there is no path, and without witnesses, it tosses the map that might lead me to finding those responsible. Do you understand?"

Tears streaked her eyes. A tear rolled down her cheek. And another one. "I had hope."

It was exactly that hope that he wanted her to keep.

One that would disappear once surrounded by his life.

Swallowing hard, he brushed away the tear that had escaped with his thumb. He held up his now tear-dabbed finger for her to see the moisture he had removed from her face. "I acknowledge your pain." Holding her gaze, he brought his finger to his own lips and kissed it. "Now it is mine."

She stared up at him, her lips trembling. Her hands jumped upward and grabbed at his arms and shoulders as she quickly leaned upward and toward him.

He stiffened. The moment he let her infiltrate those thirty-seven locks better known as his heart, there was no going back. Not given who and what he was.

She wasn't ready and neither was he.

Ridley jerked far back and removed her hands one by one from his tensing muscles that roared against his own will to cooperate. "No. *Cease.*" He couldn't breathe knowing what she wanted of him. Already. The future was already knocking on that door, demanding he not only open it, but rip off the hinges. "You're leaving in less than three days. Whether we overturn that conviction or not, you're set to depart. It's for your safety and there is no way around it. So don't complicate this."

He swiveled away in his chair, purposefully leaving her on the floor at his feet to contemplate his words as he snapped the tin's lid hard back into place and set it back into his drawer.

He slammed it shut. Much like he was slamming shut any idea that she was ready for the sort of life she was asking for. Not for another five years. She needed to crack and break beneath the weight of experience to better understand him and his ways.

Moving his chair closer to the desk, he opened a ledger and refocused.

Kumar quietly rose. She rounded the desk with a soft swish of cashmere and calico, and stood before him, running her fingers across one of the open ledgers as she angled it toward herself. "I will permit you to work."

He nodded.

She hesitated upon seeing his notes and jerked down toward

it. She waggled a finger across it as if trying to erase what she saw. "How much coca have you been chewing?"

"Pardon?"

Her brows flickered. She pointed. "This. Whatever is this?"

Unable to think, he leaned forward in his chair, tapping one of many cases he was working on and somehow managed, "Eraow acaer tupress jeren."

She gaped and then squinted. "That is not any language I know. Is it... Swedish?"

"No." She was attempting to dig out all of his mind's secrets and... he was letting her. He was letting her because he wanted that future to be his. His. "It's called a shadow language."

"I do not understand."

"Meaning, it doesn't exist. I write all of my notes in it so that if anyone breaks into this house and seizes my notes, and it *has* happened, they can't figure out what it says. If it's unusually important, I also keep additional copies of it locked in a tamper-resistant box." He pointed to a bookshelf where the safe was hidden behind. "In my line of work, you have to dig deeper than the nearest shovel can."

Looking at the words, she glanced up at him and clasped her hands. "It is as equally marvelous in its inception as it is useful. I wish to learn this shadow language. Might you teach me?"

He gave her a withering look. "No one who isn't me can learn a language in three days."

She snorted. "Cease thinking yourself to be a greater prodigy than I. A few words is not going to confuse this mind. My memory is remarkably good. How do you think I learned English? Or became knowledgeable about flora? Teach me."

"No and no. And should there be any further misunderstanding... *no*."

She stared. "Why ever not? Are you denying me the right to learn?"

This one was a girl of his veins looking to tickle her mind. "I appreciate your enthusiasm but as I told you before I have to work. Or have you forgotten?" He tsked. "So much for your memory being remarkably good."

She squinted, taking on the challenge. "As you can see, I have already forgiven you. *However...*" She tapped at her shoulder and feigned a wince. "It still hurts. I have no doubt it will turn into a sizable blister and bleed for at least a week. I have no doubt. It may even scar. I ought to have you arrested."

He rolled his tongue against the inside of his mouth. Her being eighteen showed. For she knew how to poke it. "Learning a shadow language is involved."

She brightened. "I enjoy learning. I enjoy—"

"Shadow languages take time. It took me, its creator, eight years to perfect. There is no pattern as it is created out of the ether. I more or less piece together an array of nonsensical words and assigned them to a real word to create a language."

"Demonstrate. I promise not to share its secrets with anyone."

Dig, dig, dig. Go on, Ridley. Dig that grave for her. "I can't."

She paused. "Do you not trust me?"

"It isn't that." Ridley tapped at his head hard. "This is where it *has* to stay. Because if anyone figures out I have someone other than myself who can translate all of these…" He swept a hand to the piles around them. "That someone will end up being used against me like a wiggling worm on a jagged hook called Kumar."

She said nothing.

"It's a compliment. It means I don't want you to die." Picking up a quill, he dipped the nib into the inkwell and grabbed a missive he didn't need off the desk, turning it over so he had an empty surface, he scribed: *Oleald Ekcle Surogou.*

Ridley set the quill back into the stand and pushed the missive toward her. "These are the only words you need to know. It applies to you."

She picked up the missive. "*Oleald Ekcle Surogou.*" She tapped it and then set it against her crinkled nose, peering at him from over the missive with mischievous eyes. "It says, *Be Mine Tonight.*"

He pointed. "Flirting is not advisable." Not given what went through his head earlier.

She tapped at the missive. "This is your attempt to be romantic. *Haan?*"

Romantic? *Him?* Maybe, maybe a long time ago. As a child of… ten. He'd often seen his parents whisper and laugh and even chase each other around the house while his father dangled mistletoe during Christmas.

And then they separated.

And then his mother got involved with Lord Spencer who swept her into a far happier life.

And then his father continued to do what he did best: spent his vast fortune on books and antiquities, making the rest of the house unusable, like this study. Making him, Evan, read and organize musty leather bound books each and every day while the two of them climbed over them like ants looking for the hill.

And then the murder that all too eerily whispered of a passion gone wrong given he had heard violent lovemaking and grunts and moans and thuds while he had tried to sleep in riled discomfort through the words of 'Hish! Yes! Mm! Mm!' followed by a very long silence that eventually brought the slow, slow barefoot pattering of a faceless woman creeping into his own room naked with an ax. She rendered him unconscious prior to butchering his own father.

It was as if she had wanted him to hear them fucking and live with it every time he now did.

And then Vidocq and that iron fist that refused to let him sleep unless he solved the puzzles set before him in both English and French. Which wasn't even the academy.

And then he and his profession became overly popular at a mere two and twenty when he solved his first double-homicide.

And then the women he tried to shove out the door for he hardly wanted to end up like his father: butchered well past the sternum known as the heart.

And then Elizabeth who had tried to turn him—him!—into the very thing he was fighting against: irrational animalistic passions gone wrong.

It never fucking stopped.

How did one embrace the very thing that personified what hurt most and made a man do things no man should? "Romance and I aren't related. I sentenced that codswallop to hang the moment he tried to sell me some mistletoe, but that doesn't mean I don't respect those who entertain it. Some are known to survive it."

She lowered the missive and glanced at it again, smoothing it. "One day, I will find someone who offers me that and more."

"Not everyone shares the dream of avoiding reality." He leaned forward and pointed to the missive. "It says *Freedom is mine*. It's my promise to you regardless of what happens tomorrow night. I have an arrangement with Finkle to ensure this conviction does not touch you."

Her cheeks flushed, deepening the bronze of her skin. She tilted her dark head as if the words pleased her, her full lips subtly curving. "*Oleald* means 'freedom', *Ekcle* means 'is', and *Surogou* means 'mine'."

He clapped, letting it echo in the vast study. "And those are the only words she will ever be able to translate lest she die before she gets on that boat."

She grinned, revealing adorably crooked but white teeth. Turning away, she held the missive high up over head, as if the ceiling were a person in need of seeing it. Touching her chest and forehead twice, she quietly chanted something.

Observing her, he quieted his voice. "What are you doing?"

She swung her skirts toward him and breezed back through the piles of newspapers, lowering the missive. She folded the missive twice and tucked it into her décolletage. "I was announcing my freedom to the gods. I wanted them to hear it so they can no longer deny what is mine. I also wanted them to ensure they bless you for giving me my freedom."

There was something... *magical* about her and what she believed in.

As if nothing could dissuade her from seeing the brightness of tomorrow.

It scraped at the muscles of his leather-toughened heart.

It scraped it a bit too hard knowing she thought it was real.

She leaned back toward the desk. "Now you. Scribe something for yourself. Scribe what you want most and I will ensure the gods hear it."

"We would be writing well into next year and another ten after that. How about I scribe the words 'Go to bed'?"

Giving him a withered look, she gathered his ledgers. "Cease treating me like a child. If freedom is truly mine, *I* decide when I retire. Not you."

He was done arguing. It's not like they had to be anywhere until tomorrow night.

He picked up his quill, still watching her and started paging through what he needed to do next. While still watching her, of course.

He rolled the quill against his fingers that annoyingly quaked.

He needed coca/limestone. "How much longer do you think you'll be awake?"

She methodically tucked ledgers into a neat pile and evened them out with quick hands, setting them all on the edge of his desk. She then proceeded to gather every last parchment into sweeping stacks they didn't belong in, shuffling them together like cards.

His heart flipped as his hand jumped out and slapped the stack hard, the quill rolling. "Whoa, whoa, and whoa. Do not... touch... *anything*."

She stilled in a half-bent position that continued to lean toward him over the desk, then lifted a finger and veered it like a whirling fly to his forehead. She touched it. "Is this *anything*? Or it is nothing?"

Their eyes locked.

His mouth twitched.

Her eyes sparkled knowingly. "Admit that you *almost* smiled," she taunted, waggling her brown finger at him.

To admit it would be to acknowledge that he'd be butchering men and women on the hour for even commenting on the coloring of her skin.

To admit it would be to acknowledge that her rapier mind was already his.

To admit it would be to acknowledge that he could fuck her until her soul and body ripped at its seams.

To admit it would be to acknowledge that the future was now.

He dragged his hand away from the papers and gripped the edge of the desk, allowing the hard wood to bite into his palm. "Go to bed, Kumar. When you see the carnage in the theatre tomorrow night, it will make you realize where your priorities should be. With them. Not me."

Her smile faded.

With a half-nod, she turned and wove through the mess. She paused just outside the double doors and said softly over her shoulder, "Good night, Mr. Ridley. Your devotion is humbling and I enjoyed learning about you. You are a very noble and intelligent man. I only wish you would respect yourself more by admitting a raven will never be enough."

She left.

DELILAH MARVELLE

If he wasn't careful, he'd end up becoming the very thing he was accusing Dr. Watkins of.

Knowing she was gone, he jerked open the drawer, grabbing a stack of leaves with a larger pinch of limestone. Rolling them together with trembling hands, he tucked it into the side of his mouth and chanted to himself to chew. Hard. To let the numbness in his mouth overtake the numbness he wanted to feel. The numbness he needed to feel so he didn't give into what he wanted to feel.

For it was true. All of it.

She had read him like an open book in four different languages.

He *was* lonely. It's why he thought about hanging himself. He *wanted* more than a raven to converse with. It's why he thought about hanging himself. He *wanted* to return to something other than a house filled with aristocratic treasures belonging to those beheaded and to musty books that only reminded him of lives unlived.

Death surrounded him so much that he sometimes thought of just joining it.

And yet… he wanted there to be more. He did. He wanted to find someone capable of giving him a reason not to crawl into a noose.

Someone who wasn't looking for marriage but freedom.

Someone who wanted to be their own person yet part of something.

As your associate, I wish to see your study.

Swallowing against the bitterness of the leaves, he paused, his gaze settling on his trousers.

He had missed a button.

I will continue to be the conscience you clearly do not have, Mr. Ridley.

He fastened the button back into place.

If he survived beyond five years, he'd circle back to her and revisit what he saw in his head.

It's what made him an overlord.

When others could no longer stand, he yanked on his leather boots and kept running until the leather fell off and nothing was left and *still* he kept on until he hit bone.

Or thoughts of suicide.

Restless, with his leg and boot jittering, jittering into the

118

floorboard, he withdrew his pocket watch, rotating it twice. It didn't matter that he was going on over fifteen hours of no sleep.

He'd get plenty of it given he had nowhere to be tomorrow morning or the afternoon.

He needed to know more about the logs he saw at Millbank.

Or his mind wouldn't let him sleep.

It was Thursday. Thursday, Thursday.

Past two in the morning.

Think, think, think.

Where was Pickering usually at this hour?

Opium. Den. Devil's Acre.

CHAPTER SIX

She couldn't sleep.

It felt like the longest night she had ever lived.

As if she were compiling thirteen lifetimes into a single breath she was forced to swallow.

Despite too many minutes passing, Jemdanee could do nothing but eye the lone oil lamp she had left burning. She did so in a childish attempt to ease her imaginings which were accented by countless shadows that were becoming too menacing to look at.

What made it further impossible for her to sleep was that the tightly laced and overly small corset was digging into bare skin. With no chemise beneath it and no way to reach the lacings tied and tucked and knotted to the stretch at the back, she ached with discomfort.

Still curled against the sunken mattress of the massive four poster bed overstuffed with pillows, she tugged up the layers of linen to her chin in an attempt to shield herself against the coolness of the night that penetrated her skin.

She eyed the cavernous room whose gilded and ornate furnishings reminded her of items pulled from the palaces of European kings she had seen in illustrations from books Peter had kept on his shelf back in Calcutta.

The wardrobe, which had been left open, seemed to be held into place by an unseen hand that sat in the darkness of the chest within.

She had never been one to believe in ghosts.

She thought it childish.

And yet...

Dark shadows shifted against the sparse light that fingered across the uneven floorboards and illuminated the heavy, velvet curtains around the bed. The wind caused branches beyond the window to rustle and sway, looking like countless witch-like arms attempting to find souls to drag in and eat.

Occasional creaks within her room as if someone were walking toward her bed made her do something she rarely did: *panic*.

Flipping aside the linen, she scrambled out of the bed and darted across the room. Jerking open her door, she peered out, her pulse roaring. The lurking shadows were even worse in the corridor, heading out to countless blackened rooms with smeared doors that no doubt housed things she dared not fathom.

Bones. Lots of them.

She bustled back toward the landing of the stairwell and thudded down the stairs toward the study, refusing to be alone. It reminded her of too many nights spent hidden beneath a manure cart buried in foliage in an effort to remain hidden from sight and keep others from grabbing her whilst she'd slept.

Skidding into the study, she paused at finding it empty. "Mr. Ridley?" she whispered hoarsely as if he would somehow emerge from the hip-high piles of papers and books that filled the room.

Where was he? *"Mr. Ridley?"*

No answer.

Eeeeeee. Though he had never once said it, she *knew* his father had been butchered in this house. And he was living in it. Living. In. It. Like a morbid king requiring a skeletal throne.

What if she was sleeping in the room where it had happened? What if that body and its pieces had spattered the bed and the walls of...

Jemdanee shuddered and swung around.

An elderly, bony man in a robe veered in.

"AAAAAAAAAAAAAAAAAAAAAAAAAAAAAAAAAAAAA AAAAA!!!" she screamed.

The man cringed and set his fingers into his ears, waiting for the screaming to end.

Edging back between ragged breaths that made her clutch her robe and her beating heart like she had been stabbed with a knife multiple times, she was convinced this elderly man before her was... Ridley's dead father.

Only he was real.

"Forgive the stealth in my approach, miss," the gentleman intoned, his dark eyes shadowed from age and no doubt darker things seen. "I abide by the name of Mr. Fulton and serve to this residence as butler. Mr. Ridley has stepped out for a small while to tend to business. I was asked and tasked to oversee your wellbeing. Might I assist you in something, miss?"

She swallowed, her limbs now quaking from over-fatigue. "When will... Mr. Ridley return?"

"That I cannot say. He is known to keep odd hours."

Why did that not surprise her?

"Are you in need of nourishment or tea?"

What she was in need of was assurance that she wasn't going to die.

She shook her head. "I require nothing." She hardly wanted to come across as a ninny. Too many years with Peter had softened her to the point of feathers. What was wrong with her?! Maybe a part of her knew she was sitting in the belly of a morbid beast known as Mr. Ridley.

She inclined her head in appreciation. "Knowing he will return, I will retire. I thank you for the offer of tea and your assistance, Mr. Fulton."

The man inclined his own head. "It was a pleasure, Miss Kumar."

She blinked. He knew her name. Which meant Ridley had instructed this gentleman. It comforted her. "Forgive me for waking you, Mr. Fulton."

"If only you were the one who had," he countered with the slip of a lip. "I bid you a good-night, miss. Should you require my services, I will be in the kitchen as I was instructed not to retire until Mr. Ridley returned."

She cringed knowing it. "Please do not impose yourself in that manner on my account. I will retire and advise you to do so, as well. Good-night, Mr. Fulton."

"Good-night, miss."

Drawing the cashmere robe against herself to push away the chill that seemed to linger despite it being a summer night, she turned and thudded her way up the stairs as if something else might lunge after her.

In between uneven breaths, she eyed the long corridors, then her room and Ridley's.

Deranged though it was to even think it, she knew she would sleep far better in his room. There was a dagger on his nightstand. One she had seen when she had chalked her teeth earlier.

Not that... ghosts succumbed to daggers.

CHAPTER SEVEN

Devil's Acre

People often whispered that he, Evan Oswald Ridley, was deranged.

It was true. He was.

For the devil in him was as equally deranged as the criminals he shackled up.

He reveled in slamming criminals to their knee caps that shattered beneath their screams and the eerie glory of the peace it always brought.

One could say his obsession with piecing together a past he'd never been able to unravel had turned him into a gothic champion for some and a lot of a villain for others.

His own crimes included but were not limited to destroying property, tossing delinquents out of moving carriages and over bridges, breaking the arms of men who didn't seem to understand prostitutes were still people, getting to a scene before Scotland Yard did, and pointing pistols at the heads of those he didn't like.

Sometimes he pulled the trigger and purposefully shot them in the arm or the leg.

Sometimes he did more.

For the countless times he'd been arrested for overstepping his bounds, all it took was a disgruntled missive to his contact at Scotland Yard and Finkle would stalk in and file the necessary paperwork to get him out.

For too many years he had accepted that he would only ever be married to the dead. And then he married and *felt* dead. Given Elizabeth turned out to be a bigger loon than he'd ever be, he went back *to* the dead. And now? Back to the living.

This is for you, Kumar.

Tossing his half-smoked cigar onto the cobbled street, Ridley jumped down from the iron step of his coach and slammed the door shut before the footman could get to it. Double rows of brightly lit burning lamps hovered above the opium den he knew Pickering frequented.

Yanking out a prepared roll of limestone/coca leaves, which was enough to get his pulse roaring, he tucked it inside his mouth, chewing into its bitterness in an effort to bite through what needed to be done.

The numbness against the inside of his cheek soon started as saliva dampened the dry leaves. He chewed, signaling to his footman, Shelton, to stand on the pavement behind him.

Slowing each chew, he waited for the coca/limestone to take effect.

It usually took seven minutes for it to start tapping his brain.

Much like everything in his life, he had laid out each and every minute of what needed to happen next and why. More than seven minutes had passed. For the coca now revved his pulse to full throttle. He rattled his leg, waiting.

"One minute remains, sir," Shelton announced, thudding the gold handled cane into the ground.

"Thank you, Shelton. Hold your position and the cane."

Flexing his arms, one over each shoulder, which was still sore from his boxing trainer's relentless practice a few days earlier, he widened his stance, ready.

The woman he had earlier paid to usher Pickering out at an exact time, bustled past Evan and down the darkened, gas-lit street.

Swilling the last of the coca juice that was already accelerating his heartrate and sharpening his mind, Ridley swallowed the full warmth of it and then spit the spiny remnants of the wadded leaves out.

Pain for pain, but never for self-gain.

A cloaked gentleman whose top hat was drawn over his eyes

pushed past the door of the opium den and paused, realizing the woman was gone.

The officer, whose dark mustache was stiff with wax, snapped his gaze to Ridley.

Shifting his jaw, Ridley held that gaze to ensure the man had a few breaths to adjust to whatever panic was going through that head. "If you lie down on the pavement, I'll ensure I don't touch your face."

Pickering glanced toward the entrance of the opium den where a crowd had gathered and then opened his coat, displaying a rosewood pistol attached to a holster. "Remove your weapons, Ridley."

As predicted. "You needlessly worry. I left my holster at home. After all… some men need more than a bullet." Removing and shrugging off his great coat on the gas-slit street and folding it, Ridley handed it off to his footman behind him to showcase he had no weapons at all. He pointed at the heads of every last person watching. "Go inside. *Now*. All of you."

Two men lingering nearby, eyed the massive wad of coca leaves Ridley had spit and hustled back into the den.

The rest of the men who also lingered, adjusted their collars and went inside, as well.

Pickering released his coat, covering the pistol. "What is this about, Ridley? I'm far from your usual sort of fair."

"Are you?" he rumbled out. "Why are some of the logs off by more than a day?"

Pickering dragged a hand across his mustache and shifted from boot to boot. "I thought you were the sort of man who knew everything."

Oho. "Answer the question."

Pickering gave him a look of indifference. "Unlike the rest of these constables at Scotland Yard, I'm not intimidated. You're what I call a nuisance pretending to be the law."

Ridley lowered his chin, his mouth numb from the coca and his pulse roaring. He leaned in. "At least I know how to pretend with finesse. Because you're far too busy smearing the logs and making Indian women stand naked in your back room. And for some reason, you can't even slap on shackles properly. You turned in the bolt."

Pickering dropped his voice to lethal. "Are you referring to the one with the brown tits and brown cunt I could have easily fucked but didn't?"

That made Ridley drag in a breath that burned his chest.

Cracking his hands to ready them, he breathed out, "I'm about to make The Black Raven Murder look like Jesus was having fun."

Removing his pistol, Pickering pointed it at Evan's head. "Leave."

"No."

Pickering cocked the pistol.

Ridley slowly signaled the footman behind him with four fingers.

Shelton tossed his gold headed cane on an angle and scrambled back.

Jumping aside, Ridley snatched it, and swung the head of the cane at that pistol with the grit of teeth, dashing it *downward* so hard out of the man's hand, the thundering echo of the pistol fired off.

It thudded across the far end of the pavement, announcing *he* was in control.

Pickering seethed out breaths, holding his rigid hand against his heaving chest. "Clever."

"At least one of us is." Gripping the cane, Ridley waited. "Why are you smearing the logs?"

"I have no idea what you're referring to."

"Wrong answer." Backhanding the cane *hard* across those facial bones with the swing of his body, the sound of flesh cracked the night air. "What about now? Does anything come to mind?"

"*Son of a bitch!*" Pickering keeled off to the side before jumping back toward him with a swinging fist.

Skidding aside from the swing of those knuckles, Ridley brought the entire tip of the gold cane across that mustached face with the force of a brick going through a building.

Pickering staggered and collapsed to the ground.

Standing over him, Ridley whirled the cane and lifted it up and onto his shoulders, letting his wrists dangle it in place behind his head. "You're usually on the right side of the law, Pickering. What the hell is going on? Is someone threatening you?"

"Fuck all nine generations of your ancestors," Pickering choked out.

"There may be far more than nine, but why not count them in person yourself?" Lifting the cane up and off his shoulders, Ridley tapped the pavement with it in warning. "I'm offering you what I offer everyone: assistance. Take it before I introduce you to the cane."

"I intend to report you to the commissioner. He will know of this. He. Will. Know."

Little did this bastard know the commissioner was 'Finkle' and now Ridley's other hand. "You do that." Gritting his teeth, Ridley swung the cane down over and over, despite the shouts and the grunts that the coca blurred.

Much like it always did, his mind blanked as he let the devil do the rest.

Head. Neck. Back. Back. Jaw. Head. Mouth. Face. Head. Face. Face. Face. Leg. More leg. Don't break it. Mouth. Shoulder. Back. Hard. Harder.

Why count?

Thoughts of Kumar in chains, thoughts of her wrists, her fear, her humiliation at having to stand naked before men who knew nothing of pain, made him hit Pickering harder and harder, until blood spattered and covered his clothing, the cane, and his boots.

"Sir?" the footman politely called in from behind as he was instructed to always do. "There is more than enough blood to warrant stopping. He is no longer moving."

Her eyes. Her innocence. Let it guide you.

Between evening breaths, Ridley stepped away, folding himself back into his mind, and tossed the cane back to his footman. "Thank you, Shelton," he rasped. "Wipe it down and soak it in brandy."

"Yes, sir."

Pickering slowly edged his head upward to look at Ridley from the blood-spattered pavement, his gored face, heavily gashed and swollen, his seething breaths wheezing.

Squatting casually beside him, Ridley leaned in to that bloodied face. "The only reason you're not dead, *Monsieur Pickering*, is because of one person. Me. Learn how to better fight because pistols aren't always reliable even when shot." Ridley leaned in closer, the acrid smell of fresh blood drifting from that flesh and that pavement. "Why are the logs being smeared?"

The man attempted to move away. "I... I needed... the... money. I owe the den... a thousand."

"Ah." The coca still roaring through his veins, Ridley nudged that head to get a better view of that battered face. With a gloved finger, he dipped it inside the man's blood-filled mouth like an ink well and scraped it into the pavement, in between frequent dips, writing out KUMAR.

It took a small while, given he had to keep dipping for blood and making Pickering wince.

Given the last letter wasn't dark enough, Ridley dipped it in the man's blood again *hard*, making Pickering hiss, and then casually rounded the R. "There. Read that for me. What does it say?"

Those brows flickered.

Ridley pointed to each blood letter. "K-U-M-A-R. Kumar. *This* is the name of the woman whose rights you violated. Explain to me why you thought it necessary to strip a respectable woman naked in a prison whilst purposefully turning a bolt inward in the shackles of her wrists. Explain this to me."

"I... I lived through seeing my... wife and child *burn*... due to... those... *heathens*."

"Is that what that was, Pickering? My, my. I certainly hope the blood you're dripping and the pain you're feeling will remind you of not only her pain but the pain of her people. Maybe they burned your wife and child because the government you work for burned their wives and children. Have you even given thought to that? Or do you only see your own cock hanging between your bony little legs?"

Pickering said nothing, only wheezed.

"Now that you understand my position on India, explain to me who is making you smear the logs? Unlike your ears, mine are not full of blood and I can hear you. I suggest you start talking."

Pickering averted his gaze that was swelling from the gore but said nothing.

This was going to require gentlemanly French devil finesse. Ridley snapped his fingers at Shelton. "Load his pistol, *s'il vous plaît*. Use my gunpowder and a lead ball."

"Yes and most certainly, Mr. Ridley!" Shelton swiped up the pistol and held it up and passed it to the driver.

The stocky driver, in between the smack of over-enthused lips, primed and loaded the pistol before handing it back to Shelton. "Five pounds says I'll see the inside of his skull," he chided.

"As if you have that sort of money, you popinjay." Shelton pointed up at the driver and chided back, "Eight pounds says he'll get arrested."

Ridley leaned in closer to Pickering, his own arm draped over his own bent knee. "It would seem my footman and driver appear to be bidding against you with their own wages, Mr. Pickering. Heed the warning as they have both seen it all. Do you have a name for the one making you smear the logs?"

Pickering staggered to lift his head off the pavement but still said nothing.

"I see." Taking the pistol from Shelton, Ridley whirled it and then cocked it. He set the pistol against the man's bloodied head, digging it into that temple. "Given your inability to use the brain that is swelling against your skull, I will reduce my own level of intelligence in your honor for a game called *Trios*. When you hear the French word *trios*, those ancestors of mine, which you had so boldly insulted and who are all buried in France and some without heads, will formally greet you. The hardest part of playing this game or winning it is one never knows when I'm actually going to say *trios* because I'm not one to count in any particular order. Permit me to do it in English first until I get to the French. Let us begin, shall we? Sixty. Nine. Fifty." He ensured the man heard his finger tapping on the trigger. "*Vingt-et-un—*"

"The governor," Pickering choked out. "The governor. He... he had me... smear the logs."

Ridley paused and squinted. "Why?"

"I was never told *why*. I... I did it and... and took the money."

Sensing the man was telling the truth, Ridley removed the pistol from that temple. He would ensure Finkle knew. Because something was going on. Kumar's log wasn't the only one that had been played with when he'd been rifling through them.

Too many logs were missing.

Feeling at ease with the information he had, Ridley sighed

and leaned in. "How do you feel? Do you need a ride home?"

Pickering's chest heaved, his eyes rolling to the back of his head. He went limp.

"They always do that." Realizing he'd delivered one blow too many, Ridley grudgingly handed off the pistol and wagged over the footman. "Fetch my satchel. He needs gin, laudanum, thread, needle and a few bandages."

"Yes, sir."

Tugging over his great coat from off the pavement, Ridley methodically folded it and set it beside the man's head, rolling him onto it. "You need to cease being cocky. You're the law. Represent what few do."

Pickering drifted back into consciousness and stiffened.

"You needn't worry." Ridley leaned in to that gored face and grabbed the man's hand hard to assure him. "I'll pay half of what you owe the den and offer to pay the rest if you find out more. Try to get the governor to talk. Can you do that?"

Picking's features flickered in confusion. "Why are you...?"

"When the sun rises, my friend, you will find yourself in endless pain and your soul will be cleansed because of it. Take the offer and find out more." He grabbed the bottle of gin from his Shelton. "Wait until your face heals and don't mention my name."

Ragged breaths escaped Pickering. "You will... pay... the debt?"

"Only if you stay true. Work alongside me, Pickering. You're more than this. Honor the child and wife you lost by starting anew. Nothing is ever guaranteed until we're dead. Are you insinuating you're already dead?"

There was a long moment of silence.

"I'll do it." Pickering winced. "Can I... have the... gin?"

"In a moment." Ridley uncorked the bottle and leaning toward the pavement, poured out enough to finger out Kumar's name which he had written in blood until it smudged and was unreadable. He leaned back and tilted the bottle toward those split and swelling lips. "Drink the whole thing. Judging by the damage, you're going to need about..." He surveyed the gashes. "Two inches of thread pulled through your face. I can assure you, the women will love it."

Pickering groaned.

"No, no, I'm quite serious. Women are drawn to dangerous men. Now hold still."

3:18 a.m.
221 Basil Street

When I heard her voice, I fancied I knew her, but could not be positive. After we had got about fifty paces into the wood, the man who seemed to be their commander, rose up to the person that carried me, and cried to him, set down the slabbering milksop you have behind you, and let her shift for herself.

The damn thing wasn't even properly edited.

It was going to be the first book he ever sold off that he didn't finish reading.

Christ. Slapping shut *The Comic Romance of Monsieur Scarron*, which had been printed in 1775, Ridley reached over the ledge of the copper tub he was soaking in and set it onto the stand. How the damn thing was worth even a farthing yet alone the twenty guineas a collector wanted for it went beyond his mental understanding.

Ridley edged up and up, sending a swirling wave of warm, blood-tinged water against the soapy, porcelain tub around him. He raked his drenched, dark hair out of his eyes with a few agitated sweeps and seethed out a breath.

Numb, given the effects of the coca had vanished, he stood, water streaming down the length of his muscled, nude body. A body he punished to the point of never giving himself any pleasure outside of pain.

He was used to it.

His career had seen him stabbed four times, each requiring a half an elbow of needle and thread. He'd been shot twice and stitched up for that, too, one bullet having almost hit an artery. Broken glass marred and whitened his knuckles, whispering of the times he'd broken windows to get to people who refused to open doors.

His body was a map to his own insanity and the mind that had long lost track of it.

Grabbing hold of the towel from the brass stand beside the tub, he rubbed the water from his hair. He stepped out onto the black-and-white Italian tile, blankly drying the rest of himself and folding the wet towel, draped it back on the brass stand.

The flickering light from the oil lamp within the bath chamber shifted the shadows.

Shrugging on a cashmere robe over his unclad body, he left the bath chamber and entered his room, lathering his face with shaving soap. He snapped open his straight razor. By the dim light, he scraped the coarse hairs from his jaw and upper lip, needing to look like the gentleman his mother, Marguerite, had raised him to be.

Methodically cleaning everything and chalking his teeth while humming a tune he'd once heard in France, he rubbed his face with cologne, letting it sting his freshly shaven skin, and tying the robe into place, he eased out a breath and turned toward the adjoining bedchamber.

Extinguishing the oil lamps, save the one by the *écritoire* which he always kept on, he guided himself toward his own bed into the darkened room.

He paused.

The outline of a curled female body was tucked into it, the linens up to her nose, sleeping.

Kumar had... crawled into his bed.

His bed. As if it were hers.

He lingered. Watching her sleep so trustingly, with her black hair curling out of its bundled pins as it grazed her bronzed cheeks made his chest tighten.

She already trusted him.

It was humbling. Albeit incredibly stupid and naïve.

The soft intakes of her breath made him veer in and lean in close, almost setting his nose to her nose. In between steadying intakes of breaths, he drew in her heat. A sweet, sweet and delicate heat the devil in him wanted to swallow whole.

No. Not swallow. He was never one to dash his way through anything.

The devil in him wanted to chew her slowly. With eight incisors, four canines, eight premolars and twelve molars. All thirty-two of his teeth and his tongue for whatever was left over as she slid down his throat.

Knowing full well the darker side of him was whispering things it shouldn't, he considered carrying her back to her room, but knew he needed the sleep more than she did. The heavy quake of his arms which had thrown full force into delivering the caning Pickering needed, were weak.

He'd only end up dropping her given it had been close to nineteen hours since he last slept.

And yet he lingered.

Seeing her slumbering so innocently without her knowing the violence he was capable of, one he had delivered in her name without her permission, made him feel vile and unworthy of even being in her presence.

She was the very definition of the sunlight that made his soul squint.

She was also the definition of the sunlight he wanted to warm his skin.

Respect her peace. It isn't yours. It's hers.

Extinguishing the oil lamp, he rounded the bed and slowly settled in beside her beneath the linen, easing himself close to the heat and softness of her body. A softness he needed to feel to remind himself of what he was protecting: her innocence.

Although the right thing to have done was to give her his back, the overlord in him wanted to touch a thumb to the beauty of what he never touched: purity.

It was his way of cleansing his soul.

He pressed himself into her slim backside, his hands sliding over the soft curves. Trying not to wake her, he tucked her against himself, wrapping his arms around her.

A gruff breath escaped him.

For the first time in a long time, he felt human again.

It was nice.

Closing his eyes, he faded.

Muscled arms and a muscled body weighing her own body made her startle awake in the darkness, momentarily wondering whose arms she could possibly be in.

Then she remembered.

"Mr. Ridley?" she whispered.

He stirred and then paused. "Yes?" he whispered back. "What is it?"

A shaky breath escaped her realizing Mr. Ridley was not only holding her (*whilst in his bed!*), but casually responding to her as if they had been married for twenty years.

The creaking sounds of the house disappeared knowing it.

Tightening her hold on his arms in welcoming adoration, she winced against the pinch of the corset and attempted to shift out of its burning hold. The cashmere robe that was soft against her fingers, made her ease out a breath only to note the muscle of his body and its hardness.

His Parisian cologne mingled with her breaths that made her not only melt, but sink further against him. It was agony. Agony, agony, agony.

How was it he seemed oblivious to her being a woman?

He appeared immune to her, and yet… he held her.

What if she was dreaming? "Am I awake?" she ventured.

"You shouldn't be."

What if he felt obligated to hold her? After all, she'd crawled into his bed like a ninny looking for shelter. "Should I leave?" she whispered. "Would you rather I leave?"

"It matters not to me."

She swallowed and turned toward him in the darkness, his undefined features in the shadows close behind her. "Your house makes too many sounds at night."

"It's the books," he whispered. "Some are as old as the Crusades and they're all telling stories. They try to crawl out of the pages and drag you in with warped words. The ones in the attic are by far the worst. They're piled high enough to enable you to stand on them and reach the rafters where all the old ropes from the building hang."

Dread crawled up her spine. "You would make for a horrible father if you told stories like those."

"Which is why I'm *not* a father," he rumbled out, digging his chin into her shoulder. "Now can I sleep, Kumar? Or are you going to keep talking?"

She shifted and winced against the corset. Fire ants! "Ridley?"

"Mr. Ridley, if you please."

They were sleeping in a bed, her rear to his front and he wanted to be referred to as a Mister. Hahahaha. "*Mr.* Ridley, I hardly wish to further impose, nor am I being bold or fanciful in my approach, but…"

He paused. "I'm getting bored."

She bit back a smile knowing he most probably was. "My corset."

"What of it?"

"I have no chemise beneath it."

"Yes, I know. I saw your rear when I was fastening your gown. What is your point?"

Her face burned. His casual indifference to her nudity was unnerving. "It pinches my skin."

"Welcome to life. Good-night."

She elbowed him. "Might you unlace it by a few strings? Only a few? Please?"

A riled breath escaped him as if she were asking to go shopping at four in the morning. "Now I remember why I never remarried." He tapped her. "Lie on your stomach."

This was about to get awkward.

She rolled onto her stomach, pressing her cheek to the linen and waited. Any normal woman would have darted out of the room and slept with a pinching corset. Which was as equally stupid in her opinion as lying on one's stomach asking a man almost twice her age to free her.

Ridley tugged down her robe to her elbows and unfastened her calico gown beneath and pushed back the material with calloused fingers that brushed her now exposed skin.

She could barely breathe through her parted lips knowing if this had been any other man, she would have been screaming.

Instead, her heart did nothing but pitter-patter and flippity-flop as if it were her wedding night.

Wedging his large fingers beneath the lacing, he unraveled several knots, tugging the lacing out, and loosened with several quick tugs, loosening and loosening and loosening as if he'd done it over a hundred and three times.

Which she had no doubt he probably had.

The pinching finally ceased with one last solid tug and a shaky breath escaped her.

"How is that?" he asked.

"Divine." He was the ultimate hero. He didn't even linger. Nor did he make it awkward. "I thank you."

"Thank me by letting me sleep. Fortunately, we don't have to get up in the morning or the afternoon." He tugged up the robe back over her shoulders without bothering to fasten the gown and lowered himself to the pillow beside her.

She dragged her stockinged feet against his robed leg beneath the linen and hitching up her skirts, she rolled down both stockings and yanked them off. "Where shall I put my stockings?"

He groaned and rattled her gently. "Toss it and let me sleep."

She did, her heart pounding at the realization that she was annoying him. "Forgive me. Good-night."

"Anything else?"

A breath escaped her. She closed her eyes. "No."

"Good." His arm folded around her quick and tightened as he remolded her against himself.

Her eyes opened, her pulse roaring. "How am I supposed to sleep when you are holding me tighter than the corset?"

He gently bit her shoulder, digging his teeth into her, startling her. "Let me sleep or I will shove you off... the... bed, Kumar. Don't think I won't."

Sensing he meant it, she cringed and closed her eyes again.

Unable to see him, only *feel* him, made her pulse further roar. It felt unreal and a whisper of too much more to come. If this was them now at only a day of knowing each other, she could only imagine what a lifetime spent together would be like.

It was overwhelming.

As if their souls had met too many times before to ignore each other.

This she wanted. To be protected. To be warm. To become a

flower nestled into a pot waiting for the water to flow and the sun to shine. Or in his case, she would wait until the moon did shine. The moon, when full, shone equally bright in its own way.

She loved moonlit nights as much as she did the afternoon sun.

Both served their purpose. Some flowers, like the *Ipomoea alba*, only bloomed at night when the light of the moon touched its white petals. The sunlight only closed them.

Jemdanee dragged her fingertips up past the cashmere spread of his muscled arm that held her, her throat tightening and her belly with it.

His scent penetrated her nostrils.

His feel penetrated more.

The hardness of his body made her core tighten.

His heated breaths made her own become heated.

It was as if he belonged to her.

Stealthily, she drifted his weighted hand upward and kissed it softly in reverence, allowing his velvet heat to penetrate her quaking lips, wanting to touch his skin and everything he was.

He said nothing as his large finger grazed her lip and pulled the lower bottom. He tapped at her teeth and then slowly slid his finger into her mouth and pressed down on her tongue.

Something primitive within her emerged as her pulse roared and she grew… wet.

There was no shame in it because she had made herself wet.

He hadn't forced her to be wet.

Something within her body and mind wanted to prove to him that she was ready to know real passion. The sort women rarely got to touch without labeling themselves as whores. "Rith… ley?" she asked past his large finger.

He pressed down a rigid finger on her tongue *harder*. "I'm holding your tongue down for a reason, Kumar. It's so you *don't talk*. Why is it not working?"

As if she was going to sleep with his finger in her mouth.

She tried to push it out.

His now wet finger dragged itself to her jaw and rested there, tingling her into wanting more.

One is reincarnated to live this life beyond its thread. Live it!

Dragging him toward herself with a turn, she shoved the cashmere robe off his muscled large shoulders and tried to blindly capture his mouth in the darkness, only to miss. She frantically undid the belt of his robe and unleashed the body she wanted to make hers.

His hands grabbed hers hard, but otherwise didn't appear fazed as he held her back with the shift of dueling arms he effortlessly controlled. He wove his fingers into hers and tightened them, until they were palm to palm. "What are you doing?" His voice softened. "Wrestling a bear given your size is unwise."

She cringed realizing he wasn't even physically responding to her. He was as calm and cool and collected as he always was.

It wasn't much of a compliment.

She swallowed and sank back down onto the mattress, her body burning as she released his hands. "I have desires and feelings much like any woman. Yet you refuse to acknowledge it. Why?"

He set his shaven chin against her throat. "I am acknowledging it by not permitting you to have control. Don't throw yourself at things you have no understanding of. There is more to me than even I understand. Leave it be."

She swallowed.

"Respect yourself in the way I am respecting you." His now nude, muscled body, which he didn't bother to cover up with his robe, gently pressed into her as his hands dragged into her hair, loosening the pins holding them. He raked the pins off the pillow, sending them tinkering to the floor beside the bed. "Maybe one day, when you're older and our paths cross again, you will tie the first knot," he whispered, tracing a finger down, down her back to the curve of her bum.

A shiver consumed her body as her senses roared to life with each quaking breath. What was this? Why did she feel as if throwing herself at him wasn't enough to hurl out everything she felt and wanted?

He laid himself beside her again, dragging her back against himself. "This is not the first knot, Kumar. This is rest. Something we both need."

She tightened her hold on his arms, trying to ignore her racing heartbeat caused by his unashamed nudity. A shaky breath escaped her. There were too many things happening to her head and to her body which she didn't even understand. What did he mean by knots? What did he mean by one day?

Would there be a day? When? When, when, when?

She tried to sit up. "Ridley—"

He jerked her back down against the mattress and rigidly held her against the mattress. "Learn to kneel." His voice grew gruff and ominous. "It's Mr. Ridley given I do not belong to you. Just as you are and will always be Kumar, because you do not belong to me. We belong to ourselves and not to each other."

She jerked toward him, refusing to let him command her. "What did you mean by one day?"

"As in not now." He flicked her forehead. "Cease letting your body dictate what you want. At your age, even a finger resting in your mouth seems exciting." His tone hinted he was mildly amused. "You were riled by it, weren't you?" He tsked. "Call on me in five years. In the meantime, do you need a towel for those moist thighs? Because I'd hate for you to slide off the bed and hit the floor."

Her own pride got the best of her. She shoved him. Hard.

His muscled, naked body shoved her back. Harder.

She thunked off the bed and grudgingly blinked. "*Ow*."

"Better *ow* than *now*. Let me sleep." He was quiet for a moment. "I'm sorry. Are you all right?"

She rolled her eyes. "If I were in any way wounded, I would never admit to it." Especially given she was rejected to the point of being shoved off the bed.

Did women usually have this much of a problem seducing men or was it only her?

Grudgingly crawling back into bed in the darkness, she collapsed onto the mattress beside him and gave him her shoulder and bum.

She was determined to push out any awareness of him.

He slid her back hard against himself. "I didn't mean to shove you off the bed," he murmured, smoothing her hair. "I simply haven't slept in over eighteen hours. I'm barely functioning."

Jemdanee's stomach sank knowing she hadn't even considered him. She deserved getting shoved off the bed. Though she wanted to apologize to him by whispering it, she decided to let him sleep.

He had more than earned it.

Her breaths remained uneven in the darkness. She chanted to herself to count through different gods to help her sleep. There were more than enough to exhaust her.

His breaths soon faded and his arm loosened its hold, hinting he was asleep.

She'd never known anyone to fall asleep that fast.

A shaky breath escaped her as she closed her eyes and tried.

She. Tried.

CHAPTER EIGHT

The scent of a sweet, leafy cigar tugged her from the long lush sleep she had succumbed to. She *streeeeeeetched* against the smooth linen surrounding her. Sunlight poured in through a massive window, making her squint.

The sound of a page turning made her blink.

She paused, realizing she was staring up at the velvet brocaded curtains of Mr. Ridley's bed. Remembering all too well how she had deliriously thrown herself at him, she cringed. Sitting up and dragging the linen to her chin, she veered her gaze to the leather upholstered chair set beside the window where Ridley sat.

He was fully clothed in grey and black, a charcoal cravat knotted and tied with a ruby red pin glinting against the sunlight in which he sat. With a half-smoked cigar resting between large fingers and a book set on his crossed knee, as his lowered eyes intently followed the words whilst slowly drawing the cigar to his lips, he exuded a sophistication that made her almost sink into the mattress with a breath she could hardly hold in.

Waking up to him made her feel ravishing.

"If you require more rest, feel free to do so," he intoned, never once lifting his gaze from the book. "It's almost two in the afternoon, but we have nowhere to be until tonight." He drew in on the cigar, inhaling smoke that caused the tobacco to gently hiss, then blew the smoke out, still reading.

She quickly propped herself onto one side, attempting not to openly admire him yet failing to do anything but that. With the sun brightly blanketing in and his dark chestnut hair swept back with tonic, he no longer looked so imposing.

He looked debonair. Like a gentleman basking in his own sophistication.

The house didn't look quite so imposing either.

Daylight certainly changed one's perspective.

Trying to find something to say, given she felt a touch awkward about last night, she smoothed the linen around herself. "What are you reading?"

He didn't look up. "*The Cure of Old Age and the Preservation of Youth* written by mathematician and physician Roger Bacon, printed in 1683. It's worth two hundred and fifty guineas, but I'm attempting to get four hundred for it from another collector."

She bit back a smile, realizing he was in the business of more than investigative work. "You aren't at an age to be reading books about curing youth. Maybe in another five years given that appears to be the time you have set for us." She tilted her head. "Shall we agree to meet in Calcutta in five years?"

He dragged in more smoke. "Are you insinuating you would wait five years?"

Was that an offer? Or was he teasing? She couldn't tell.

She sat up and propped her shoulder toward him, trying to exude the sort of grand sophistication he required. "If I am promised something worth waiting for, why would I not?"

He said nothing, merely drew in more smoke. Turning a page, he kept reading.

She sensed he was avoiding the conversation, yet here he still was in the room, clearly needing and wanting to impose his presence. He could have easily taken him book elsewhere but didn't.

She eyed him. "Are you angry with me about last night?"

"No." He kept reading. "Why would I be?"

This one might as well have said yes. "You are."

"If I were angry, Kumar, I wouldn't be sitting in this room out of fear for you."

She scrunched her nose knowing it. "Is it really two in the afternoon?"

He gave her a withering look. "I'm not known to lie about the time." He set the book onto the small side table and tapped the ash of his cigar into the ash pan beside him. He leaned back with his cigar, his gaze methodically skimming the entire outline of the linen she was buried under.

Searching her face, he patted his knee. "Come to me."

She pinched her lips and eyed that knee. One would think he were calling over a pet. "Why?"

Pulling in a long breath of smoke, he released it through his nostrils. "Because I asked you to. Are you insinuating after I rejected your advances I am now keen on seducing you when I could have done so last night? You didn't stop me, Kumar. I stopped me. Now come to me."

Her face burned. Despite common sense, she scooted out of bed and trailed toward him with bare feet, her unhooked gown and loosened corset slipping from her torso. She kept dragging both up and paused before him, searching his rugged features in an attempt to gauge what would happen next.

Setting the cigar between his teeth, he tapped his knee.

She swallowed, turned and seated herself on that hard knee, letting it dig into her bum.

He removed his cigar from his lips. "Do you smoke?"

It wasn't something she usually admitted to given it was frowned upon. "*Haan*. I smoke *bidis*. I brought four bundles with me, but they were confiscated by Peter when he found them in my luggage on the way over." The troll.

Ridley held out the cigar. "I firmly believe in the equality of men and women. Otherwise, there will never be peace. Here. For you."

He'd be the first man to offer her such a grand gesture of equality.

Needing to take off the edge of not having smoked in days, she quickly took it from his fingers. She drew in the earthy, sweetness of the tobacco smoke, letting it pool in her mouth before easing it out with a glorying breath. After everything she'd been through, it was a kiss of heaven. She tugged in more and eyed him, easing out another breath. "A more glorious moment I have never known. I thank you."

He watched her lips. "I thank you," he dipped his voice.

Why did she sense he was enjoying this? She fingered the large cigar, trying not to think about the fact that all of this was rather... phallic. She paused.

"Again." His deep tone hinted at a strained need.

Her fingers now trembled realizing his gaze was still trained on her lips. She took another quick puff, gathering a mouthful of smoke. Turning her face toward him, she purposefully blew the sizable cloud of smoke at his face. "I am on to you, Mr. Ridley," she tossed. "This is not at all about offering me equality given I am sitting on your knee. You, sir, are enjoying this a bit too much."

His amber eyes clouded in the smoke she had blown at him. "What if I am?" he rumbled out, holding her gaze. "I think you're beautiful."

Her pulse skittered.

She had invited the dragon out of its lair and could hear the tail scraping the gravel.

Daft as she was, she didn't mind. For he and this and her and this was the most excitement she'd had since... climbing abandoned temples without any sandals.

She knew how to balance herself without falling.

Reveling in the idea of such a powerful, dashing man being in *her* control, she set the cigar slowly between her lips, ensuring her entire mouth rounded the end of the cigar ever so invitingly. She dragged in a heated puff of tobacco. She even took the tip of her pink tongue and dragged it across the end of the rolled leaves she had just puffed on.

Staring, he reached out and took the cigar, bringing it to his own lips. Holding her gaze, he stuck it between his teeth, biting down on it hard enough to make the rolled leaves crinkle. "What sort of a virgin are you? *Hm?* What sort of a virgin revels in toying with men almost twice her age?" he asked from between his teeth.

"I was raised differently from what your British society would approve of, Mr. Ridley. My mother was a basket weaver and though she did her best to shield me from the rabble around us, I saw too much to pretend I wasn't one of them. I will admit I have done things in my youth I wish I had not."

He searched her eyes. "Like what?"

She averted her gaze, cringing at the troublemaker she'd once been. The troublemaker she still was. For here she sat on his lap,

DELILAH MARVELLE

her gown sagging off her shoulders, smoking his tobacco.

With the cigar still clamped between his straight teeth, Ridley's large, calloused fingers turned her chin toward himself. "Tell me. What sins could one with eyes like yours possibly have? Are you saying you fucked someone?"

Lowering her startled gaze to the pin in his cravat knowing how casually he said the word 'fuck', she tried not to feel the heat of his gaze or the heat of things she remembered. "No. I... I have never... no. There was a hovel where a certain woman paid me a rupee to stand at her door to warn her if her husband was coming given she prostituted herself without him knowing. *Maa* and I needed the money, so I..."

She felt guilty about it to this day. That poor husband. "I would sit by the draped door and whistle when I saw him coming down the long corridor. That gave men in her hovel time to crawl out through the mud wall window in the back. Sometimes, when I got bored, I watched out of curiosity. It was as disturbing as it was entertaining. That woman had no shame. She would even let men put eels into her." She shuddered.

"Yet you watched."

"I was bored."

He slowly shook his head, his features offering a form of pained tolerance. "Do you know what you are, Kumar? *Angustia.*"

That didn't sound like a compliment. "Meaning?"

"It's Latin for trouble. T-R-O-U-B-L-E."

She poked his muscled shoulder. "I know how to spell trouble."

"I don't think you do." He leaned far back in the leather chair, jostling his knee for emphasis and continued smoking with the tilt of his head. "How did you get involved in phytology?"

It would seem he was curious to know more about her.

It was darling. Most men didn't even know what phytology was. Then again, Mr. Ridley was not most men. "I was always taking trips into the surrounding jungles with Peter whilst growing up in India."

She leaned toward him and wedged out the cigar from between his fingers, shifting against his knee. Taking several regal puffs, she handed it back to him, enjoying the intimacy of their words and the cigar they were sharing. "I was about nine and had been in his care for several months when I had accidentally

146

plucked the shiny leaf of a *rhus acuminata* from between the stones of an abandoned temple we were visiting."

"Is that a form of poisonous sumac?"

Of course he would know. "Yes. 'Tis native to India. The oil on that sharp edge created a severe reaction of boils on my hands that had burned and itched like demons trying to crawl in for a week. Any normal child would have cried and never gone back into any jungle. I, on the other hand, gaped at it in reverence and returned to collect more. For the power yielded by that seemingly insignificant and small leaf came to represent what few saw in it: magic. Much like the rash of poverty that had marked my skin and taken my mother, I was humbled and inspired by a mere *rhus acuminata* to leave my own mark on the world. I wanted to understand it.

"So I started collecting, sketching, documenting and dissecting every seed and leaf and plant found in the jungles and unveiling its potential. Peter was impressed enough to hire a prominent Parsee teacher to navigate me through the world of botany, and soon, it turned into a passion of having crates of endless exotic plants being shipped in from other continents."

Ridley eased out smoke, his shaven jaw tightening. He searched her face intently before asking in an overly even tone, "Are you insinuating the pain you endured at the hands of that sumac wasn't enough to deter you from understanding it? Does pain fascinate you?"

She made a face. "Not at all. Pain is simply part of life, Mr. Ridley, and I have never let it keep me from what I wanted. In truth, we dip ourselves in pain the moment we are born."

He thoughtfully dragged in more smoke. "So true." He let a misting circle drift toward her throat, creating the illusion of a collar.

She sensed there was more meaning in it than she cared to acknowledge.

His arm slipped slowly and tightly around her waist and dragged her closer, as if resigning them both to the reality of a situation neither had any further say in. "I had the servants bring up hot water for the tub a half hour ago. We should bathe you."

She dug her fingers into that broad shoulder he had propped her against, his heat melding into her own. Why did she sense he was offering to bathe her?

Her entire body burned like the red cigar tip pointed at her. She eyed him.

Dashing out the cigar into the ash pan beside the chair, he dragged her legs over his one arm, wedging his hand behind her back and rose, lifting her up and into his arms effortlessly. He straightened to his imposing height that now took her up toward the low ceiling.

He rounded the chair and carried her into the adjoining bath chamber.

Her heart pounded as she clutched at his shoulders. She tried to read the expression on his face but it remained what it usually was: unreadable. "You are not actually going to bathe me, are you?"

Not that she minded, but... her poor heart!

Striding into the massive bath chamber, which echoed all around from the impact of his booted foot falls, he set her down before the still steaming water and straightened. "I should hope you know me better than that by now," he said in a low tone, dragging her unraveling braid away from her throat and skimming his hand down its length to its end. His rigid fingers grazed her bum, following its curve to her crack, which he edged a finger into and pressed, pushing the fabric inward.

He stepped back. "Do you need assistance removing your gown? Or can you reach everything on your own?"

Her legs quaked, barely holding her up in place, still feeling the graze of those rigid fingers on her rear as if he'd wanted in with the fabric he'd pushed.

The amount of restraint this man had was something to be respected *and* feared.

Especially feared.

Though her own physical desire for him was base, she knew herself well enough to admit that if she were to fall into his arms, she would be giving him far more than her body. She would be giving him control over what mattered most to her: her mind. "I can manage."

He pointed to a freshly folded towel on the brass stand and a carved bar of soap set on the ledge of the copper tub. "Take your time." He strode out. "I'll be reading."

She swallowed, disappointed in him for not acknowledging the intimacy they both wanted to feel. Those fingers on her rear were an indication of more than a mild interest.

"The water is getting cold," he called. "I suggest warming it up by getting in."

"You are *angustia*," she called back, knowing it had to be said. How can it not be said? "Any other man would have done a dozen other things to me aside from reading. Why did you not stay?"

"Because every tile in that bathroom would have cracked."

"You can afford to replace them."

"I'm not worried about the tile," he rumbled out from the other room. "I'm worried about that rear I touched."

Jemdanee set a trembling hand to chest, feeling as if she was going to suffer heart failure. "Your level of restraint is disturbing."

"Who says I have any left?" His voice broke with riled huskiness. "What do you want from me, Kumar? What in hell do you think you are going to get?"

She half-expected him to dart in, her breaths uneven.

He didn't.

Trying to steady her mind, she eventually said, "What does any woman want from a man? To feel wanted and needed. To feel part of something bigger in a world that makes us feel small."

There was a moment of silence. "You are small, Kumar. Damnably small and therefore all too easy to hurt. I don't want to hurt you."

The softness of that tone hinted he meant it.

She swallowed, feeling a mutual adoration for him. "I'm not without strength. I still live because I have strength. More than most."

He said nothing.

A part of her knew that once she left London, she most likely would never see him again. Why did she already ache? Why did the thought of not seeing those ambers eyes or that overly serious demeanor drag her into wanting more? "Might you at least kiss me?" she ventured. "Once?"

His boot hit the floorboard twice. "Kumar, I'm still human."

That strained voice hinted of his need. It was sweetly draining. It meant he wanted to. "I sometimes doubt you are human, Mr. Ridley. You appear to have built an altar of refinement, distancing yourself from those around you, but I sense it is an illusion meant to hide who you really are."

"Bravo. Do you need me to clap?"

She rolled her eyes. "What do you hide?"

He shifted against the chair, creaking the leather. "The very thing all men hide."

"What would that be?"

"The devil."

She refused to believe that he harbored any demon within him. Not given everything he had already done for her. Not given the way he continued to protect her from even himself. "I doubt you let him rule over you."

"What little you know. He rules over me as if I were the clock and he the key. Most clocks are set to run for eight days before having to be wound. He turns that key far enough every time, straining the coils and the gears to a point that if anyone touches the hands... pop."

Something about the way he said, dragged a bony finger down her spine. "You speak of the devil as if he were real."

"Oh, he is," he chided. "He chants to me to overstep bounds. It's what he wants. In fact, he is chanting to me right now. *Chanting*," his voice dipped.

Her throat tightened. She eyed the door. "What is he chanting?"

"If I tell you, Kumar, I would have to do it."

She swallowed. "I trust that it would not be anything I would fear."

"Only because your youth makes you think you're invincible, when in fact, it only makes you stupid." He hesitated. "The water is getting cool. Why are you not bathing?" A thud against the wall resounded within the bath chamber. "Remove your clothing."

She lingered, endlessly disappointed in his inability to seduce her.

His tone hardened. "Remove your clothing, Kumar. Strip."

She almost needed the wall for support.

With quivering fingers, she tugged off the already open back of her calico gown, letting it rustle and whisper to the marble floor. Keeping her gaze on the open door, she shimmied out of it and wedged down the overly loose corset he had undone last night.

She now stood naked, her skin on fire. "I am unclothed."

"Good. Slip into the water," he instructed. "Is it still warm?"

Glancing toward the open door, she scrambled into the large copper tub and sank into the depths of the warm water that splashed up to her chin. A breath escaped her lips against the wet warmth. Was he going to walk in?

She wanted him to. "It is still very warm."

"Good." He was quiet for a moment. "Wet your hair."

"What if I do not want to?"

"I'm not going into that bath chamber, Kumar."

"What if I want you to?"

"Wet your hair."

It was a subtle command. One she hoped would bring him to her. She slowly slid down beneath the surface of the water, cocooned in a moment of silence, her eyes open in expectation that she would see him standing above the tub watching her.

He wasn't there.

She bubbled out air from her lips, wondering if she held her breath long enough, would he run in and rescue her? Of course he would.

Needing air, she slid back up out of the water, her breaths ragged as if he and she had been making love. She waited for the sound of his voice. "Now what am I to do?" she softly teased him.

His deep voice turned sensual, sending a ripple of awareness through her. "Lather yourself."

Dragging in the cool air of the bath chamber, she gripped the wedge of soap and with a trembling hand, touching her nose to it.

The crisp scent hinted it was the same soap he had used on his own body.

The wetness between her thighs had nothing to do with the water.

She now knew why women allowed themselves to be seduced.

It made the body feel it was being remolded and reborn into a greater purpose.

One meant to be worshipped.

Glancing toward the still open door, she slowly rubbed and lathered the soap over her brown arms, throat, her breasts whose nipples had hardened and tingled at the very thought of him walking in at any moment. She dangled up each foot, rubbing soap on each one before veering her way to her legs and thighs. Though her legs were unsteady, she stood with a splash, and with circling motions lathered the soap across her belly, her rear, which he had touched, and then used her hand to soap between her thighs using the wedge she knew had been between *his* thighs.

"Are you standing?" he asked.

She stilled. "Yes. I am."

"Grip the edge," he intoned.

She did, willing him and wanting him to come to her. *Come to me.*

"Release your need. The one I hear in your voice." A huskiness lingered in that ragged tone. "Find your nub. Do it knowing I acknowledge your desire. Do it knowing I want you to."

He was becoming the voice in her head and the very thing she wanted to gasp to.

Gripping the ledge hard with one hand, she gave into what her body wanted and needed and frantically fingered her nub. She watched the open doorway, her core tightening from the release she so desperately wanted.

All whilst thinking of him. His cologne. His amber eyes. His muscled body. His length. The one she wanted in her mouth and in between her thighs.

Her fingers grew slick from her rising pleasure. Disbelief overwhelmed her knowing she was letting him control her body without him even touching her or seeing her.

"Breathe without restraint," he intoned. "Breathing hard and harder will constrict your core and bring you to what you want sooner. Quicker. Gasp for it."

She gasped against the overly rapid intakes of her rapid breaths that now heightened the sensations. It hurled her toward the chasm she wanted to fall into. She willed each breath and each crazed gasp to be heard within the echo of the bath chamber in the hopes that he would lose control and take her.

Unable to hold onto the peak she wanted him to see and hear and feel, she gasped, letting it sweep at her like a high wind from every mountain.

"Who are you thinking of?" he asked.

"You," she whispered.

"Who do you want in the tightness of that cunt?"

"*You.*"

"Who are you willing to bleed for?"

"You," she choked out.

"Am I worth the pain?"

"Yes!" She flicked faster, her core tightening beyond what she could hold. It came too fast for her to breathe as she called out, "Ridley!" She staggered against the pleasure that momentarily blinded her.

She wobbled and sank back into the water, letting the soap float away from her body much like the world was floating away with her soul.

There was a moment of silence followed by his choked, rasping breath that rose and rose.

She paused as she eyed the open doorway in disbelief.

She sat there unmoving in the lapping water and listened.

His body shifted against the creaking leather chair as his quaking breaths grew more labored.

Kali. On. High.

He was pleasuring himself. As if he could no longer restrain the control he had over the power of their attraction. She sank into the water and peered over the copper ledge of the tub, a part of her knowing she had driven him to this. Even worse? She was *reveling in it*.

The sound of a well-wetted hand moving quick against his cock as he dragged in over-controlled ragged breaths filled the silence. He grunted.

She brought her quaking knees together feeling as if she were climaxing again and with him.

Long seething and regimented, savage breaths became timed against moist sounds.

Her face and her body were on fire, heating the water she was sitting in. She would never be able to look at another man again without hearing those breaths. *His* breaths.

She dug her fingers into her burning cheeks, waiting.

Waiting.

Waiting.

He kept going and going, those moist sounds now frantic and needful and riled and spastic. What sounded like a boot slamming into the side table sent it crashing, shattering glass that sprayed past the door and into the bath chamber.

The wrong side of her brain wanted to scramble out and see him doing it.

Instead, she set her chin against the ledge of the tub and imagined him in his glory.

A thud, thud, thud hit the chair harder and harder, tremoring the walls as if he were bucking his muscled thighs and the thickness of his rigid cock well beyond what the chair could hold.

She clacked her teeth against the edge of the tub, feeling as if he were thudding his entire length into her and filling her womb with his seed and their future.

The chair hit the wall.

A long guttural groan and seething breaths through nostrils and teeth filled the air.

Silence now settled itself.

Keeping her own upper teeth still wedged against the tub, she eyed the doorway.

There was a rustling of clothes and the shifting against the creak of leather. After a moment of silence, he said, "I'll be in the study."

He rose and wordlessly stalked past and left the room, closing the door behind him.

She giggled and went under water in complete disbelief.

She had somehow managed to seduce Mr. Ridley.

Not even an hour later, after she had dressed with the assistance of the chambermaid who arrived at the pull of the bell (how lovely), Jemdanee breezed out, her freshly washed hair braided.

She officially felt like a woman. And not just any woman. One capable of bringing the strongest of men to his knees: Mr. Ridley.

It was glorious.

Determined to find him and wrap her arms around him to show him the unending adoration she felt, she alighted before the closed doors of his study.

She eased out a breath, chanting to herself that this changed everything yet nothing. Turning the latch of the door, she paused.

It was locked.

She cringed. So much for it changing anything.

She knocked gently. "Mr. Ridley?"

He didn't answer.

She couldn't imagine that a man like him would feel awkward.

If anything, that was for her to feel.

She knocked again. "Mr. Ridley?"

He didn't answer.

Jemdanee hesitated, rather surprised he would sulk about what just happened between them. "The doors are locked from within. So I know you are in there and that you can hear me."

He said nothing.

She pressed her cheek to the cool surface of the door and tried to be consoling. "You need not apologize or feel guilt," she offered, knowing full well any other man would have just veered into that bath chamber and spewed it on her or shoved it into her. "I never do anything I don't want to and I wanted to."

There was a thud against the desk. "You're too damn young to know what you want." He was quiet for a long moment, then softened his gruff voice. "I'm not avoiding you. I have to finish these damn notes given I never did." He hesitated. "Feel free to wander about the house and open every door. Take whatever book you want. Read. Make my home your home until I'm done."

She bit back a smile.

It appeared she had earned more than his pleasure.

She had earned a measure of trust. "I'll be upstairs should you finish your notes early, Mr. Ridley." She grazed her fingers against the wood, wishing he would come out. When he still didn't, she decided it was best to give him the time he was asking for.

Exploring the house would not be without its merit.

It was yet another way of getting to know him.

Making her way back up the stairs, she wandered down the vast corridor, determined not to miss a room that might whisper more of who he was.

She veered toward the first door and opened it.

Her eyes widened as the scent of must and dust swept at her like ghosts looking for a body to possess. Leather bound books of all sizes were stacked unevenly against every wall from floor to ceiling, covering old furniture and tables and sideboards that had been stacked with as many books as it would allow without toppling. The shelves of the bookcases were bowed beneath the weight of too many books, books, books. The entire floor to her knee were also stacked with books and no reasonable manner in which to enter that room without knocking something or everything over.

She decided to shut the door.

"Mr. Ridley, I worry about you," she muttered, half wishing he could hear her.

She went to the next door.

Opening it, a large stack of books toppled. She cringed. Glancing down the corridor, she wedged herself inside, trying not to knock anymore over and knelt against the bundling of her skirts. She carefully gathered the dozen she had knocked over, but her elbow hit another stack and her foot did another, thudding more books to the ground.

"This is not going so well." She stacked, smoothed and patted them into random piles which she slid toward the wall and away from the door.

A sound from the other side of the room she was in made her gaze snap up.

Chaucer sat perched atop of a stone bust of what appeared to be Napoleon.

How. Fitting.

Chaucer blinked and with a wobble offered, "*Faaaawwwwwk. Fawk.*"

She burst into laughter, her eyes widening. "Poor Chaucer. Are you attempting to repeat vile words your master has condemned you to hear?"

With the rise and spread of wings, he flew toward her, circling once and then alighted onto a stack of books beside her, glancing up. "*Caaawww.*"

"That would certainly be a more appropriate use of your language," she chided. Wanting to touch that dark head, she slowly, slowly held out her hand, holding his gaze, wondering if he would let her touch her. "Might I pet you?" she softly asked.

He clicked.

"I have no idea what you said, but I will attempt to trust that you will not lunge." Holding out her forefinger, she gently grazed the softness of his feathers, surprised that he was letting her touch him.

"He never lets anyone touch him," a deep voice said from behind her. "No one but me. Consider it an honor."

She gasped and almost smacked poor Chaucer in doing so.

Chaucer flew up and darted toward the open doorway, landing on the shoulder of... Mr. Ridley.

A shaky breath escaped her.

Ridley leaned against the doorway, Chaucer still propped on his shoulder. He eyed her. "I want to apologize for what I did."

She smoothed her calico skirts against herself in an attempt not to squirm beneath his steady gaze. "I should be the one apologizing."

Ridley shifted his jaw. "I rarely lose control. Not like that."

"Human nature is known for its lack of control, Mr. Ridley."

Petting Chaucer's head with a large hand, he held her gaze. "And that is what makes us dangerous to ourselves and the world. Our lack of control."

They said nothing for a long time.

He scanned the room and pointed to a pile of books tucked within a sizable glass encasing. "Those came from King Louis' personal library out of Versailles."

Her lips parted. "How is it you have books from the behcaded French king?"

"My father was one of the few Brits who went into France during the Reign of Terror. Morbidly, it's how he met my mother. He entertained himself and her by attending estate sales across France, purchasing items that in my opinion, should have never been bought. I've attempted to contact certain families with the assistance of Vidocq who is still in France in an attempt to return whatever I can, but too many were left unmarked, erasing who it belonged to. So I sell it, hoping someone might treasure it more than I."

Jemdanee wove her way through the piles of books and furniture toward where he stood in the doorway. She lingered close.

Chaucer flew up and disappeared down the corridor.

Ridley continued to hold her gaze. "He senses danger."

She gripped her skirts. "Ridley...?"

"We can't." He turned and stalked down the corridor.

She cringed and bustled after him. "I would never judge you," she offered. "Taking pleasure in each other is not the worst thing we could have done."

He stopped but did not face her. "Understand, Kumar, that I

157

have the devil in me and he is French."

Whatever did that mean? "Assure him I am not offended."

He glanced back at her, his features strained. "Your soul is twisted to even jest."

"I grew up seeing the world for what it is: twisted."

He swiped his mouth and tugged his waistcoat into place. "Are you at all hungry?"

She perked. "Very much so. Yes."

He swung away and wagged his hand. "Come. You and I will dine at a table I only reserve for myself."

Hurrying after him with the rustle of skirts, she alighted beside him, almost humming at the prospect of being invited to see every corner of his life. "What sort of table is it that you only reserve it for yourself?"

"It came out of France during an estate sale. It belonged to a certain Marquis de Sade who has long since departed."

She eyed him. "Was he an agreeable man?"

His tongue rolled around the inside of his cheek. "There is a woman here in London by the name of Madame de Maitenon who claims de Sade was more of a gentleman than a demon. Of course, she herself is a courtesan which may skew her own perception on what defines a gentleman."

"Ah." She followed him down the sweep of stairs and into a dining hall whose doors were closed to the adjoining parlor.

Rounding an inlaid carved wooden table, he pulled out a chair and angled it for her, waiting for her to be seated. He inclined his head. "Please."

A true gentleman despite what he did earlier. She seated herself regally. "I thank you."

"My pleasure." He yanked on a calling bell cord beside the entrance and rounded her, pulling out a chair for himself. He sat and slid a hand across the surface of the table. "Few get to see it."

"I feel so honored." She smiled and leaned toward the table to observe the intricate carvings laid beneath glass. Her smile faded. "There is a man eating the head of a goat whilst buggering a woman who is… using her foot to… bugger a man who is whipping a woman." She eyed him. "I believe this is where I lose all understanding, Mr. Ridley. I prefer not to set a plate on this, for as I had mentioned to you before, I am a vegetarian," she quipped.

He heaved out a breath. "That particular scene hardly personifies me. *This* is what I am referring to. Isn't she beautiful?" He tapped at a wooden carving of a woman who was sensually draped in ropes from foot to throat.

Jemdanee eyed it and him. He thought a woman choked by rope was... beautiful?

His finger traced it, his voice fading. "I only point her out to those I trust."

Which hinted it meant something to him.

She leaned in and angled her head to better look at it. The twisted look of anguish on that contorted face and sneering lips hinted the woman was trying to free herself but couldn't. A serpent bit into her throat. "Do you truly find her and this beautiful?"

Ridley half-nodded. "I used to sit at this table as a boy. Usually alone, because my father travelled and my mother had her own circle. Given I refused to associate with many people when I was younger, for I was awkward and shy, I read books to her. Unlike everyone else in my life, she remained unchanged. She always welcomed me with the same expression and never walked away. She was always here. Waiting. As if the ropes kept her in place. As if not being in my presence caused her anguish. The sort of anguish I have always felt toward everything in life."

Her throat tightened knowing it.

Steps echoed into the room. "You rang, Mr. Ridley?" the butler asked.

Ridley glanced up and rose. "Yes, Fulton." His voice warmed. "See to it that Kumar receives whatever it is she desires out of the kitchen. I have a few missives to write." He angled past the butler, stepping out into the corridor.

Jemdanee almost knocked over the chair in an attempt to keep him from leaving. "Ridley?"

He swung toward her and blankly held her gaze. "'Tis Mr. Ridley, if you please. What is it?"

She swallowed, sensing something had changed. "Are you not joining me for a meal?"

"No. I'm not hungry."

"Then why did you...?"

"You have honored me by sitting at a table that rarely has guests. That was the only meal I required. I will see you later tonight. We depart at twenty after ten. Enjoy your meal and instruct Fulton on anything else you may need." With that, he inclined his head and disappeared.

Trying to better understand him, her gaze veered back to the figure of the woman he had pointed out. The one wrapped in rope and in anguish.

He thought her anguish to be beautiful.

Rope. Knots. Ridley.

Jemdanee swallowed, sensing he had been silently communicating with her as to his innate desires. She set quaking fingers against the flat of the glass above the woman's anguish.

Whilst she wanted to dash after him and shake him into telling her what he found beautiful in it and why, she sensed an attempt to confront him too strongly would yield nothing but his displeasure.

If he felt shame in it, and clearly he did, she dared not further wound that shame.

She would honor it by waiting until he willingly unraveled that stubborn fist.

A fist that would eventually tire and relinquish its hold on every secret he kept.

CHAPTER NINE

Well-fed and well-rested though she was, there was no further denying that Mr. Ridley was an outrageous man who had taken her to be a *Kumar* too far.

Too. Far.

Jemdanee grudgingly adjusted the oversized wool cap she was forced to wear down to her nose over her braided hair. She shifted against the equally oversized male coat and trousers she'd been stuffed into in the name of 'justice'. Fake black whiskers had even been applied with beeswax beneath her nose.

It reached past her chin.

For *clearly*, as an Indian, she wasn't hairy enough.

"*Haaaaallo*," Chaucer offered from beside her, peering up at her. He clicked as if laughing.

She peered down at Chaucer. "I will mind you to keep that clicking to yourself. I am fully aware of how ridiculous I look and hardly need it pointed out by a raven."

Having a boot-sized bird chiding at her in English and sitting on the seat in a black lacquered carriage as if it were a human passenger on its way to a theatre full of dead bodies was as equally morbid as it was outrageous. "Inform your dark prince I am not at all pleased with him," she added. "Inform him. Click

161

at him twice and swat a claw at him for me."

Ridley's rugged features rhythmically appeared and disappeared into the shadows of the night as light from passing lampposts filtered in through the carriage windows. "It could be worse," he rumbled out. "You could be dead."

Coming from him, that was anything but original. "Sometimes being dead prevents us from seeing things best left unseen." Her whiskers flapped against her words. She pointed at its annoying length. "Do you even see this? It hangs well past my lips and moves every time I say anything." It kept flapping with each word she spoke and tangled against her lips.

She pushed them out with the flick, flick, flicking of her tongue and with a *pfffffff*. "No man keeps whiskers *this* long. Not even in the Orient where the emperor's court demands it."

A muscle quivered at his jaw. "Facial hair has been symbolically used throughout history to change one's identity for gain and *we* are gloriously partaking in that gain given I wasn't about to further insult you by powdering your face white. You should thank me."

She stuck out her tongue.

His boot hit hers hard. "Ey. None of that. I require maturity from here on out. Start. Building. Maturity. Or tomorrow will never come. And cease grouching about something that is protecting your life. Everything you are wearing is preventing others from seeing what they should: you. It's an illusion and goes back to what you were earlier saying about pigs and stallions. They'll point to a stallion and think it's a pig."

She gasped. "I am insulted."

"By what?"

"I am *not* an animal. How dare you call me either?"

"I wasn't—"

"It was not your analogy to use. It was *my* analogy. An analogy I used with respect. Do you have any idea how many white British men have referred to me and my people as being animals?"

His features flickered. "Kumar. Cease. That wasn't what I was—"

"Be mindful of how you speak to me."

His voice softened. "I will. I'm sorry."

It was something. "Be mindful."

"I will."

"Be mindful or I will take out the rope from your coat pocket and repeat what I did last night."

He lowered his chin. "I think you are now disrespecting me."

"There are times you men earn it."

"There are times you women earn it."

"Oyo. So I am finally a woman in your eyes, am I?" She tut-tutted. "What did it take? My being dressed like a man or that we took pleasure in each other?"

He stared. "What the hell has gotten into you? Do you need a sword to go with that tongue?"

She rolled her eyes and clumped her booted feet together. A part of her was annoyed that he'd avoided her all day only to shove her into male clothing. "Everything is too big."

"Or maybe you're too small," he countered. "Use the glory of the mind I know you have and cease being a child about this and everything."

And it was back to her being a child. "My being a woman did not last very long, did it? It ended after the soap."

He said nothing.

Knowing it had to be said, she blurted, "Are you afraid the ship in my harbor will be seized by your pirate?"

"What?"

She cringed. "Does my being a virgin keep you from touching me?"

"Ah." He dug into his coat pocket, removing a cigar from his leather casing. "Did you want one?"

"No. I fear I would only set fire to this mustache."

"You probably would." He struck a match and lit it, tossing the match and puffed on the cigar to further light it, the tobacco hissing. "In reference to your earlier question, you can say some pirates aren't known to leave survivors."

And it was back to cigars and death for this one. "Some pirates willingly sink with the ship."

He released smoke through his nostrils. "Yes. It's called marriage."

She tsked. "I did not ask you for marriage. I do not want marriage. Marriage is what women do when they have no career and I now have one. With your nine books, I will open an apothecary store in Calcutta with Limazah. He and I are of the same soul. Limazah made me the botanist that I am today."

His jaw and face tightened as he drew in more smoke. "Did he?"

Was that a glint of jealousy? She couldn't tell. "You need not be jealous of Limazah."

He released smoke through his teeth. "Then why mention his name?"

"For he is—"

"I'm at an age where I don't play games and I advise you to adhere to do the same."

This one was being cryptic. "Cease. Limazah is my Parsee teacher. He is eighty and equally wise. Much like you. Very, very old but wise."

He gave her a withering look.

She grinned. "Will you visit me in India? Will you visit the apothecary shop when I open it?"

"Maybe in five years."

Her smile faded. "Five years? It only takes four months by way of boat to cross over."

His tone darkened. "And another three dozen years to keep us both under control." He stared her down. "I can assure you, Kumar, what happened between us was me being incredibly tame. That was me ensuring you didn't get hurt. Why do you think I kept the wall between us? Because I do things that make the word 'fuck' look like the rosary. You don't want this. You deserve better. You are better."

Her face grew hot. "You appear angry about the adoration I feel for you."

"Angry is not the right word. Your attempt to osculate a deranged man fourteen years older than yourself is better defined as stupid."

"You are not deranged." She hesitated. "What is… *osculate*?"

"Mouth to mouth. A kiss."

This one clearly thought kissing *was* stupid. "One would think I tried to replace two of those s's with two l's."

"Kiss. Kill. Given who I am, it's all the same."

"Death starts to lose its meaning when it becomes all I hear. Death this and death that. Death, death, death. Deeeeeeeeeeeeeeeeeeeeeeeeeath. Death appears to be your lover."

He drew in more smoke, the tip of the cigar turning red.

"You're fortunate I have a sense of humor."

This one had a morbid way of showing it.

She could either continue trying to scale that immovable brick wall or... she could try to make him smile. She preferred the latter. "I will attempt to do the impossible."

"Is that so? How? By garnering some maturity?"

"Hahahahahahahahaha. *No*. I will make you smile."

He averted his gaze. "Can we not do this?"

She waved toward him, wanting to bring him cheer. Outside of her plants, bringing cheer to others was what she enjoyed doing most. "Watch. Watch, watch."

He grudgingly veered his gaze back to her.

Heartily smacking her lips, whilst flapping the mustache, she leaned far back and sprawled her trouser clad legs across the length of the carriage out toward him. She widened her knees far apart and scratched at the flap, sniffing loudly. "*These British men call me Kumar, but only because they fear me and my*...." She paused, realizing the stockings she had generously stuffed into the flap of her trousers for the purpose of a cock had fallen down her... left trouser leg.

He blew out smoke. "There goes your investment."

She burst into laughter and pointed to it. "I did not even plan that!"

"Yes, yes. Entertaining. I'm beginning to believe you aren't eighteen but closer to eleven."

She giggled. "How are you not laughing? Why do you never laugh or smile?"

Ridley rolled his cigar between fingers. "Maybe because we're on our way to a murder scene, Kumar." His voice strained. "Whilst you laugh, I wish to assure you, death and the stench it brings is real. Of course if that amuses you, by all means, laugh. Laugh until your nose bleeds."

Jemdanee cringed, her amusement fading until it was... gone.

Gone. Like *maa*.

She eased out an anguished breath, trying not to think about the past that always hovered but one she sought to keep alive. "I am not by any means being disrespectful," she admitted, eyeing him. "Laughter is what saves the parts of my soul which the world seeks to take. Finding moments of joy between too many hardships was the gift *maa* taught me to cherish when she was still a part of my life. It did not mean she or I were by any means happy, for we had very little and there were too many days food was sparse, but it was more comforting than cradling what everyone else did: tears. Whenever I cried, she would tickle me into a giggle, insisting it was all the gods wanted to hear. Whenever others shouted, she would tuck her veil into her ears and make faces. It was who she was and I loved her for that. She brightened a room that rarely held any light. For without humor, I doubt I would have survived everything I did. Especially now that I no longer have Peter." Her voice cracked despite her not wanting it to. "I am alone in this world again as I was when I was eight. I have no one."

His rugged features softened. He searched her face and her eyes. "If you ever need anything, Kumar, regardless of where you are in the world, you have me and I will get to you. Forgive me in my constant analytical judgement and by all means, cradle what little you have left of your mother. Smile. Even if the rest of the world thinks it's morbid. You've earned that right. People think I'm morbid, too. Hell, I know I am. We can be morbid together."

A part of her was honored hearing him say it.

Sticking the cigar into his teeth, he swiped up the stockings that had rolled to the floor and held it out. "Do what all men ought to do and keep it in your trousers," he softly chided.

An exasperated breath escaped her, fluttering the mustache, knowing it was the most she'd ever get out of him regarding a smile. She grabbed the stockings and stuffed them into her flap.

She glanced toward Chaucer who stared at her unblinkingly whilst rocking. He looked unnerved. "Poor, poor Chaucer. What you must see from the sky above is what truly darkens your feathers to soot. How do you manage to be inspired enough to fly in a world such as this?"

Chaucer clicked.

"You must come to India," she openly conversed, reaching out and grazing her fingers across his wings and head. "We have jungles."

"Ey." He pointed at her head with the cigar. "Cease attempting to steal my bird."

"To bring your poor bird to a murder scene is what I am commenting on. He does not need to see such vile things. He may molt."

He lowered his chin. "It isn't that I want him to partake in a supper and a theatrical. I simply prefer not to keep him in the house by himself. He is the only true associate I have and follows me everywhere, even into the cellar of the house. And if I'm ever bold enough to close a door to keep him out, he'll stand outside it and peck at the wood informing me I'm being rude. He gets incredibly agitated when I'm not around and goes straight to stripping wallpaper. Sometimes, even books. Which costs me *money*."

She lowered her own chin. "Perhaps you ought to set him free. He should be with nature. Keeping him in that house is cruel. He only has a parlor, your study and your room and mine to fly in. He deserves more. Does he not? Might I take him with me to India? Would he not benefit from a life amongst vegetation and other birds? If I take him with me, then I will be *guaranteed* you will visit."

A low whistle escaped Ridley as he tapped on his shoulder.

Chaucer perked and hopped up onto his seat, his knee and then onto his shoulder. Holding her gaze, he touched the head of his bird that nuzzled his hand.

His tone remained velvet. "I can assure you, Kumar, I have repeatedly released him to the sky to offer him the freedom he deserves. More than once I have locked every window to inform him he is free of me and able to leave anytime given I am not an easy soul to understand or please. Yet he not only comes back, he taps at the window to the point of cracking it for he knows I offer him what the world cannot: everything. That, to me, is the sort of unending devotion I want and that is why he is my closest confidant and true friend. For he offers me allegiance and fidelity without question as to who and what I am in a world that offers none. Something I have yet to receive from anyone. Especially a woman." He stared.

Jemdanee sensed window cracking loyalty was what this one wanted. Yet he'd pushed away her arms the moment she attempted to offer her own. She swallowed, noting the way he continued to watch her whilst Chaucer settled himself more comfortably onto his shoulder.

She wrung her hands. "If devotion is what you seek, Mr. Ridley, then why do you refuse to permit us the opportunity to explore what we could mean to each other?" Her tone was overly serious, even for her liking.

He said nothing.

She picked at the wool on her trousers. "Is it because you think me too young? Or do you not find me attractive enough given I am not of your culture?"

He averted his gaze, dragging in a breath of smoke. "Men like me have long grown bored of trying to define attraction. Nor is osculation necessary to the existence of one's persona or mind. I look for pieces of what I need and put them together. I look for cracks I can fill with rope."

That didn't sound like a compliment. "Last I knew being broken leads to an inability to be of much use to anyone."

"That is because you have no understanding of real life, Kumar. You have yet to live it apart from others to permit yourself to grow and break not by the whims of others but yourself. Because being broken isn't always a bad thing. In fact, it enables us to strive for more knowing there are pieces missing from who we are. That, in turn, enables us to find better pieces we can fit into those cracks that have failed us."

Her lips parted. "If I were to experience any more of this life, between my mother, the hovels, Peter, people and their judgment of me and my culture and now *murder*, there will be no pieces left of me to gather."

He dashed out the cigar into the ash pan on the arm of the seat. "The right man will know how to put you back together when it's time."

"Are you insinuating you are capable of being such a man if I wished it?"

He grabbed the walking stick from the seat beside him and angled the gold-headed cane. He unsheathed its length, revealing a thin sharp blade within it, startling her. "We return to the topic of what is most important: your safety. It will ensure you don't end up in *real* pieces." He sheathed it hard and set it into her gloved hands. "Any questions?"

This one enjoyed his weapons and being cryptic too much.

She drew in her legs and leaned her hands and chest forward against the head of the walking stick. "Yes. I do have one. When will you *osculate* me?"

He stared. "Ask me before you leave for Calcutta tomorrow night."

She pulled in her chin. "I leave for Calcutta tomorrow?"

"Yes. Tomorrow night. You'll be escorted to safety by Finkle's best whilst I do what I do best: finish this case without interruptions."

Her stomach dropped. "What if I find the source? Will that not enable me to stay longer?"

"No. For the outcome might not be in your favor and I refuse to take that chance. You leave tomorrow night. That was etched into stone well before I yanked you out of that prison."

"What of Peter?"

He no longer met her gaze. "He will follow you in a few weeks, unharmed. You may choose to address him at a time when you are situated in a realm of your own where he cannot manipulate you or your mind. Whilst we may never see each other again, I wish to offer you this parting advice: You need to be your own person, Kumar. You need to belong to yourself first before you can belong to anyone else, especially someone like me. Do you understand?"

She nodded and softened her voice. "*Haan*." She hesitated. "Though it would be morbid of me to say our time together was pleasantly spent, I have endlessly enjoyed getting to know you and thank the gods for bringing you into my life. I have not known you for very long and yet my soul whispers of more. Why is that? How is that possible?"

His expression was tight with strain. "Because great minds can see past the jargon."

Is that what he thought this was? A meeting of the minds? "Will we survive the jargon to perhaps see each other again?"

"In five years."

"You will forget about me in five years," she grouched.

"Quite the opposite, Kumar. It will give me time to think about the things I will miss."

She bit back a smile, sensing he meant it.

The horses whinnied as the carriage rolled to a stop.

The glass window at her elbow revealed a looming, three story building whose glass windows were dimly lit from inside.

Her stomach squeezed knowing what awaited inside.

The carriage door swung open revealing a dimly lit pavement.

The footman unfolded the steps.

"Mentally prepare yourself for the worst and expect it will be twice that." Ridley lowered his head, to keep his top hat from hitting the door of the carriage, and jumped down onto the pathway.

Chaucer flew down from the seat past her and hopped down each stair and onto the pavement, waddling his way past the footman.

Because that was normal.

She grabbed the satchel of copper instruments she required, which Scotland Yard had earlier confiscated from her, but one Ridley had returned. She stood, cane in hand, and was about to extend her free hand to the footman, when she realized she had no free hands.

The cravat the chambermaid had affixed around her throat too tightly seemed to be choking her further into grudging submission.

Hopping down onto the walk without any assistance, Jemdanee widened her stance, hoping to garnish a measure of approval that she was playing the part of a man quite well.

Ridley only moved to the already open door of the theatre, his great coat billowing around him as Chaucer flew up and alighted perfectly on his shoulder.

It was like witnessing the gods of justice descending onto earth.

She drew in a steadying breath at the thought of it, and strode into the large foyer lavishly graced with black and white marble tile.

A constable stoically closed the door behind them.

"This is Mr. Limazah," Ridley announced in a deep tone, gesturing toward her. "He will be conducting observations of the bodies as arranged."

Jemdanee lowered her cap, as she'd been instructed to do, and walked past a man bearing a wooden baton whilst wearing a domed blue hat that, in her opinion, made him look like an idiot.

No wonder criminals didn't take any of these constables seriously.

Ridley removed his top hat, smoothing the sides of his hair, and stalked onward, signaling they were done.

Her stomach squeezed as she tightened her trembling hold on the carpet bag in her gloved hand. The idea of seeing more than one dead body was unnerving.

She followed Ridley past elegant, round alcoves displaying a series of bronze and white stone busts of dignified men propped on Roman-like columns.

Her eyes followed the wood railing that trailed the wall toward an oversized landing that led to various doors upstairs. The theatre boxes.

"Widen that stride," Ridley tossed back at her as he mounted the stairs. "Remember everything I earlier told you. Breathe through your mouth the moment you enter that box."

Trying not to lose the cap on her head, she sprinted up after him, the coat weighing too heavily to her liking. It was tangling with her legs.

Ridley strode past the landing down a wide corridor and disappeared.

Low, male voices drifted toward her.

Jemdanee drew her brows together and followed him through a large rounded entryway leading into side doors, its arched ceilings bearing elegant ribbon plasterwork and a long row of windows on one side.

She veered into one of the boxes draped with heavy, brocaded curtains.

The cadaverine, putrid smell of rotting flesh mingling with citrus and foul garlic-like odor and vomit made her gag. She almost heaved as tears overwhelmed her. She gagged again, acid running up to her throat as she frantically set her sleeve to her nose, Ridley's deep voice crawling into her head.

Breathe through your mouth.

One breath. Two breaths. Three. She couldn't smell it half as much but she could still taste its acrid scent on her lips.

How did Ridley do this?

How did he... disconnect himself from a reality that went beyond horror?

The glow of candles in sconces set on gilded mirrors refracted an eerie gloom in the box. Several linen sheets soaked with vomit covered the expanse of the floor that had been cleared of its cushioned chairs that were supposed to overlook the balcony of the auditorium. Two bodies that were outlined beneath those vomit-soaked sheets, appeared to be contorted into demonic positions. The expensive satin heels, belonging to a woman whose face lay buried sideways beneath, peered out of one end of the sheet, spread apart as if the woman had attempted to run from her own symptoms.

It could have been anyone's mother.

It could have been *her* mother.

Her eyes burned and she almost sobbed. To give herself strength, she lifted her gaze to Ridley who stood on the farthest side of the box.

A gentleman with piercing black eyes whose skin was heavily scarred with pockmarks whispering of a childhood illness, finished his conversation with Ridley, his voice fading. With the flip of a collar from his evening coat, which he set against each side of his jaw, he angled around the covered bodies and stalked past her and out the door of the box, disappearing.

There was no doubt who that had been.

Finkle! She scrambled out into the corridor and called out, "May the gods bless you!"

He paused, his broad back to her, but didn't turn. "You have Ridley to thank, Miss Watkins. Not me. Find something so I can point this at the Barlows." He raised a black-gloved hand, acknowledging her and with the shrug of his coat, kept walking.

Two men were putting faith into her talent and in doing so, saving her life.

She had a chance to not only save herself, but unravel this horror to bring it peace.

You survived many nights beneath a manure cart, watching the feet of others pass by, hoping they didn't see or grab you. The terror is the same but the outcome is different.

Turning, she chanted to herself to remain calm and entered the box again. She kept breathing through her mouth to ensure she held onto her stomach and didn't retch.

Ridley pointed. "We only have two hours. He'll be downstairs waiting for anything that will enable him to take this case from me." He removed his great coat from his broad frame and tossed it out into the corridor behind her, yanking on a pair of leather gloves. He wagged his fingers toward her. "Give me your coat. You don't want it touching anything. Especially given the poison."

With trembling hands, she set down her carpet bag near the door of the corridor, as far from the feet of those unmoving satin slippers as space allowed. Removing the oversized male gloves from her hands, she shoved them into the pocket of the coat and removed that, as well.

She held them out, her hands trembling despite trying to steady them.

Leaning toward her, he grabbed the coat and tossed it onto his own in the corridor. "Do you need a few more moments to adjust?"

As if any amount of moments or breaths taken through her mouth was going to change what was beneath those sheets. She shook her head, still breathing through her mouth and set her cane against the wall behind her, trying to steady the trembling in her hand.

Ridley gestured toward an ornate sideboard against the wall. A decanter of wine and still-full glasses were set onto it beside an ornate silver tray laid out with a display of segmented oranges, both peeled and others still in its round entirely with its peels intact. "If one follows the pattern of the display, fourteen pieces are missing from the arrangement. Which means, however many they ate between themselves, still resulted in a bizarrely quick death that suffocated them before they could make it to the door. According to witnesses, about a half hour after the lights had dimmed and halfway through the theatrical, the sounds of their shouts and angst occurred as fast as the death itself. They didn't make it out of this box, which is unheard of even for arsenic. It's something far more lethal."

And rare.

Jemdanee veered toward the display, trying to focus in the same way he was, despite the bodies lying behind them at their feet. She kept breathing and breathing through her mouth, scanning the segmented oranges. Countless flies that had attempted to partake in the display were on it dead.

It affected the flies that usually avoided the bitterness of any toxic alkaloids.

There was no visible film or discoloring.

Think. Think, think, think. What could be *that* elusive and *that* powerful?

She turned. Kneeling near the door, she unstrapped her bag filled with instruments she usually used to dissect leaves and rising, turned back toward the bodies. Walking toward them, she gestured toward the sheet nearest her to signal that she was ready for the first body.

She swallowed, still breathing through her mouth.

Ridley adjusted the leather gloves he was wearing, then angled in and leaned down. Carefully folding over the linen sheet, he pulled it away from the contorted and bloated, bluing face of an elderly woman wearing a carmine-colored velvet gown. The rigidness of her body and the twisting positioning of that outstretched neck whispered of far more than the effects of a body rotting.

It whispered of an unimaginable suffering brought on by poison. Too many poisons contorted and stiffened the muscles of the body with the pain it brought.

It didn't help with her assessment.

She gestured toward the other sheet, attempting to remain calm.

Ridley unfolded the other and also pulled away the linen sheet, setting it aside to reveal a gentleman as equally contorted as the woman.

Jemdanee stepped back toward her carpet bag and reached in, yanking on tighter fitting leather gloves, fitting each one over her fingers before repositioning the instrument in her right hand. Turning back, she squatted beside the body. "Some poisons can remain on the skin after it is ingested. Have you or anyone else touched them?"

Ridley squatted beside her. "No. I never do. I usually use a yardstick. Though most of these morons don't even do that."

Contact. "Has anyone fallen ill after touching them?"

He paused. "One. He was retching the very first day we came in."

"How long after?"

"Less than hour."

"Did he live?"

"Yes. He likened it to heavy nausea and eating something he shouldn't have."

They were in England. In London, of all things. *Anything* could have been imported and brought in through the docks. England itself had countless poisonous plants.

Too many. *Aconitum* was but a single genus in England of over two hundred species of flowering plants alone. What if she couldn't help? What if she found nothing?

Panic seized her. She couldn't breathe. She couldn't—

"It's all right," Ridley whispered. "Hold onto your mind knowing it's still yours. Think of nothing but what you know and love. Greenhouses. Fresh air. Plants. India."

It was as if he knew.

She half-nodded, mentally sweeping herself back to a calm knowing what was waiting for her when this was done. Home. India.

Taking a copper scraper, she used her gloved fingers to carefully wedge open the mouth of the elderly woman. It easily slackened. She squinted and noting the woman had dentures, lifted them up and away from her gums to see if the remnants of anything from the orange was visible.

Nothing. She lowered the dentures back into place and scraped at the teeth, removing the thick film on it. She held it up to observe it. She had once found leaves between the teeth of a dog who had chewed through vegetation he shouldn't have. There had been enough of that vegetation for her to decipher it then. Maybe...

Ridley searched her face, leaning in. "What are you looking for?"

"Fibers from any other form of vegetation outside of those of an orange."

He squinted. "Would you be able to determine anything from it?"

She lowered the instrument and eyed him. "Only if the strand is large enough. I have to scrape each crevice in their mouths in the hopes of finding something." Anything. Two hours wasn't going to be enough.

Removing the dentures, she tried not to cringe as thickening liquid from the woman's mouth followed the dentures out. Jemdanee resumed scraping each and every darkened crevice between each human tooth and moved over to the gentleman and did the same with his mouth and yellowing teeth.

An hour passed.

Her neck and back and arms ached from stooping. Her eyes burned knowing she might as well be looking a single droplet of water in an ocean.

She rose and tightening her hold on the copper instrument, she quickly stepped around the bodies and returned to the oranges, determined to find something. "I require the scalpel from my bag. Might you fetch it?"

Ridley veered toward the corridor, removed it and angling around the bodies, extended the scalpel.

Still breathing through her mouth to the point of her lips being dry, she positioned the oranges and sliced through one. She sliced through the unfolding, pulping flesh of each segment, looking for an anomaly. Any slight discoloring. Any thickening.

After dissecting all fifty-two small segments and still finding nothing, she started grabbing what little was left of the display. Whole oranges. The ones still in peels.

Five.

Rotating each one carefully and slowly, to see if it had been punctured, but finding nothing, she used her scalpel to slice into the first one, dismantling it down, down, down to the inner peel, until nothing but shredded pulp and skin remained.

Nothing.

The second.

Nothing.

The third had a small break in the peel. A hole.

Odd. It didn't appear to have been done by an insect. Her scalpel sliced into it. Something stopped the blade, pushing back the metal.

She paused and frantically removed the scalpel and manually opened the flesh finding... a broken tip of a quill. Her pulse roared. "Ridley," she rasped in disbelief. "I found something."

He angled in close. Using his gloved finger, he nudged it free from the pulp and lifted it toward the candlelight above their heads, angling it. "Son of a bitch. It's hollow."

"What does that mean?" She peered at it, trying to understand. "None of the other oranges had it. Why does this one?"

He lowered it and set it back into the pulp. "Because it wasn't supposed to break off. They were stabbing quills dipped with poison into the oranges. Much like an ink well to paper delivering a missive." He slowly set the orange onto the tray and picked up the remaining two whole oranges, his brows coming together. "Were any of the other ones you dismantled punctured? Did you make a note of it?"

It was a good thing she had. "All of them were pristine, save this one. Only this one had a small hole burrowed into its peel."

"Huh." Inspecting the remaining two whole oranges closely, while running his gloved fingers over them, he set each one before her on the sideboard. "Dismantle these two, as well. Slowly. See if you can decipher any tunneling that we might be missing."

She nodded and slowly, slowly used the scalpel to break down each orange, carefully wedging apart the flesh more carefully than she had the rest. She followed each vein and the whitening edges and the pulp itself for each one. "Nothing. They are pristine, like the others were."

Ridley squinted. "Only specific ones were poisoned. Which means…" He shifted his jaw. "The server knew which ones to lay out. Gibbons knew. That son of a bitch was instructed, because he usually boards with James Barlow at Cambridge. It means we might have an actual witness we can break. One who could identify what I know to be true: Emily and James Barlow decided to end Emily's engagement to Mr. Rubenhold through force, given their parents refused to desist, eliminating not only Mr. Rubenhold and his family, but their own parents who had life insurance policies put in their children's names. *Voilà.*"

He jerked toward her, leaned in and down and set his forehead against hers. *Hard.*

She stilled, her forehead and nose set against his heat and cologne.

"This is me digging into everything you are." He swung away, stripping his gloves and jumped over the bodies, tossing the gloves into the farthest corner. He stalked out into the corridor and disappeared.

Jemdanee lingered in the eerie silence of the box, her own heartbeat making her all too painfully aware that hers was the only heart left beating in that room.

The two bodies with their mouths open, stared blankly.

She swallowed hard and quickly took the soiled sheets and covered them to give them whatever dignity they had left. "May your souls be reincarnated into better paths full of promise and happiness," she whispered.

The flapping of wings swooped in, startling her.

Chaucer casually alighted onto the sideboard and started scooping at the oranges, eating.

Her heart popped. "*Chaucer!*" she boomed, running at him,

waving her arms at him in the hopes he hadn't swallowed the poison *or* the evidence. "Chaucer, *nahin*!"

Chaucer darted past her into the vast open space of the auditorium and disappeared with a swoop below. He clicked.

She frantically skid toward the sideboard and eyed the oranges, noting the broken quill tip was still there, but... several of the oranges were *missing*. "Kali save him."

No. No, no, no. No!

Grabbing the velvet curtain of the box, she gritted her teeth and using whatever strength she could, she ripped it down with her weight, popping the rings from the pole until it fell. She covered the sideboard completely with its weight, to ensure Chaucer couldn't get to anymore. Stripping her gloves, she whipped them into the corner and jumped over the bodies, sprinting into the corridor.

"Ridley!" She couldn't breathe knowing what was about to happen. "*Ridley*!" she sprinted, feeling the beeswax on her upper lip unfastening against the moisture beading her lips as tears blinded her. His bird. She sobbed knowing what was about to happen. "*Ridleeeeeeeeeey*!"

His muscled figure jumped over the railing of the open stairwell above where he'd been talking to Finkle and thudded onto the landing several feet before her. Rising to his full height with the wide stance of boots, he removed both pistols and stalking around her, aimed each behind her, waiting.

She almost slapped him in between her sobbing as she shoved his arms away. "There is no one! No one! 'Tis Chaucer! *Chaucer*. He..." She gulped breaths. "He swallowed... some of the... oranges."

The heated crisp scent of his peppery cologne surrounded her, momentarily erasing the smells she wanted scrubbed from her nose and mind.

Ridley swung toward her, lowering his pistols which he shoved into his holsters. His rugged features wavered. Turning, he sprinted past her and back toward the box, disappearing inside.

She covered her mouth with a trembling hand, the stench of death still overwhelming her as she sobbed and sobbed. Citrus. Garlic. Vomit. Blood. Skin. Blue. Feces.

Chaucer.

She fainted, her body and head hitting the nearest wall.

CHAPTER TEN

Women.

They overreacted to everything.

No matter how old *or* young they were.

Chaucer circled him in curiosity as he carried Kumar's limp body into the carriage, ensuring her cap was pulled over her nose. Angling her carefully into the carriage, he draped her onto the seat and then signaled to Finkle over his shoulder. "Even if Gibbons offers testimony, she can't stay. She has to go. I'll sign off on any and all witness papers. Any idea on what could be happening with the governor and the logs?"

Finkle muttered something. "I have no doubt I already know. He could be lining up certain female prisoners for sexual favors in return for plea bargains and God knows what else."

Ridley jerked toward him. "Jesus. Prosecute the son of a bitch."

"I plan to. It's the third governor we've had to resign due to criminal endeavors. Are you interested in running for governor?" Finkle chided.

"That isn't even funny." Ridley pointed. "Keep my name off the ballot and get on Gibbons. We need that confession."

"I'll send Parker over to crack him. Go take care of the girl." With a smirk and the incline of his head, Finkle disappeared back inside.

Ridley whistled up at Chaucer who was sitting up on a lamp post.

Swooping down into the carriage, Chaucer landed onto Kumar's hip, tilting his head at her as the footman closed the carriage door behind them.

Ridley fell back against the seat in exasperation and tossed the coats from his arm and her carpet bag onto the floor. "That there, Chaucer, is someone who was *very* worried about you. Fortunately, you're indubitably smarter than you look and swallowed the right ones. That is why you're *my* bird. You're brilliant. Like me. *And…* like her."

Chaucer hopped closer to her shoulder, grazing his beak against the waistcoat she wore, rubbing his head into her, as well.

"Worry not," he offered. "When she wakes up, she'll be a year older." Leaning forward, he skimmed his hand across the softness of the small brown hand dangling over the seat. "Well done, Kumar," he murmured. "I hadn't even thought of dismantling those full oranges. My nose was too close to the bark to see the ax."

Her head popped up, her mustache hanging off to one side and the cap over her nose.

Chaucer alighted onto the floor.

Ridley leaned back against the seat and waited for the cap to come off so he might glory in seeing what he knew would one day be his: her.

She scrambled to sit up, shoving the cap up. Her blue eyes darted down to Chaucer. Her lips parted. "He lives? *How*? He ate the segments. I saw him!"

"He ate the pulp from the untouched whole oranges, bless his raven heart. If cats have nine lives, my bird has eleven."

She sagged against the seat. Tugging at the mustache from her upper lip, she flinched at removing the last of the beeswax and then tossed the mustache. "I do not like this profession of yours." She cradled herself against the side of the carriage and closed her eyes, easing out of a shaky breath. She turned her chin inward. "Might I sleep?"

He half-nodded, knowing that his dark, dark world was not a place where one like her could exist or survive. "Of course." He softened his voice, unbuttoning his coat. He quickly removed his weapons from his holsters and set them into the casing beside him, securing the latch.

A part of him needed to hold her. *One last time take my knee…* "Come to me." He patted his knee. "You will rest better here. Come."

She shook her head and kept her eyes closed, curling herself further into the seat.

His throat tightened sensing she was already carving out her own little life like a caterpillar weaving itself into a cocoon.

A cocoon only one could fit into.

That flicking flame of a future he saw, the one he had vividly glimpsed all but an hour earlier whilst watching her intently scrape teeth and slice oranges in the name of delivering justice alongside of him, was… gone.

For all he heard in his head were screams.

Her screams.
Her sobs.
Her terror.
Her angst.
Her misery.

Everything that defined him.

Did he want this life for her or any woman? Ever?

A life of very little laughter or joy? Ever?

One he had sentenced himself to forever given it was how he was? No.

He'd never been that selfish and that was why he continued to be alone thinking of nothing but the rafters in the attic and the ropes that whispered to him to cross over to a life where death became one's friend, not one's enemy.

The following morning,
9:42 a.m.

There was too much to do and although his body needed *rest*, he knew coca, coca, coca could get him through this endurance *test*.

181

So he chewed. Twenty leaves and a good dose of limestone was enough to get him through it.

"See to it she continues to rest and has everything she needs," he instructed the butler, handing off the entire lined up staff of footmen a pistol. "I'm heading over to Scotland Yard to sign off on papers and won't be back until the afternoon."

"Yes, Mr. Ridley."

"Don't answer the door to anyone whilst I'm gone."

"Yes, Mr. Ridley."

"Tug every last drape in this house shut so no one from the street might see her."

"Yes, Mr. Ridley."

"*Don't* let her leave the house or open a window. Don't let her go near a window."

"Yes, Mr. Ridley."

"Feed her."

"I will, sir."

"Bathe her so the stench of that theatre is no longer with her." He pointed at the butler. "Not you, mind you. No male servant in this house is permitted to see her in a state of undress. Not even when she is lying in bed resting. Is that understood?"

The butler blinked rapidly. "I should hope you know me better than that, sir. The chambermaid will oversee her in that."

"Good. Treat her with the respect of nobility." He paused. "*Better* than nobility."

"Yes, Mr. Ridley."

"There is one last gown in the trunk for her to wear." The last one he would ever see her in. "Have the chambermaid fit her into it. She also needs a better fitting corset. Have one of the maids borrow her one."

"Yes, sir."

Ridley hesitated. "Count out ten thousand pounds in coins from the cellar, put it in a leather satchel and lay it on my desk." He'd have to contact more collectors and sell more books.

"Yes, Mr. Ridley."

Tugging on his great coat, and latching on his leather belt with his pistols and blade, he stalked out. If he had stayed, he would have only sat outside the room she was sleeping in. He hardly needed a reason to do it after he hardly slept last night in the hopes she'd come running into his room. She didn't.

He dragged in a long breath of coal-tinged air and jogged down the stairs toward his waiting carriage. Despite his stride, in the distance, he already noted… *trouble.*

Though not at all the usual sort. Boys.

He scanned the expensive waiting carriage, noting no one else was in it or waiting other than a driver. He slowed. This ought to be fun.

Three lean-bodied youths with burlap sacks on their heads who barely reached Evan's broad shoulder approached. Each of their white gloved hands pointed a pistol, their varying colors of eyes barely visible through uneven cut out slits.

All the flintlocks pointed at him were… ornamental.

The pristine barrels bore no signs of having ever been fired.

None were even cocked and there were no triggers.

One could say, he was cursed to be smarter than nine-two percent of the overall population, be they young or old.

He chewed his coca, wincing at the tanginess of the limestone that overpowered the twenty leaves he'd rolled in. "How goes your day, boys? I didn't realize I was intimidating enough to warrant four pistols." He didn't bother to reach for his. Yet.

Instead, he ticked through their appearances like the puzzle pieces that they were.

Expensive coats. White silk cravats.

Done up by servants.

Knee-high leather boots of Italian make.

Never seen dirt or the road or a single scuff.

The closest youth tapped his arm and draped out a sack, gesturing to Ridley to put it on.

It was hilarious. They were being so mindful and polite.

How could he *not* entertain this?

He didn't have to call on Finkle until noon. Which meant he had time for what he loved most: a puzzle. He took the sack.

"*Sir!*" His driver and the footman jogged toward him, their pistols pointed at the three young boys.

The boys snapped up their hands in unison and one of them sobbed.

That was all he needed.

Ridley held up a quick hand and waved off the driver and footman with the burlap sack he still held. "No need, Shelton. If

I go anywhere, feel free to follow at a distance. Otherwise… no. Go. Go, go, go. You're scaring them." He hardly wanted to be known for making children cry. His reputation was sordid enough.

The driver and footman eyed each other and slowly departed, heading back to the coach, while still glancing back at him.

These boys clearly needed him, but didn't want the world to know given the burlap sacks on their heads.

Returning his attention to the three youths surrounding him, Evan chewed his coca and rattled the sack. "So I take it you boys want me to put this on and join in on the fun?"

They nodded in unison.

Given the expensive make of the ornamental pistols whose brass were stamped with *Hewson*, this had the aristocracy slathered all over it. How droll. Their weapons were no doubt from display cases belonging to their fathers.

This crowd was straight out of Eton. "Permit me a moment." He shook out the wool sack that matched the ones they wore, noting the *Sturminster Newton* mark that was found in high-scales kitchens, then yanked the sack over his own head, blanketing himself in darkness.

The scent of grain penetrated his nostrils as he decided to further amuse them. "You might want to remove my pistol and blade. That will ensure I don't hurt you. Because if this goes beyond two hours, boys, I *will* use both weapons for I hate being late."

Hands frantically patted his pockets.

"Ey, ey, *careful*." Ridley stilled their hands. "Unlike your weapons, my pistols are primed and loaded. Slow. And set them *carefully* onto the pavement so my servants can retrieve them."

They paused and then slowly, slowly removed his pistols, then the blade from the leather belt attached to his waist, setting them on the pavement with a soft clack, clack, clack.

Someone now slowly took his arm and he was led and guided up and into a carriage.

Evan landed on a cushioned seat in exasperation and set himself into the farthest corner, letting his shoulder hit the side of what was a private coach. The seats were velvet. "Did you need me for an investigation? Or is this a school assignment?"

When none of them spoke, he sensed they were too panicked

to talk.

Not a school assignment.

The carriage slowed approximately eighteen minutes later. He did his best to count given he couldn't see and his watch was buried in his pocket.

A small hand grabbed his hand and he was carefully guided out of the carriage with a surprising amount of graciousness.

It was charming.

Silence surrounded him as he was guided up eight stairs, into an echoing room and… into a creaking chair.

"Might we tie you, sir?" one boy asked.

How kind of them to ask. "To what purpose?" he countered. "I prefer we continue to be civil and talk."

"We cannot speak about what plagues us until you agree to be tied. Those are the terms. Otherwise, you might get angry and we…"

He sensed it would ease them into what he wanted them to do: talk.

How was it his life always evolved around a rope? "Of course. Go on. Have at it."

Roped thudded the floor as he was now being tied.

They carefully knotted more and more thick rope around Evan, ensuring his arms were at his sides and that each muscled leg was strapped tight against the chair to keep him from moving.

How very off-putting that this was being done to him by several young boys. "I do have to be somewhere by noon."

"We will ensure to it that you are, sir. We will even have the driver take you to wherever you wish to go."

It was like arriving to a dinner party and being escorted to a finely set table. These were the days when being an investigator was not only entertaining, but all too easy. "I thank you kindly and will most likely take you up on that offer. Now what is this about?"

There were a few whispers between them.

"…how do we…?"

"You do it!"

"I am not as well-spoken as you. *You do it*."

At least they were *attempting* to organize. "I'll speak to the oldest. Which of you would that be?"

The one nearest him cleared a throat. "That would be me, sir." That boyish voice cracked in an attempt to be manly.

The tone and language was *very* upper crust. About one year off of being at Eton. "A pleasure to formally meet you. What is this about? How did you know to find me?"

"Everyone knows where to find you, Mr. Ridley. You post your cases in the newspaper every week and we follow your adventures. Our favorite thus far was when you threw a procurer from a bridge for refusing to testify."

Ah. The Limmer case. He got arrested for that one. "I didn't realize I had a following." He rattled his head against the burlap sack, bending it toward them. "Do you mind? The smell of grain is a bit strong and I'm chewing on something I shouldn't be chewing on in front of children. More importantly, I prefer to see who I'm talking to. Might you?"

"With pleasure, sir." The sack slowly came off, cascading his dark hair into his eyes while revealing an empty room with one cracked window and missing plaster.

An abandoned building.

How original.

The three youths were still wearing burlap sacks, the slits of their eyes so unevenly cut out, one of them even dipped downward.

All done probably with a pair of scissors they stole out of their governess' own sewing box. Whilst he was never known to laugh, this made him want to reconsider it. "Is there a reason you boys brought me here? We could have easily settled this back at the house."

One of them pointed his blade. "We didn't want anyone to know we were talking to you. You are also twice our size, sir, and twice more in everything else, including wit."

He wasn't going to brag or argue. "If you follow my adventures in the broadsheets, surely you know I wouldn't hurt you. I only go after criminals."

They were quiet.

Interesting.

"We tied you, sir, should you... succumb to anger."

Double interesting. "Why would I get angry?"

They fell into silence.

Evan paused, noting a gold signet ring on the hand holding out the blade. While he couldn't make out the engraving, given the direction of the ring was turned, it was resting on the same finger that had been missing from—

Male of about eleven. Freckled white skin in state of blue darkening, brown eyes, brown hair, lean, four feet and ten inches. Notable indentation of the skin on the left, fourth finger evocative of a large ring no longer present.

The Clover Stack boy.

They were the same age.

Setting his shoulders against the bindings, Ridley let his mind rifle through the case in his head. *No calluses on either hand and nails unusually clean, indicating wealthier station despite frayed trousers.* "I promise I won't get angry. I'm strapped to this chair and tied, remember? Which means I can't hurt you. Now what would you like to talk about?"

The one with the blade leaned in, turning the hilt. A thistle crest revealed itself. "We are asking you to close the investigation into *The Clover Stack* that was shared with newspapers."

Bold. "In return for what? My life? You'll have to offer me a bit more than that. My life isn't worth as much as you think it is."

The youth pointed the dagger with a trembling hand. "If you think we are not in earnest, Mr. Ridley, we are. Our lives depend on it, and as such, we will show you that we are to be feared."

That tone indicated the boy wasn't quite certain.

It was time to gauge their behavior. "By all means," Ridley countered. "Show me. It's important we understand each other. How serious are you? Hurt me. Come on."

"I…" Still pointing the dagger, he hesitated and then slowly and carefully, carefully dragged the blade across Ridley's hand, with a trembling hand. "*There.*"

The pressure of the cold blade pierced a small angle of the skin, yielding a pinch but nothing in the least bit extraneous. It was obvious this poor boy had never even cut his own finger on parchment, yet alone that of others.

For effect, Ridley winced and hissed out an exaggerated breath for effect. "I am undone. I may require stitching."

The youth glanced at the blade and frantically handed it off to the one next to him. "Get rid of it! *Get rid of it!*"

One of the others shoved him hard. "Whatever are you doing?! We are attempting to get out of this, not into it! *You dolt!*"

Another grabbed the blade and frantically threw it out with a clatter into the corridor behind them. "Leave it there. Leave it!" He sobbed.

These three clearly weren't intent on ever becoming professionals.

In fact, he had no doubt they were only desperate to hide what was becoming all too obvious.

An accident. He softened his voice to ensure they didn't feel threatened. "Why did you leave him beneath a clover stack? Was he your friend?"

They all grew quiet.

Ridley noted they were all wearing the same thistle ring. The same burlap sacks. The same ornamental pistols. They *were* all friends. His heart squeezed knowing it. "Did you boys have some sort of club?" He further softened his voice. "I've always wanted to be part of a club. What did you name it? Did you have a name?"

There was a moment of silence.

"The Thistle club," one quietly offered, turning his ring. "Charles named it. He… how did you know we had a club?"

It was like being ten again and running down the street with a book in his hand, trying to keep up with other boys who only ever left him behind. "I'm incredibly good at guessing." He eyed them. "Consider me your newest member and a true friend. I need you boys to talk to me. I need you to tell me what happened and why. It's important. Did you hurt him?"

"No! Never!"

There was a shaking of burlaps heads.

"He was *our friend*! He…" A sob escaped one of them. "He fell from the window."

Teeth untouched, yet jaw, side and back of skull fractured. Nostrils heavily coagulated with blood and uneven bruising on right shoulder and entire side. Broken ribs, shattered pelvis and dislocated shoulder all on same right side, indicating possible fall from an elevated height.

They were telling the truth. "Whose window? Why did he fall?"

They all grew quiet again.

Ridley eased a slowing breath through his nostrils, his leg jittering from a need to keep up with his thoughts and his body that were speeding through coca. "Why did you decide to cover it up? Why didn't you call for your parents or servants? Hm?

They would have helped and could have helped you."

The youth adjusted the hood to ensure the eyes aligned better. "We didn't know what to do. None of us even wanted to be there, but Charles insisted. He *insisted*. He wanted to see her."

"Who?" Ridley prodded.

"Lady Stanton. He wanted to see her in a state of undress and… fell from her window."

This crowd might as well have been thirty. And yet another reason why women were pistols waiting to be shot by men who didn't know how to fucking handle them: with care. "I see. So now you think you're going to make it all go away by holding ornamental pistols to my head and cutting me with a blade? Was that the brilliant plan?"

They said nothing.

Jesus. "I need the clothing he was in that night and anything else you removed from his person, including the ring he was wearing. What did you do with the ring?"

Several eyes widened.

"How did you know he was wearing a ring?" one of them echoed.

They were all so innocent. That was what made this as incredibly heartbreaking as it was sad that it had to end in the death of one as equally innocent as them.

This is why he did this. To protect faces like theirs that were forced to hide beneath burlap sacks out of fear. "When you're on the right side of the law, you see things a bit clearer." He tapped his thigh that his arms were bound against. "I appreciate everything you shared with me, and now I'm asking that you boys cut me loose. All right? I'm not angry. Far from it. The good news is you won't be in any trouble. The bad news, you'll have to tell the boy's father and give testimony in court."

They shook their heads and kept shaking and shaking it.

"*We didn't do anything*," the closest boy with a velvet blue coat pressed. "*We didn't kill him!*"

Ridley eased out a steadying breath, trying to control the tone of his voice so it didn't strain, confuse or scare them. "I know that and I'm not accusing any of you of such. It was an accident and the burden laid upon each of you has already been too great. Let me help you. All I ask is that you untie me so we are able to finally lay your friend to rest. He deserves that much, don't you think? Was he not your friend?"

The boys looked at each other, burlap sacks shifting.

Momentarily leaving the room, they picked up the blade from the floor, and closing the door, they whispered to each other.

Through ebbing pulses of silence he heard snatches of their conversation.

A choked sob escaped one of them. "…the right thing…"

"I told you we shouldn't have disrespected his memory! *I told you!*"

There was a moment of silence and the door reopened.

One by one, they filed back in.

Some of them sniffled beneath their burlaps.

The leader of the four, who appeared more composed despite the trembling of his hands, lingered. "We will return with everything you need."

Return? He slowed his chewing. "Ey. I appreciate that you boys were so pleasant and cooperative given my days usually are never quite this glorious, but I need you to untie me. All right? I won't hurt you. I promise."

They paused.

That was *not* the sort of reaction he wanted.

He stared them down. "Is there a misunderstanding I ought to be aware of?"

"We should speak to our fathers first. We may need a solicitor."

Only the aristocracy would feel so entitled! "I didn't realize you boys even knew what a solicitor was." He hardened his voice. "I need you boys to untie me. *Now.*"

"We will. We will! *After* we talk to our fathers." The tallest of the three walked over to the door, letting the others leave before glancing back at Ridley through the slits of his hood. Dark eyes held his. "I am ever so sorry about cutting you." With that, he closed the door.

Jogging steps echoed as they hurried to leave the building.

What the fuck just—

Violently trying to loosen the binding ropes tightly holding him, while clattering the chair he was tied to, he stilled and looked down. The ropes weren't even budging.

In fact, the knots were the best he'd seen in years. Military style.

The sons of little bitches actually knew how to trammel a man.

And they took the blade from the floor, so he couldn't even—

Ridley grudgingly listened as their coach clattered away.

Fuck. Fuckity, fuck, fuck, fuckity, fuck.

At least it wasn't a complete waste of a morning.

One less file on his desk.

Unfortunately… he had no use of his arms or his legs and had to get to Finkle before noon to sign off on witness papers for Kumar's case.

Fuck! He paused. His driver.

His driver wasn't going to be able to find him.

Shite! Spitting out the coca past his shoulder, lest he choke on it given what he was about to do, he gritted his teeth and thudded the chair across the floor, each jarring effort straining muscles. He continued to methodically lift and drop himself and the chair in increments, ensuring he didn't topple over.

It took… a… lot… longer… than… he… wanted… it… to.

He *finally* clattered into place beside the dirt-streaked window, his chest heaving from the amount of effort it had taken merely to get to the window.

He paused as an all too familiar black lacquered coach with his driver and footman jostled past the window and out of the square, clearly intent on catching up to the *other* coach that had already left.

Ridley thudded his head against the glass pane that might as well have been real *pain*. "Why did you let them tie you? Why?" He groaned. "This is what happens when you get too cocky, Ridley. *Oh, yes. Remove my belt, boys. Tie me to a chair, boys. I'm solving a case, boys.* Only… I'm now the case! *Fuuuuck!*"

Given how decrepit the outside buildings were, strewn with trash and broken windows, it was obvious very few people were going to walk by. Fuck again.

Minutes crawled on and more and more minutes devoured the last of him.

He *hated* not doing anything.

It was a waste of his mind.

His leg rattled and rattled and rattled in an attempt to calm down as the coca effects didn't seem to slow down. In fact, they were speeding up and his pulse seemed to thicken his veins.

Not good. Not good, not good, not good.

He eyed the window, his breaths uneven, trying to figure out if there was a way to break the glass and then use the glass to cut his restraints.

It would require a lot of bleeding on his part.

He paused.

A young woman scrambled out of a carriage as she made her way into the square. Her skin glowed with a soft rich caramel tone as thick black hair pushed out in untamed ringlets against its bundled state. And in her hand was a curtain rod.

He dragged in an astounded breath.

It was Jemdanee.

In public.

With a curtain rod.

Whilst her name and likeness was plastered on a brick wall just across the street.

Fuck! Fuuuuuuuuuuuuuuuuuck! Where the hell were the servants?! *Fuck*!

She wore the same oversized calico gown he'd fastened her into in prison. It flapped and ballooned against the whistling, summer air.

Hell and well and there goes the bell and its funeral knell.

He might as well... make use of her and get them the hell out of sight.

Ridley tipped his chair closer to the cracked window, trying to follow her movements, his legs quaking and rattling against his will.

While crossing the desolate square toward him, she grew annoyed by the expanse of the dragging fabric bundling her limbs and with the puff of golden cheeks, while repositioning her sword, she gathered the gown high enough to expose frayed wool stockings that were sliding down shapely ankles and leather boots.

God save me from becoming my own greatest fear.

She paused beneath his window, glancing around with the curtain rod.

It was almost amusing. Almost.

He thudded the wall beneath the window with his boot. "Kumar. *Kumar*!"

She blinked and jerked toward him with the rod, startled at seeing him strapped to a chair while peering down at her.

Their gazes locked.

The base of his throat pulsed. Hell on earth and damn her all over again for she might as well have been the one to have bound him.

With that curtain rod in hand, she climbed up on the iron railing to better peer up at him.

He now felt like a lion strapped to a cart awaiting a safari with an audience.

Bearing it with the set of his jaw, he fully recognized his own humiliation and that the only reason why she was even out in public with a fucking curtain rod and without a veil to cover her face to protect her from a lynching was because of him. *Him.* Him and his cocky ways and his fucking coca and his need—

"I'm *usually* on the other side of this window."

Keep saying it, Ridley. Coca, coca, coca.

Her fingers tightened against the railing she held with one hand. A strong breeze made her flinch as her thick hair lost several pins, causing a curtain of locks to unevenly fall around her shoulders and past her waist.

Jet-black hair rose and fell against the wind, making her features all the more striking. Set against the rod she held, it was like beholding Madame Justice.

His jaw worked, annoyed for noticing how gorgeous she was. He didn't want to be attracted to her. He didn't want to turn her life or his into a passion-spilling, skin-splitting mess that would turn him into the animal she didn't deserve.

He grudgingly stared at her, waiting. "Assistance would be appreciated."

"*Array haan!*" Tucking her skirts around her legs, she climbed up higher onto the railing and teetered toward the window, loosening one of the iron bars. She gripped the ledge where a piece of a bent pipe rested and after peering past him into the room, she blinked at him through the cracked window.

"Are you bound and alone?" she half-whispered in that heavy accent. "Or will you require me to slash a dozen throats?"

He gave her an exasperated look, attempting to straighten against the ropes binding him.

He couldn't move. "Your enthusiasm is much admired, but there is no need to slash a single throat. It's just you and me and the building. And rope. Lots of rope." God was mocking him.

"Are you hurt?"

"No." His leg rattled in an effort to try to throw off the roaring of his pulse and whatever was left in his veins. His pulse wasn't coming down. In fact, it was going up and up and he knew it had nothing to do with her. It was the coca. He had saturated the limestone with too many leaves. "'Tis merely a good lesson and will ensure I never play with children unless I'm fully armed," he sped out the words, almost unable to hear himself saying it.

Edging closer to the window, she teetered against the railing.

His gut flipped. "*Don't*— You'll fall off! Climb down. For fuck's sake, *climb down*. Go around. Go to the—"

"Cease telling me what to do whilst using foul language." Those soulful pale blue eyes that shone through a cracked glass in the middle of nowhere. "I have climbed abandoned temples higher than this." Leaning toward the window, she positioned herself and lifted the curtain rod high over her head with uneven breaths.

He was so startled at the realization of what she intended to do, he snapped his head away, barely in time for the impact. The shattering of glass exploded within the room, spraying him as the warm afternoon wind whipped through, filling his breaths with coal-tinged air.

She kicked at the remaining shards of glass still attached to the window to make more room for her body, using the handle of the curtain rod to chip and dash away the rest, then climbed through and jumped down onto the floor with a graceful thud.

If love had a name this was it. "You could have used the front door. It wasn't locked."

She straightened, thudding the tip of the rod into the wooden floor. "You needed me sooner."

If he had married this one back in 1820, his outlook on life probably would have made him a better man. Only... she would have been nine. "I appreciate the urgency. Might you untie me?"

"*Haan.*" She leaned in. "I saw the faceless ones approach you from the chamber window. I was worried and had your other driver and footman follow. They have all of your weapons. The ones you left on the pavement."

He was endlessly impressed. "The servants weren't supposed to let you out of the house."

She pinched her lips. Glancing off to the side she said out of the corner of her mouth, "The butler pinned me to the wall and refused to let me pass, I therefore had to…" She tapped the end of the rod, indicating she had used the hilt. "His nose will need tending."

No. My very mind will need tending.

Kumar, run. Run before I crush every bone in your body in an effort to seize you. "What you did was incredibly stupid," he bit out, refusing to listen to his mind that was no longer being rational. "*Incredibly.* You could have been hurt. Someone could have seen you. You also forgot to wear my cap down over your nose. Where the hell is it?"

Jemdanee lowered her chin. "Would you prefer I leave for an hour and retrieve it, Mr. Ridley?" Her tone indicated she was displeased with him for not thanking her.

Back to the girl he knew. "No. That won't be necessary."

She pointed the tip of the rod to his chest. "Are you not going to thank me?"

For what? For taking the only thing I have? My mind? It's all I have. "I thank you."

She set her chin, clearly pleased. "I wish to hear more of this gratitude. I wish for you to call me *Jemdanee*. No more of this Kumar. Or I will not untie you."

He was tied and she was insisting. The overlord in him grumbled. "Jemdanee it is."

"Might I call you by whatever your parents named you? You never told me. What is it?"

"You're overstepping your bounds. You'll only ever get that name when you're lying beneath me, which won't be for another five years."

She rolled her eyes, then glanced toward him and veering in close, started unraveling and tugging against the ropes angled behind the chair, wedging and pulling them free one by one by one as she rounded him, her tangle of black curls wagging before him.

The bursting glorious heat of her being near permeated his being, overwhelming his senses. He swallowed and almost buried his face and his nose into her hair and that penny soap scent in half-anguish, wanting to fall into her for being the first woman to actually… save him.

She stripped the last of the ropes and paused. Her eyes widened as she grabbed his hand with soft fingers and cupped it. "Life escapes you!"

"Cease being dramatic." He squeezed her small hand hard, wanting to remember this moment and its warmth as he would have to carry it with him for a long time. "It's a scratch. That said, I want to thank you." He softened his voice. "Thank you for…"

"Not being a child?"

"Yes. That. I…" The room felt like it was swaying.

Edging forward and back against his skull.

It was the coca.

It was speeding up his heart beyond what he and his chest and his mind could bear.

Though a profound weakness slammed itself into his body, sinking deep into the bone from too much coca, his riled mind was much stronger. It had always been. It had to be. He pushed himself up from the chair knowing he had to get her out of the public eye.

His vision dimmed, making him realize he got up too fast and his ankle turned and—

He collapsed to the floor, stunned as his mind blanked and his body suddenly thudded and thudded and thudded, his head and his skull and his arms and his legs hitting and hitting and rattling in a blur he couldn't control.

"*Ridley. Ridleeeey*!" Frantic hands held him down and down against the thudding that didn't end. "Breathe. *Breathe!*"

He couldn't see or breathe.

His body, his head, his arms and his legs continued to *thud, thud, thud*.

His greatest nemesis had at long last come to grip his skull into compliance and what it wanted most: his mind. *Thud, thud, thud.*

He lost consciousness.

CHAPTER ELEVEN

On both knees beside him, Jemdanee sobbed knowing he wasn't responding. "*Ridley?*"

Blood gushed from his nose, his eyes rolling to the back of his head.

Trying to remain calm and rational, she hovered over his lips.

There was heat.

His breaths were short and labored, but they were there.

He was still with her.

She frantically unraveled his cravat and slipped it out from beneath his neck. Rolling the silk, she tucked it in and against his nose. The blazing moist heat of his forehead burned her hand.

All that mattered was that the seizure had stopped.

Scrambling to her booted feet, she skidded to the window and screamed out to Ridley's driver and footman, "*He requires assistance!*" She pointed toward the direction of the door, lest they attempt to scramble through the broken window. "The door is open! You will need to carry him out!"

The two men thudded down onto the ground from the coach and sprinted from the street and up the long stone stairwell of the building and banged open the doors into the abandoned house.

"He is still breathing, but requires a physician." Her throat tightened. Peter. Peter had dealt with coca/limestone seizures.

He'd saved a man from it once. But how was she, a fugitive, to get to him?

"Lift on the count of two, Shelton," the driver instructed, one grabbing Ridley's booted feet and the other beneath his shoulder. "One and… *two!*"

Both men lifted Ridley up with a grunt, staggering with gritted teeth as they attempted to shuffle him back out the door, their feet skidding against the swaying, limp weight.

Pulse roaring in between more tears that blinded her knowing what might have happened had she not followed him, Jemdanee jogged around them and held the door wide open. It was in moments like these that she realized, she was only as strong as the weight the gods had given her.

"Move slowly," she offered, knowing it was the only form of assistance she could give. "He suffered a seizure and will most likely endure more. I therefore advise you both to be very careful with him. Do not drop his weight."

The driver glared. "Don't you be talking at us as if you were master, you heathen of a slave. I can damn well carry him and more. Christ, you damn well got him into this row given his need to yank you from the misery you call a life!"

A sob escaped her. Ridley had indeed left the house to sign her witness papers. To save her.

The two men turned sideways on the top landing of the stairs and were about to descend when Ridley's body violently thudded. He jarred out of their arms and down the sweep of stone stairs spanning several feet.

She screamed and shoved both men in an attempt to lunge after him.

Ridley's body thrashed down onto the last stone ledge, the sound of bone cracking.

In a droning blur that erased everything but Ridley, she fell beside his bent leg that continued to thrash against his seizure. His gagging made her realize he was choking to death on his own tongue and couldn't breathe.

Chanting to herself to remain calm, she tucked his head between her knees hard, squeezing it into place. Having nothing else to keep him from gagging, she set all four of her fingers into his mouth, which she forcefully widened and held down his tongue as he bit and bit and bit his teeth into her fingers to the bone.

She sobbed through it as her blood swelled from her own fingers, the searing pain ripping straight from her hand to her jaw. Knowing his life depended on her ability to hold onto his tongue, she sobbed and hissed her way through it, pressing her fingers down harder and harder, willing him to live.

Too much blood was coming from her fingers.

He would suffocate from the blood, not merely his tongue.

"I will not fail you, Ridley," she choked out. "I... will... not... *fail you!*" she roared, pushing her strength and will through her own voice.

Ridley stilled.

"Jesus Christ." The two men hovered, eyes wide. "What the devil is wrong with him?"

"Be he possessed?!"

She sobbed and sobbed, removing her severely gashed fingers from Ridley's slack mouth lest he choke on all the blood pouring from her fingers. "We cannot... m-move him," she choked out, unable to breathe against the pain blinding her. "W-we need a doctor! A doctor!"

Shelton pointed rigidly at the head of the driver. "Get your bloody arse into that seat and ring for the nearest one lest I backhand you for giving her the lip you earlier did! *Go!*" he boomed.

The driver sprinted, scrambling into the coach.

Ridley remained eerily still, despite his chest heaving and his eyes fluttering.

Jemdanee continued to cradle him and his head between her thighs to keep his skull safe, knowing the seizures might continue. She sobbed, feeling helpless. As if she were eight and unable to find her mother. Unable to breathe. Unable to find the will to do anything but sob.

"Miss. *Miss.*" Shelton knelt beside her, snapping off his cravat. Taking her hand gently, he bandaged it quick and hard. "A braver soul I have never met than you."

She sobbed again, but not from the throbbing of her blood-bitten fingers, but the throbbing she felt within her heart. One that appeared bound to a man who had ultimately saved her from the wrath of London's judgement.

She lowered herself to Ridley's chest, kissing it in prayer and reverence. "O Shiva, watch over him. Shiva, he needs you.

Shiva, he is worthy. Shiva, I will gift thee whatever you ask. Save him. Save him and I will guide him to a better life. One he deserves."

In between her chants and willing her strength of faith into him and this moment, she held onto Ridley, refusing to look at the leg whose bone protruded, goring his trousers.

She squeezed her eyes shut past more tears, chanting and chanting until the gods responded and brought forth the doctor he needed.

Midnight

With a bandaged hand and trembling fingers that had been carefully threaded from the gashes of Ridley's teeth marking them straight through her skin to the bone, everything still throbbed but was equally hazy from the laudanum she had been given. She tucked the quaking bandaged hand against her chest and waited and waited against the wall outside of Ridley's bedchamber where the physician had been setting his bone over an hour earlier.

She had been waiting for too long.

Too. Long.

The door opened, making her stumble toward it.

An elderly gentleman sighed, removing a bloodied apron and bundling it. "The rest lies within the hands of God."

Ridley needed more than one god to save him from what she had seen of his leg. "Might I see him?" she choked out. "Is he conscious? Might I go to him?"

The surgeon nodded. "Yes. I set a bottle of laudanum for the pain at his bedside. See to it he takes it every few hours and ensure his leg is not over elevated. I will call on him in a few hours."

She nodded. "I thank you."

He eyed her. "Given he demanded to know, I have already

shared the grim assessment. He will never walk again."

She sobbed. No. No, no, no, no. Noooooooooooooooo.

Gently squeezing her shoulder, he nudged her toward the door. "He is heavily sedated, but conscious. You may speak to him briefly, but I advise you to let him rest. He needs rest. Not these tears."

With the left hand that wasn't bandaged, she swiped at her tears and nodded. She slowly angled past the open door and into Ridley's bedchamber, which reeked of acrid blood and the burning nostril stinging of ethanol alcohol.

Ridley's head was rolled toward the pillow, his eyes squeezed shut against the trembling of his fisted hands that gripped the newly laid linens that surrounded him, covering his quaking limbs. His damp hair clung to his forehead, his strong jaw unshaven as he bared his teeth to permit slow takes of breath through them and flared nostrils. Scrape marks from the stone he'd hit and bruising covered his face and hands.

She hurried toward him, feeling the agony of every breath he took, and lingered beside him. Wanting to take his hand, but fearing it would hurt him too much, she only leaned in. "Mr. Ridley?" she whispered, leaning in closer, so she might better see every inch of him and that face and that he knew she was with him. "I am here. I am with you."

He opened his eyes, staring at her as if he didn't know who she was.

Her lip trembled, praying he had not lost the one thing that made him who he was: his mind.

His amber eyes lowered to her hand and paused. "What... what..." His breaths were uneven and no more words seemed to emerge.

She didn't need to hear the words to know what his mind was thinking. "'Tis nothing. I cut myself on some glass." She hardly wanted to pile any further guilt he no doubt felt.

"You... ought to be... more... careful," he rasped.

Despite barely seeing through tears, she nodded and smiled for him. For she knew a smile is what he needed now more than anything. "It was rather silly of me. I promise never to do it again."

He lifted a hand to her face, grazing moist fingers across her cheek and dragging it down to her lips. "No... tears. I am... unworthy."

Little did he know how worthy he really was. Shelton had spent the last hour doing nothing but praising his employer, Ridley, over the countless times over these many, many years Ridley had endangered himself for the sake of others.

It was a wonder he was still breathing. "You are worthy of more than my tears. You are worthy of my devotion and my kisses and even my heart if you will it." She leaned over him and gently pressed her lips to his forehead.

"No." He rolled his head heavily away from her and stared blankly at the linen. "I am... undone. Without the... use of my... leg... I..."

She almost grabbed that head and shook him. "If you cannot see your worth, Mr. Ridley, how am I to respect you?" she choked out. "You appear to respect everyone more than yourself. *Why*? I told you about the effects of coca/limestone. Why did you...?"

He continued to blankly stare at the linen. "I... didn't... want to be... in my... head... anymore."

She prayed this was the laudanum overtaking his tongue. For this would not see him through what lay ahead: surviving. She seated herself on the bed beside him and tucked herself as close to him as she could without ensuring she hurt him.

He snapped his gaze to hers, his chest heaving. "Leave. You have seen... how... vile... my intentions are... toward... you."

She shook her head. "I saw nothing vile about how lonely you are. That moment of pleasure you gave to me and took for yourself against the burn of my cheeks, I will gladly give to you again. Especially given all that you have done for me. And even if you were to push me from this bed as you did last night, I would stubbornly crawl back into it, as I did last night. I would crawl back into it for a man who sought to save me—*me*—an Indian whom he did not know, from the world. I will forever honor that and you. Never feel shame for the desire you have for me. I am honored by it. For I hold an equal desire for you, Mr. Ridley. Surely, you know that." She brokenly smiled and attempted to use her good hand to graze the hair from his forehead.

He pushed away her hand and closed his eyes. "I cannot... rest... with you... touching me."

Swiping at the tears that refused to desist, she nodded. "I will let you rest. Sleep." She dragged herself off the bed, wincing against her own pain, and trailed toward the door. Glancing back at him, a soft breath escaped her.

Just as she was about to leave, he rasped something.

She paused and turned back to him. Her fingers tightened against the frame of the door she held open at seeing him staring after her. Her heart squeezed. "Yes, Mr. Ridley? Was there something you wanted to say?"

His throat worked visibly. "Your... money... is... downstairs in the... study."

Damn him to hell for thinking of money at a time like this. She almost sobbed, but for his sake, she remained calm. "I thank you. Was there anything else?"

He half-nodded. "I want you... to know... that..." He winced and seethed out several breaths through gritted teeth before evening his breaths again. "You... would have... been... the one had... I... been... a different... man."

Tears blinded her. She swallowed, knowing full well what he meant. He was acknowledging their connection. The one she knew he had felt all along but one he had attempted to hide and bury due to him being what few men were: heroic. "When you are well again, Mr. Ridley, and I know you will be, for you are the strongest of men I have ever met, promise me you will not break the bond we have made. Fate has brought us together for a reason. We must respect that reason and allow for this to become what we both deserve: more. Promise me. For I wish to offer you that."

He stared, his chest heaving.

She softened her voice. "I am not by any means insinuating anytime soon. I acknowledge that I am young. I acknowledge there is far more of life I need to see and live, but whilst I seek to live that life, I can and will be devoted to you and whatever bond we now share."

A muscle flickered in his scraped and heavily bruised jaw.

"I will stay in London," she offered. "With you. You need me and therefore I am staying."

"No." He glared. "I can't... have you... destroying... yourself... in my name. *Never*."

Why did he refuse to embrace the connection they made? Did he fear himself that much? "I can be as stubborn as you," she pointed out. "I will tap the window until it cracks and if you still refuse to open that window despite my beak bleeding..." She held up her bandaged hand. "Then I swear unto you, Ridley, I will make you bleed in turn and I will make you crawl, too. For you cannot make us both suffer for the bond we have found in each other. That is wrong. You will walk again and I will help you."

His nostrils flared. "I will... ensure you... do not... destroy... yourself." His chest heaved.

She softened her voice, refusing to rile him. He needed this time to heal. "Rest, my dear, dear Mr. Ridley. Rest knowing I am but a bell's pull away and will not leave your side."

He said nothing.

She lingered, then edged out and closed the door.

Pressing her cheek against the coolness of the door, to keep her body and mind from swaying, she whispered through the haze of laudanum, "The gods introduced us for a reason. May that reason guide us to something far greater than either of us could have ever imagined."

She remained at his door, cheek pressed to it for a very, very long time, wishing and willing him to heal. If twenty minutes had passed in a blink, she would have believed it.

Veering away from the door, she paused at realizing two men, Finkle and a round-faced man she knew quite well were standing at the top of the landing of the stairwell, lingering.

It was Peter.

Though she would have normally thrown herself into the arms of the only father she had ever loved, knowing of his betrayal, she sobbed and quickly turned and jerked open the door to Ridley's room, determined to stay with the one who needed her more: Ridley.

She closed the door behind herself and trailed over to Ridley and paused.

An emptied bottle of laudanum lay in his unfurled large hand, his lips parted and his gaze blank.

The screams and screams that tore from her lips were no different than tearing off every finger, every toe, every hair, every piece of skin from her body.

CHAPTER TWELVE

10 minutes earlier

In a delirium he couldn't control, and knowing he had to save her from himself and the waste of a life he now and would forever be, Ridley dragged over the writing box that had been set beside him and crookedly and unevenly wrote Jemdanee a letter.

Forgive me for saving us both from a life of pain.
Ridley

With quaking hands, he nudged that bottle of salvation toward himself and gripped the glass. He uncorked it and quickly drank the entire bottle of stinging liquid of laudanum refusing to live with the devil who resided in his head.

The one who would no longer be able to walk.

The one who wanted her despite the voice of justice that reminded him she was only a child.

The one who wanted to fill her small womb with his seed until he could see it drip.

The one who would have never stopped taking what he wanted from her until their souls ripped.

The one who wanted to make her into what no woman ever should be: a bondwoman.

Ink smeared the page and the world blurred as he eventually stopped responding even when someone screamed and screamed and tried to shake him.

He had purposefully drank every last drop to ensure it ended before it started.

Ridley could hear shouts from the servants and men, but it sounded so far away, he was convinced he was already buried underground in a casket where he belonged. Dead.

Unfortunately... he... came... back.

Why was he back?

Thud, thud, thud.

Strapped to a bed to limit his movements as his body healed, he only ever saw a shadowed face when food was spooned into his mouth, when he was being shaved or when he required assistance with the chamber pot.

Thud, thud, thud.

He was in his own home only it didn't feel like a home anymore.

It felt like a prison.

Thud, thud, thud.

The flap of wings circling over him and the curling of feathers against his neck might have been Chaucer, but it might have been death.

Thud, thud, thud.

Most of the time he stared up at the ceiling through the swimming effects of his own pain that blurred reality. He felt as if his father's own butchered body still lay two walls down, whispering him to come. He was dying.

Thud, thud, thud.

Despite fighting, he came back again and again edging in and out of reality until...

Bam!

A gentleman dressed in a linen cravat and green morning coat leaned over the side of the bed, smelling of castor oil. His bushy hair was combed back with tonic, his mustache waxed at its ends. Dark eyes momentarily held his. "Mr. Ridley. It's good to see you are finally aware and fully conscious. Do you know who I am? Do you remember?"

Ridley blinked, trying to focus.

His head.

His body.

Fuck. What did he do?

"My name is Dr. Watkins."

Jemdanee. He had abandoned her. He had abandoned her out of fear of what he'd do. Fuck.

"Your arm, if you please." Dr. Watkins leaned in closer. "Are you able to move it?"

Ridley wordlessly held out his arm while lying in bed.

"Few things in life astound me, but you, sir, should be dead." Pressing fingers against Ridley's wrist, Dr. Watkins leaned over and placed a small cone-like instrument against Ridley's bared chest.

It was cold. Much like he felt knowing he was being tended to by a man who had treated his Jemdanee like an animal in need of breeding.

She'll never forgive you if you unleash who you really are.

After leaning in close to listen to the beat of his heart, Dr. Watkins leaned back and sighed. "Despite what could have been a lethal intake of laudanum that was supposed to help you heal through the broken bone you suffered, your heart appears to be beating at a normal pace again. I had used a tube to empty the contents of your stomach shortly after it happened, which helped.

"As for the rest of you… you had endured severe multiple seizures over the course of several weeks. Some lasting as long as twenty minutes. Your leg is healing incredibly well and no gangrene has set in against the binding. Given the amount of damage you sustained to the muscle surrounding the bone, however, you'll never walk again."

Despite his continued haze, Ridley already knew what that meant as he had faced it prior to drinking the laudanum.

He was a hero no more.

At thirty-two, *he* was sentenced to a life that would end what he loved most: his career.

His inability to walk would announce to every mother fucking delinquent that he, Evan Oswald Ridley, was a stronghold no more and that he was *weak* and that with a single sweep could be toppled over like a domino unable to stand on its edge.

No longer would he be able to sprint, hop over walls or grab collars.

He'd be confined to a bed and a chair.

It was too much. "Leave," he rasped against the dryness of his throat. "I don't want the likes of you tending to me. *Leave*."

"You have certainly made a mess of things, Mr. Ridley. All of your own doing." Dr. Watkins held up the empty glass bottle of laudanum and tapped it with a large, calloused finger. "Much like the coca/limestone, no more of this or you'll end up dead. These apothecarians and doctors here in London don't know medicine. *This* does not heal. It poisons. It will therefore be removed from your bedside and regiment and replaced with water steeped with ginger. Drink it on the hour and no more coca/limestone or you *will* be dead."

The coca and the laudanum he could live without, but... *Jemdanee...* Jem... da... nee...

She was his new coca.

It was yet another reason as to why he drank the laudanum.

To save her. To save her from himself and what he wanted: her.

Ridley tried to sit up against quaking arms, unable to hold onto his pride, despite knowing his leg was unusable. He needed to apologize to her. For he sensed she had found him. Much like she did when she followed him to the abandoned building.

For she was his little raven. The one that tapped at the glass, wanting in. He swallowed knowing it. "Where is she? I have to see her. I have to apologize to her for what I did."

A large hand firmly eased him back down. "She left for India a few weeks ago. She insisted I stay with you and oversee your healing. She tasked me to deliver these into your hands." Dr. Watkins gestured toward the bedside table where a sealed parchment and a small green bottle sat atop of it. "She wishes you well and good-bye."

'I can be as stubborn as you. I will tap the window until it cracks and if you still refuse to open that window despite my beak bleeding...' She held up her bandaged hand. *'Then I swear unto you, Ridley, I will make you bleed in turn and I will make you crawl, too. For you cannot make us both suffer for the bond we have found in each other.'*

She was punishing him. She was punishing him for having punished himself. And she did so by leaving. By making him breathe knowing he now couldn't.

Though it felt as if a sword had been impaled into his brain knowing she was so far out of his reach, despite the damnable breaths he still took, he now knew what his path was without even touching her letter.

There was no changing it.

The real Ridley was coming for her.

Dr. Watkins grew quiet. "You take your profession far too seriously, Mr. Ridley. A bit of advice when 'investigating' and 'incriminating' others. Vile accusations are no different than committing murder."

The man leaned in close, his nostrils flaring. "If your leg wasn't already broken, I would break it again because I specialize in setting and breaking bones. Because I never wanted her to know the truth of the disease I was born with. Yet because of you I was forced to say it. Because of you, I was forced to expose my vile shame to the only person who ever mattered to me. I have *never* lusted for children. I am what you virile men call a *Molly* and *a Peter*. But my profession and my faith in God has always been far more important to me than who I bed, and therefore I have taken a righteous God-loving path and don't associate with men. Never even touched one and never will."

Ridley's lips parted.

Dr. Watkins looked away. "The ring you had stripped from my waistcoat after my arrest was a gesture any father would make to his daughter." A breath escaped him. "When she was twelve, she begged for a ruby ring which I thought too ostentatious for a child. Every year thereafter, she continued to beg for that same ring. I therefore saved for it and wanted to surprise her with a trip to London given she had never been. Whilst I had no hope professors might see her potential, I still wanted her to *feel* important given the amount of rejection she has endured in far too many facets of her life. To her people, she is too light, and to our people, she is too dark. No one wants her, not even those who claim to be of her caste. I feel the burden she endures every day. And you... *you* tried to erase what little hope I have given her by making her believe the only person who loved her was a lie. You, who are blinded by darkness in the name of a justice you no longer represent."

A shaky breath escaped Ridley's lips. His throat and chest *burned*. For in the name of justice, and his need to grab every last collar, he had become the very thing London and all of its people and its newspapers were good at: gossip in the guise of a righteousness that was never there.

"Forgive the crass assumption," Ridley finally offered, trying to remain calm yet unable to. "It wasn't my intention to hurt her. I was attempting to protect her."

"I recognize that." Dr. Watkin's smoothed his mustachio, his brow creasing. "Despite my own grievances, and that she now knows the truth, you did do more for her than anyone has in a long time. She is safe and the conviction was overturned due to your faith in her innocence. And for *that* I thank you and that is why I stayed to oversee your healing. She is a miraculous individual full of light set against high winds, is she not?"

Ridley didn't need to be told twice as to where this was going. "I didn't touch her." *I wanted to but I didn't. I fought the devil in her name and couldn't even die doing it.*

Dr. Watkins stared. "I never insinuated you did. She told me everything. I merely wish to understand what it is you, a man of your age, want from her. Define it and I will try to understand."

How fitting. God was officially sitting at his bedside. He'd barely been conscious for ten minutes and the guilt was setting in. "I am an unconventional man in nature, Dr. Watkins. Much like you are. I hide in the shadows for a reason. I belong there."

"Let us permit this conversation to be kept between us men. Which I am. Should there be any doubt about the arms I am known to break." His tone hardened. "I will not permit her to become what too many white men do to her people. The only association I will ever permit is one of matrimony. Do you understand?"

Ridley eased out a breath, trying to think through the haze. "Setting aside that she is far too young to even—"

"Is that all you see? An age? I can assure you, Mr. Ridley, her soul is as old as any river given all that it has seen. And much like a river, she continues to flow and bubble clean despite what people throw into it. For she clings to what few people ever do anymore: *the glory of tomorrow*."

That voice faded. "Prior to landing into my care, she was living beneath a manure cart subsisting off of rotting apricots she chewed well-beyond the pit's bitter center in an attempt to feed herself. She had been living there for over a month after the death of her mother who had been raped and butchered by a group of Bengali men who were determined to show women in that district what associating with white men resulted in. I never told her, because the truth changed nothing. She is and will forever be an orphan, regardless of what I give her, so if I can lessen that orphan's pain, as a doctor, I will do it. *Never* tell her. Never tell her lest the last of her smiles die. Save her."

Ridley closed his eyes, sinking into the pillows and the bed around him. He felt his soul sway with a pain he hadn't known since his own father had been butchered.

Their souls were now mates.

Mates bound by the pain of life.

She who had saved his life twice.

She who broke her beak doing it. "Why did she leave? Does he letter explain it?"

"I do not know what she penned, Mr. Ridley, but there were a multitude of reasons as to why she left. Your attempt at suicide was not something any human ought to witness. It altered the state of her mind."

Ridley swallowed knowing it.

"Aside from that, she had little choice but to leave. She went from being infamous to a celebrity overnight after it was made known she not only rescued you from death, but found the broken tip of the quill at the murder scene which led to the confession of a manservant who had been hired by the Barlow heirs to do the poisonings. The journalists and crowds were making it impossible for her to have any peace. Men were climbing up the bannisters to break windows."

Christ. The usual. "You didn't send her alone, did you?"

"What sort of a guardian do you think I am?" Dr. Watkins gave him a pointed look. "You needn't worry. She was escorted by the best Scotland Yard had to offer to oversee her trip back to India. In fact, she will be living with the Governor-General, who is a good friend of mine, at the Government House in Calcutta until further notice. It is my attempt at giving her a sense of normalcy and independence. She will be overseeing their vast array of greenhouses on the grounds and will be paid incredibly well for her duties. She is thrilled about the prospect of earning an actual wage."

The tightness in his throat was unbearable.

India was too far.

He had to get to her.

Before his little raven flew off to be with someone else.

He'd sooner break that someone in half and bury the bones.

For they were bound.

He dreaded her letter. "Is she waiting for me? I need to know."

A disgruntled breath escaped Dr. Watkins as the clattering of instruments being gathered filled the room. "Damn you for thinking she would and no," he bit out. "She has given you up and did nothing but cry. In fact, she did more than that. She fed and bathed you after your attempt at suicide and well before that, when you suffered your initial seizure in that abandoned building, she saved your life by placing her own fingers against your tongue to keep you from choking. You bit into them so deep and so hard to the bone, she required threading through all four fingers."

A shaky breath escaped him as Ridley momentarily closed his eyes. Her hand. It hadn't been glass. She had endured the wrath of his seizure in his name to save him from death.

Something no woman had *ever* done for him.

How could she let his soul soak into hers and then let him go? How could she?

Thudding the side of the bed, Dr. Watkins sighed. "One would think she had swallowed the Bhagirathi-Hooghly river in an attempt to pour it all back out in your name. Sobbing the way she did isn't something she does for anyone. Not like that."

Ridley gripped the linen draped around his broken body. *My little raven.* "Did she cry?"

"You appear to take pleasure in that."

That was what the demon in him. He wanted tears for proof.

Dr. Watkins shoved his remaining instruments into his satchel. "Love is all that girl ever wanted and if you cannot offer her that, let her go as she has already let you go. 'Tis fairly obvious you prefer to bring her harm."

Selfish though it was of him, given that he now lived, and knowing what she had done for him, he refused to do it. Why would he let her go? Why would he let go of the one who had entrusted her life into his hands with a smile? Why would he let go of the one who had kept him from falling into the arms of his greatest enemy: death? Why would he let go of the one who still knew how to laugh despite the world trying to make her cry?

That was the beacon of an unbreakable mind that refused to bend.

Like his.

Sitting up, Ridley winced against the stabbing, shooting pain seizing his legs. *Jesus.* He breathed in and out, in and out through nostrils in a shaky attempt to control the writhing. "Is it possible I could walk if I… *strengthen my leg?*" he hissed out.

Dr. Watkins lingered. "That I do not know. Most likely not. You sustained quite a bit of damage. It's nothing short of miraculous that it didn't have to be amputated."

Ridley almost took a fist to his own skull knowing it was his own doing. "I have to walk. I have to." To get to her. "Even if it means I'll stretch every bone and muscle, I have to—"

"I suggest easing the torture and rest. For rest is something you have denied yourself and your body for far too long under the guise of coca. Heed the warning and rest."

Dr. Watkins held out an old book, tilting its thick spine toward him. "Given your mind appears to be like mine and is anguished whenever it is sentenced to the death known as rest, take this time to learn her ways and reconsider offering her what she deserves: more. Take comfort in knowing the independence you graciously encouraged her to embrace is now hers. Let her cradle it without either of us becoming what she no longer needs: a parent. What she will need in time is a husband. She may deny it, but she only ever talks about how one day her children will learn the art of botany alongside her."

Children.

It was inevitable that in time, such a wild spirit as hers would look for a man to fill her womb with exactly that. A choice outside of him. A life outside his reach. A man who would possess her and treat her like a pet. Stroking. Caging. Hiding her behind the glass windows of a house.

Never. "I have found marriage does not create a bond between men and women, Dr. Watkins. In fact, it erases it. For a man is given a mere piece of paper that states a woman belongs to him, when in fact, there are never guarantees in that. I prefer my guarantees to be written in blood."

The blood she poured for him.

That was their contract.

Ridley eyed the book bearing the gold lettering *India*.

Only he and he alone was strong enough to ensure her skies were never darkened by any permanent night. Only he and he alone was strong enough to guzzle poison in her name. Only he and he alone could find the strength to walk on a leg that was unwalkable.

What other man would do that for her?

For she deserved to be carried over far more than a muddy road to ensure her slippers didn't get soiled. She deserved to be worshiped and given an altar. One made of rope.

She would get that.

Whether she married another or not.

Whether she loved another or not.

They were bound and he would rip down every wall to ensure she knew it.

Like she had first wanted.

Regardless of what that letter said, he wasn't letting her go.

Dr. Watkins set the book on India beside him. "I found it amongst your father's collection. There was a total of thirty-two books on one shelf, all of it on India."

Ridley's gaze lifted to Dr. Watkins. There were so many in the house, even he, who had tried to organize them and go through them, had been unable to touch a fraction. He paused. "Did you say thirty-two?"

"Yes. I hope you don't mind, but given the amount of hours I've spent in the house while tending to you, I've been rummaging through what is without a doubt the most impressive collection of antiquities I have ever had the pleasure of seeing. You actually have medical books of Celtic origin. And the ones on India are equally marvelous."

It was a sign from his father.

India. It was where he was supposed to go. It was where he was supposed to be. With her. Thirty-two books on India and he, Ridley, was the age of thirty-two. His father had once told him that if there was ever another side, he would arrange the books with a sign.

This was that sign. Protecting her and seizing her for his own was his right. His. Right. "Take them. Take any." Leaning over to the side table and with quaking limbs, he dragged her letter and the small bottle and set both onto his lap. Still leaning over, he opened the drawer, biting back a pain-ridden wince. "There should be... a thousand in bank notes. Take it."

"I prefer not to—"

Ridley rattled the night stand. "She mentioned you no longer have your inheritance. Permit me to thank you for overseeing my recovery. *Take it.*"

Dr. Watkins hesitated, then slowly gathered the bank notes and folded them into his pocket. "I appreciate your generosity and will send it to my elderly mother."

Ridley leaned toward him. "Do you require more?"

"No. God has blessed me with a position in India I will have to return to soon." Dr. Watkins took up his satchel and walked to the door. He opened it and glanced back at him. "A certain Mrs. Berkley is waiting downstairs in your parlor. Your former wife, I believe. She has been visiting almost every day and has been waiting for you to regain consciousness. Shall I sent her in?"

Ridley hissed out a breath. "I'd rather you break all two hundred and six of my bones."

"I doubt it would help. That one refuses to leave."

"Oh, I know it. Once married, always married. Even after a divorce."

"So much for that piece of paper you complained about, Mr. Ridley."

"It's not the paper I ever complained about."

A breath escaped Dr. Watkins. "Are you wanting me to send her away?"

Ridley lowered his gaze to his hand and to the wedding ring he still wore and with the grit of teeth, wedged it off. He was done insulting himself. He hadn't failed her. She had failed him.

Jemdanee was proof of what a woman should be. "No. Have her come up."

"I will. Rest and I will call on you again in the morning. The servants know to peer in on you on the hour without the pull of the bell." Dr. Watkins closed the door.

Barely breathing against the haze that still gripped him and the deep, deep throbbing within his muscles and bones, Ridley gripped Jemdanee's letter and rotated the wedding ring between pulsing fingers, letting it bite into his skin one last time.

He stared at the door, numb.

Any moment.

Any moment.

Any moment.

Any moment and…

The door slammed open, shaking the room.

A tall woman wearing a blond, curl-ridden wig tied with black ribbons stepped into the room. Dressed in expensive, black velvet cinched at a very tightly corseted waist that brought it to an unnatural eighteen inches, she sashayed in with the flaunt she'd always been known for. She tapped a cane against her full skirts.

Because she wasn't imposing enough. *Good-bye, Bloodnut.*

Her green eyes scanned the room as if it were far more interesting as her pale freckled nose scrunched in amusement. "At least the furnishing has improved."

Fuck this. He was going for what he really wanted. All things soft, all things understanding, all things kind and moldable. *Jemdanee.* "Why the wig, bondwoman? Are you hiding termites, the men or the grey?"

She gave him a withering look and swept toward him, her heels clicking. She lingered beside the bed, the scent of vermouth permeating the room. "You may not believe me, but I was worried about you. It reminded me that I actually cared."

"A pity you didn't apply that to our marriage."

She tsked. "You had my permission to backhand me. Why didn't you?"

He heaved out a breath knowing he was the only mature one left in the room. Which wasn't saying very much given his stupid, stupid attempt at suicide. "What do you want?"

Taking her cane she poked his leg. "Is it still broken?"

He winced against the searing pain that went to his teeth. "Elizabeth, *for fuck sake!*" he roared, the real Ridley barreling to life. He glared, his nostrils flaring. "*Kneel.* Kneel, or by God, I *will* backhand you." He snapped up a rigid hand in warning, taking on the teeth she needed. "Try me."

She paused and drew away the cane, puckering her lips. "You always were too delicate in nature." Her tone indicated she believed it. She grudgingly lowered herself to the floor beside the bed, kneeling on his command, her bewigged head now below his. "Am I to be punished?"

The mocking tone alone made him glad she ran off with other men.

He lowered his hand, edging himself back into a calm he rarely, rarely lost. "That would give you too much pleasure. Your punishment will be to remain kneeling until we are done."

A breath escaped her. "You and I both know that compared to my tastes in all things leather, you were always too much of a gentleman." She eyed him and sighed. "If I may be permitted to say it, you look incredibly well given you had almost died four times."

He couldn't even walk away from this. He had to sit here with ripped muscles and a broken leg and listen. To her. "Say whatever you need to say and take the wig out."

Rolling the cane against the edge of the bed with her hands, she met his gaze. "Is it true?"

"What particular truth are you looking for and why?"

"It appears you have unhinged that massive iron door you once locked despite that black, black vow you made to me that you would turn away every last woman until death took your breath. Apparently, death has come in the form of an Indian woman. A certain Miss Kumar. I read it in the papers."

Word certainly had spread fast.

"They are known to get certain things right." He held up the ring. "Your tombstone has fallen and gone *crack*. Bury it along with your shame. Never call on me again. I now belong to another."

She sighed, slowly taking the ring with black gloved fingers. She dragged it against her palm and then tucked it deep into the wrist of her leather glove. Her voice softened. "I regret I held no understanding of what my tastes in leather required prior to our marriage. I hurt you and I regret the punishments I bestowed onto you without your permission."

Morbid though it was, he knew she was apologizing as best she knew how. "Your overlord acknowledges that. Go."

"Am I permitted to stand?"

The sooner she left, the better. "Yes. Go."

She rose. "Might I respectfully kiss your head and touch your hair one last time?"

"No."

"I was never one to listen." Leaning down over the side of

the bed, she kissed the top of his head. She brushed away his hair from his eyes and straightened. She laid the cane beside him, tilting the handle, which was the black iron head of a raven. "I had this made for you. It arrived this morning."

Because he wasn't dark enough. "Take it away. I refuse to carry any part of you."

She lingered. "You will not be carrying me, *but him.*" Flipping open the head of the cane that belonged to the beak of the raven, she carefully withdrew a small black feather. "Your Chaucer refused to eat despite my attempts to feed him and was found lifeless at the foot of your bed two weeks ago. Unlike me, he stayed with you to the end."

A suffocating sensation of disbelief tightened his throat.

His vision blurred as he turned his head away to keep his pain from breaking his own sternum. A tear traced down his unshaven cheek. He swiped at it rigidly with trembling fingers, knowing Chaucer was gone.

He hadn't even been given a chance to… nuzzle that loyal head one last time.

He wanted to rip his own bones out at having murdered the only one who had ever followed him blindly into every adventure they had ever shared.

A bird. A playful, intelligent bird who had depended on him for more than food but for company. In his blind need to play god with time and coca, he had failed the frailest of creatures: his Chaucer.

Elizabeth tucked the feather back into the beak and clicked the raven head of the cane back into place. She set it gently beside him. "Without your permission, for I believed your wellbeing was at stake, I removed all of the coca and limestone from this house. I also respectfully buried Chaucer given you were in a state of unconsciousness. In doing so, I briefly returned to being the woman you once knew and loved."

Ridley slid his hand toward the cane and with a quaking hand, gripped the head of what would forever be Chaucer. "Where did you bury him?"

"With your father."

A choked sob he sucked in deep and kept in lest he appear weak, penetrated his chest and quaked it. He'd finally become what no man should: a dark knight without a torch.

Her hand brushed his head. "On to new adventures, my love. I vow I will cause you no more pain. I swear it."

He swallowed and scrubbed each eye, refusing to show weakness in front of a woman who had knowingly tried to break every bone in his body without any compassion. Her tending to Chaucer's memory, whispered of the one he had first married. The one who was now and forever dead.

He sniffed hard and numbly flipped open the book Dr. Watkins had given him, setting Jemdanee's letter onto it, ready to read it the moment he was alone. "I will keep the cane with gratitude for the preservation of my Chaucer, but in this moment, Elizabeth, I bury you. Every last piece of me will be gathered and placed into the bare hands of one who might be able to make use of it." *Jemdanee.*

Elizabeth tilted her head, her green eyes tauntingly brightening. "You always did opt for the easy way out."

His fingers tightened against the binding. "I never raised a hand to you, Elizabeth, and I am asking you not to let me."

She lingered. "Will you be taking this Hindu as your bondwoman?"

"She isn't one of us."

She paused. "How do you intend to transition her into being yours? Does she know?"

"I hinted at it, but in her honor, I am more than ready to bury what I am."

Her lips parted. She tapped the book. "Evan Oswald, heed these words. To bury yourself even for a minute is wrong. I recognize you blame me for the failure of our marriage, and I will not argue that I deeply betrayed you by taking others into my bed, but there was a reason I did. One I never told you given I feared to say it. Might I finally say it knowing I mean to heal you not punish you?"

His jaw worked as his fingers dug into the leather binding. "I was always one to listen. Unlike you."

She inclined her head. "I acknowledge that and have since grown." A breath escaped her. "My gift to you is that you offer less words and more passion. Show whatever woman you take what you never showed me. For the intelligence of your words and their deeper meaning and the compassion and protection you offer cannot replace the physical passion you refuse to give out of fear of yourself."

She was quiet for a long moment. "I regret telling you that I was raped as a child after we had married. I regret it because it changed everything between us and you refused to give me what we once shared: teeth-clenching passion. In the remaining months we were married, it was *I* who forced your hand to touch my thighs. It was *I* who forced you to 'osculate' given you refused to impose. It is *I* who climbed onto you as I forced you to penetrate me and give us both pleasure. For you only ever saw one thing: *my pain*. And whilst I admire that you wanted to protect me from that pain, as you can see, I am far stronger than you thought me to be. For I am embracing what I have always been and what I have always enjoyed giving to others: *pain*. It is not a sin."

A suffocating sensation crawled up his throat, overtaking his mind. "Pain is a destructive path, Elizabeth. No one knows that more than I for it only grows. Be wary of it and the power you attempt to hold over others whilst using it."

"It is only destructive when there is no control behind it, and I assure you, I have long since learned from the greatest master of control: *you*. A master who broke his own rules and knelt to coca like a governess to her employer. You, Evan Oswald, have an incredible soul of unending strength and generosity, but you need to cease being too much of a hero. Or you will break not only yourself but the very people you claim to save and love. Did you not physically want me? Did I not appeal to you and the mind you feed with only books?"

Despite the pain she had caused him, he offered, "It was never that. You had simply endured enough at the hands of those men at a very young age and I hardly wanted to join in on the perversion."

She dug her nails into his shoulder. "No woman can believe she is loved without feeling it."

He swallowed. "The world would burn if I ever gave into what I really felt. Drinking a bottle of laudanum pales to what I can do. Hell would be on earth."

"Hell is already on this earth, Evan Oswald. Do not think you are saving it. If you do not unleash who you really are and the passion you feel, you will lose more than yourself, you will lose whatever woman you seek to claim. Much like you lost me."

He stared her down. "Forgive me for saying it, Bloodnut, but you were never strong enough to endure my love. You snapped beneath the weight of it the moment it landed on your weak soul."

She lingered, blinking rapidly as if he'd slapped her. "I acknowledge that." She no longer met his gaze. "We play the part one last time in honor of what had once been. Might I be given permission to depart, my overlord? Might I be given permission to let your rule be vanquished so I may now rule over others?"

"Yes. Do both. We are done."

A tear traced down her cheek. She pointed to it. "Might you take the tear from my cheek and swallow it one last time?"

"No." He still had the taste of Jemdanee's tears on his lips. "I have already swallowed the tears of another."

Her lips trembled. She turned, rustling back toward the door. She opened it and glanced back at him. "I did love you in my own way. You gave me what no man ever did: understanding. I hid myself and what I am from everyone, including my brother. But I never hid myself from you. You never let me and for that, I will always love you. You do know that, yes?"

He didn't look up. He couldn't. Because it was over. And when something was over, one never looked up or back.

She softened her voice. "May your tale have a fairy."

She closed the door.

Ridley shifted his jaw and dragged in an evening breath trying to hold onto the only thing he had left: his mind. A mind that had seen him through this much. A mind he refused to fail again.

He slowly flipped through the book Dr. Watkins had given him and settled his gaze on Jemdanee's letter. Without any of the calm he was known for, he frantically opened it and unfolded it, his gaze falling on perfect penmanship. Perfect. Like he expected it to be. Perfect. Like everything that defined her.

Mr. Ridley,

I write this knowing we are at an impasse. I wish you happiness and a long life spent in the joy I know you will never feel. Your lack of self-respect is not one I can respect. I will forever be grateful for all that you have done for me, but it will never erase the horror you forced into my arms. I am worthy of more and I hope one day you will believe you are, too. I leave with you a bottle of jasmine oil as it is known for its healing qualities. It is the only part of me that will ever touch your skin again. I attempted to console Chaucer and feed him, but he only lunged at everyone who dared to go near him as if we were the ones to have harmed you. I hope when you are coherent enough, you will cradle him knowing he will be the only creature to be so blindly devoted to your ignorance.

May we meet in another lifetime under better circumstances,
Kumar

A lone tear traced down his cheek.

One he felt no shame in crying.

One he owed her and one he owed himself.

For she at her mere eighteen had a taught a man at two and thirty that without self-respect, no life was worth living. She was right.

But that didn't mean he had to stay wrong.

He gently kissed her name, ensuring he didn't smear the ink and set the letter onto the pillow beside him. So she might lay with him in bed every morning and every night.

Taking up the small green bottle, he uncorked it.

The sweet crisp scent of a flower he'd never had the pleasure of smelling in person whispered of the cool beauty of the night she had been in his arms. It made him ache. Yet it also calmed him.

Touching his finger to it, he tilted the bottle just enough to let a small drop of oil graze his skin. Corking the bottle, he set it on the pillow next to her letter and with a quaking hand, smeared the oil against his upper lip beneath his nose, to ensure he smelled nothing else.

Nothing but her.

Eyeing the writing box set beside him on the bed, he dragged it over to himself, wincing against the effort.

The first letter he wrote was:

Quincy,
You should feel endlessly honored to know you are the first person I am writing since emerging from the gates of unconsciousness. Given I am unable to tend to the duty myself for what may be a while, might

you be so kind as to call on Mr. Pickering for me? I owe the bastard a few books. Call on me to take them and in turn, I will ensure an extra one or two are set aside for you. That way, you cannot claim I never paid you.

To the brotherhood of the whip,
Ridley

The second letter he wrote in French was:

Vidocq,
For the time being, I am retiring from the investigative field in honor of the fact that I did not die and now must give myself time to heal. As we have always agreed to never send missives beyond three sentences, I wish to thank you for this cap you so generously bestowed unto me nineteen years earlier, but regret to inform you, sir, I have no further use for it. For I now have a new motto: Protect my little raven.

Cordialement,
R.

The third letter he also wrote in French was:

Mère,
No one knows more than I how often you worry, and I thank you for having overseen my coffin nail of a life with your unending love these many years despite the hardships I have bestowed onto you, which included nearly hanging myself by a rope in the attic when I was younger. I cannot imagine the horror you felt as a mother and I still carry it with me to this day and now have stupidly infringed that same suffering on another. I acknowledge that I am who I am in my compassion because of you. I am currently bed-ridden for what may be some time. Worry not, for I am recovering, but I would nonetheless be honored if you would cross the distance between France and England and sit at my side. It is my hope that you and Lord Spencer are as happy as you both were when I left Paris.

Your son in soul and breath,
Evan

The fourth letter, which took him a few more moments to compose, he wrote:

Jemdanee (Do you see, little raven? You are Kumar no more),

223

I am still in possession of a skull because of you. Whilst you might not find it to be a compliment to cradle, I assure you, my skull means far more to me than the rest of this broken body and thus it is the equivalent of what might be my heart. The one that is waiting to beat again with far more than self-respect. 'Tis a humbling reminder of what you have come to represent in a single breath. The short time we have spent together was to me A Midsummer's Night Dream, and I vow to write far more than these words in future correspondences. I will find the countless expressions and phrases and remarks that would best personify the indescribable. For you are exactly that: indescribable. Though you appear to have abandoned me for reasons I understand and decidedly deserve, I refuse to accept never seeing you again. I will come for you. I will come for you standing as a man should and you will fold me into your arms in honor of all that I have done for you. We are bound. Wait for me and I vow unto every breath you take that as soon as I am strong enough, I will be at your side. Nothing will keep me from delivering that promise and proving to you that I am capable of being more. You wanted this bond, you pleasured yourself in my name, and given the blood you poured for me, I kneel to being yours.

Always.
Your humble servant and overlord,
Evan Oswald (disregard Ridley)

It was the first of seven hundred and thirty seven letters.

Over many months that had turned into a year and then two years and three and a few months, Ridley fought to fight past the pain of his broken body and worked to make it stronger with massive iron weights his arms and his legs dragged.

All the while, his bed and his room and his books and his think ropes created a new altar. One of unending pieces of *her* life that turned into *his*. Though she never once responded to any of his letters, he knew she was making him crawl.

It enabled him to walk.

To celebrate that he had made it the wardrobe of his room with his Chaucer and cane, he wrote Jemdanee a letter he intended to deliver to her in person. He folded that letter into leather, creating a casing to protect the words he had written. He then set that leather casing against his bicep and wrapped that bicep in rope, knotting it into place twice to ensure he carried it at all times.

One knot represented her. The other him.

He only ever removed it when bathing.

In doing so, she became what he swore no woman would ever be to him again: his.

THE END OF BOOK 1

The Whipping Society Saga

FEATURING MR. RIDLEY & JEMDANEE KUMAR
throughout all three books

BOOK 1. MR. RIDLEY
BOOK 2. THE DEVIL IS FRENCH
BOOK 3. REBORN

ABOUT THE AUTHOR

USA TODAY best-selling author Delilah Marvelle is the winner of the *RT Book Reviews* Reviewer's Choice for Best Sensual Historical Romance of the Year and had *Booklist* name *Forever and a Day* one of the Top 10 Romances of 2012. She loves researching the grittier side of history that gets omitted by too many historians and collects vintage and out-of-print books that allow her to delve into the underbelly of forgotten history. Aside from writing, she is also the co-founder of the Historical Romance Retreat, which brings the world of history and romance alive for readers! You can visit her website at www.DelilahMarvelle.com or visit the Historical Romance Retreat at www.HistoricalRomanceRetreat.com.

CPSIA information can be obtained
at www.ICGtesting.com
Printed in the USA
FSOW01n1534150317
31950FS